PRAISE FO

Sugar

"An irresistible mixture of humor and heart . . . fabulously funny, _Sugar_ will leave you satisfied and wanting more."

—Heather Gudenkauf, _New York Times_ and _USA Today_ bestselling author of _The Weight in Silence_ and _These Things Hidden_

"_Sugar_ serves up a winning combination of wit and heart in pastry chef Charlie Garrett, who reluctantly becomes a reality TV star. But as she tries to balance her ex-boyfriend, who is now her boss, and an intriguing man she just met, she soon discovers that sometimes the sweetest things in life are the most simple. _Sugar_ is an addictive and delicious pleasure, meant to be savored."

—Liz Fenton and Lisa Steinke, authors of _The Year We Turned Forty_

"A mouth-watering delight of a story about love, work, and yes, dessert! Like a perfect pastry, _Sugar_ is a book to be devoured."

—Jamie Brenner, author of _The Wedding Sisters_

"_Sugar_ is a deliciously relevant novel about one chef's struggle to balance the insatiable desire of food celebrity while remaining true to her craft. I ate it all in one sitting and loved it. _Sugar_ satisfies in every way."

—Lei Shishak, author _Beach House Baking_ and owner of Sugar Blossom Bake Shop

"_Sugar_ hits the spot! A ménage à trois between dramatic reality television, the merciless Michelin star chef's competition, and a heart-fluttering romance. When Kimberly Stuart creates the marriage of true love and luscious pastry, the pages melt like chocolate between your hands. As an aphrodisiac chef, this is a must-read!"

—Chef Fed, creator of FEDish and Love Bites

sugar

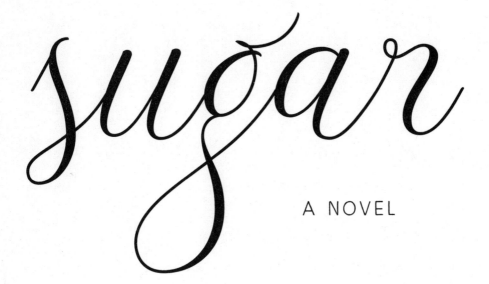

sugar

A NOVEL

KIMBERLY STUART

Skyhorse Publishing

This is a work of fiction. Names, characters, places, and incidents are either the products of the author's imagination or used fictitiously.

Skyhorse Publishing books may be purchased in bulk at special discounts for sales promotion, corporate gifts, fund-raising, or educational purposes. Special editions can also be created to specifications. For details, contact the Special Sales Department, Skyhorse Publishing, 307 West 36th Street, 11th Floor, New York, NY 10018 or info@skyhorsepublishing.com.

Skyhorse® and Skyhorse Publishing® are registered trademarks of Skyhorse Publishing, Inc.®, a Delaware corporation.

Visit our website at www.skyhorsepublishing.com.

10 9 8 7 6 5 4 3 2 1

Library of Congress Cataloging-in-Publication Data is available on file.

Cover design by Laura Klynstra
Cover photo: iStock photo

Print ISBN: 978-1-5107-1413-7
Ebook ISBN: 978-1-5107-1414-4

Printed in the United States of America

To Marc, always

1

WITH another shift almost completed, I wondered for the millionth time if the restaurant business attracted a disproportionate number of insane people. I glanced at the oversized clock on the wall and saw the hands reaching for one in the morning—dawn would be creeping into Manhattan in a matter of hours.

Folding a damp towel into a precise square, I took a look around my pastry station. After the scrub job I'd just done, I needed a postintimacy cigarette. I narrowed my eyes and inspected the corners and crevices of the pastry station, looking for any remaining streaks or stains, and then ran my set of scouring toothbrushes under scalding hot water. Satisfied, I turned off the faucet with my elbow and stacked the toothbrushes in rainbow order on a drying rack. Five more minutes and I would be on my way home. The sweat prickling the back of my neck was just starting to cool, and I could practically feel the hot shower that beckoned me from my apartment three subway stops away.

The waitstaff had finished serving the second seating, tidied up, and clocked out. Hours ago, Executive Chef Alain Janvier had abandoned the kitchen of L'Ombre, one of New York's most prestigious restaurants. Embracing the perks that came with being the boss, he slid home in the comfort of his vintage Corvette. Even many of the line cooks had finished prepping their stations for the following day and had begged off, figuring any loose ends would keep until the next shift. I remained, tottering on exhausted legs and looking like every "before" picture of every TV makeover show, but remaining behind nonetheless. I wouldn't leave until the job was done. Done and gleaming.

But in one moment, my fantasies of the new body scrub that smelled like pomegranate and jasmine; the promise of a few hours' sleep in a clean T-shirt that had never seen the inside of a commercial kitchen; the room-darkening shades of my tenth-floor apartment in Soho—all that disappeared. My boss, the talented but unstable pastry chef Felix Bouchard, began yelling his head off. He was on the hunt for blood, and I was unlucky enough to be the first person he saw as he rounded the corner from the storage room.

"Who took my baby?" He spoke with the intoxicating sensitivity of a French serial killer.

Felix Bouchard had graduated with high honors from Le Cordon Bleu, Paris. Before coming to L'Ombre, Felix had worked as pastry chef for a slew of Michelin-starred restaurants in Europe. He had served his famous apple butter crêpes with marsala-laced vanilla sauce to the former president of Yugoslavia. He had been honored twice with a James Beard Award and had been nominated for it many times. Felix was unmarried, had no family to speak of, and hadn't been to a movie theater in seventeen years. But Felix was not a man without love. In fact, Felix's love for one particular object was unparalleled.

"Who took *my baby*?" he said again.

I peered through the metal shelving separating the pastry prep area from the rest of the kitchen. The dishwashers were barely visible in the fog of steam rising from the industrial sinks. The humidity was fierce, and the few of us who remained looked as if we'd survived a tropical Armageddon.

"She is gone," Felix said. His comb-over had dislodged from under his toque. No amount of Aqua Net could defend against the air of the kitchen.

I snapped shut a container of spindly vanilla beans, marked the container with my trademark yellow painter's tape, and cleared my throat. "What are you missing, Chef?"

Felix narrowed his eyes at me. In my early days at L'Ombre, before I'd earned the right to boss around a few underlings myself, I'd once saved

Felix's ample arse during a Valentine's Day disaster by running down the block to Sal's Grocery to buy a box of sea salt. This was the first in a long line of logistical rescues I had performed on his behalf throughout the many years that followed. His present sneer suggested he had no memory of these events, or of the indentured servitude I offered him every single day.

"Charlie, I am missing my knife. My best knife. My favorite knife. The one gifted to me from the great Jacque Pépin, may God bless his soul!" Felix bowed his head on those last words.

"Did Pépin croak?" Only I heard the muffled voice of Carlo, my favorite and most irreverent of the line cooks as he emerged from the fog over by the dishwashers.

"Chef Bouchard," I said, "we don't have your knife. Right, guys?" I turned to the guys on the line. Rudy looked like he wanted his mom. He shook his head of red hair with vigor.

"Not a chance, dude," Rudy said. "I'm way too scared of you."

Felix was almost distracted by the compliment. "Thank you. But where is the other line cook? The new one. Blond. Pale. Pimples."

I turned as Danny came whistling down the hall. He stopped by my side when he saw everyone staring at him.

"Chef Bouchard has lost his knife."

"I do not *lose* my knives!" Felix erupted, jowls flushed and quivering. "Someone has *stolen* my baby. She is six inches long. Nothing is her equal for slicing stone fruits and scoring *pâte sucrée*!" He started to panic, rummaging around people's stations, provoking complaints and exhausted tempers.

Danny cussed quietly. He looked shaken. Then he spoke, his voice low and struggling to compete with the noise from Felix's scavenger hunt. "Chef Janvier asked me to run to the walk-in for butter at the end of the second seating. The carton was sealed . . . and I wanted to get right back to Chef . . . I was in a hurry, so I—"

The kitchen had grown quiet. Felix stepped so close to Danny, he could have hugged him, though that would have violated his personal code of avoiding tender human interaction.

"Why are you whispering?" Felix spoke *sotto voce*, eyes trained on Danny's.

Danny pulled a knife from the pocket of his apron and handed it over. "I'm so sorry. I was going to—"

Felix moved too fast for anyone to stop him. His cut was clean and shallow, across the inner, fleshy part of Danny's forearm.

"Do *not* touch the baby," he said, already wiping the knife clean.

A tide of protest enveloped Felix as he ambled back to his corner. The staff was so vocal in their disapproval, no one heard Danny drop to the floor.

I scooped the butterfly bandage wrappers into a neat pile and dropped them into the rubbish bin under my counter. Standing over the pastry sink, I scrubbed up again, washing off the smell of the Band-Aids, an objectionable odor that reminded me of the murky depths of public swimming pools. I watched as Danny, still looking pale and squeamish, inspected my handiwork.

"The wound is shallow," I said. I snapped a paper towel off the roll above the sink. "It should heal fine. You don't need stitches, but I'd still keep it covered, especially when you're working."

Danny looked up, his lower lip quivering. "I cannot believe him. What kind of a freak slices open someone's arm because he wants his toy back?"

I sat on a stool opposite Danny. "The man spends fifteen hours a day crimping and whisking and performing odd rituals, all in the name of pastry perfection. I know it's no excuse, but conflict management isn't exactly high on Felix's list."

Danny shook his head. "No one in culinary school tells you that the restaurant business can be so . . . so violent!" The poor kid had started at L'Ombre just a few months ago, but already he had developed some sort of heat rash on his neck. Stress, I guessed. I had been out of school for almost a decade, but I might as well have been the kid's elderly grandmother. Grandmothers had seen it all, and so had I. Right then, I was more impressed with the blister forming underneath one heel of my new chef's clogs than I was with Danny's rose-colored view of the world.

Danny inhaled shakily, eyes still on the bandages on his arm. "Psycho. I'm telling Chef Janvier tomorrow." His eyes sparked with defiance. "I know they're friends, but he has to see reason. People shouldn't be able to stab other people at work and get away with it."

I pondered that statement, my gaze scanning the exposed ceiling pipes above us. "Hypothetically, all of what you say is correct. But unless you can make forty-five covers of sixteen different desserts by tomorrow night, I'm guessing the best you'll get is a pat on the back and a free pack of cigarettes."

"You coming, Nurse Garrett?" Carlo called from the back door. "I want to get home before I have to be back in this place."

"Be right there," I called back.

Danny frowned as I pulled on my coat. His eyes were somber. "Chef, have *you* ever been stabbed at work?"

I restrained myself. My first instinct was to laugh at Danny's question. "No, I have not." I began buttoning my emerald green wool coat, a recent and indulgent purchase made in an effort to survive the last dregs of this interminable New York winter. "But I have a lovely collection of burns up and down my arms. And once I saw a chef have a nervous breakdown during rush and strip down to a pair of nasty, raggedy red underwear while he sang 'The Macarena' to a pot of squid."

Danny's eyebrows had lodged up north of his fringe of bangs.

I tugged my bag from my locker and pulled on my mittens. "And, one time during a practicum in culinary school, my favorite pastry prof got so frustrated with a slow student's pace that he took a ball of kitchen twine and started running circles around her. He had her arms totally pinned before he was discovered by the headmaster and fired on the spot." I shook my head. "Too bad, because that man made the most exquisite phyllo I'd ever tasted."

When I looked down again, Danny was slumped over my counter, his forehead planted on the stainless steel. I lifted his head with careful hands and slipped a tissue underneath before letting it rest again on my clean countertop. "Go home and get some sleep. Things will look much better tomorrow."

"It already *is* tomorrow," he said, his voice muffled by his arms.

I sighed and felt the arches of my feet object as I walked to the back door where Carlo was waiting. Danny was barely of drinking age and he still had neck acne, but he would learn, just as we all had.

Carlo and I forged through the cold edge of early morning, and I was grateful for my warm coat. He was headed to the BM5 bus to Brooklyn, and I was catching the 6 train to my apartment in Soho.

"Poor kid," I said after walking a block in silence.

Carlo grunted. "Hazing. Just part of the game, *mami*."

I nodded from within the cocoon of my woolen scarf. "We have weird jobs."

Carlo's laugh sounded more like a bark. He punched me on the shoulder before turning into the wind and walking toward his bus stop. "That is an understatement. *Hasta lueguito, amiga*."

"Say hi to Lupe for me," I called, but I was pretty sure my words were lost in the gust of wind that lifted them away.

A scant few hours later, my alarm clock sounded, and I awoke under protest. As I extracted one hand from under my down comforter and reached for the snooze button, I remembered again how much I hated that clock and its Chihuahua-like chime. I shivered and then plunged my hand back under the covers. My eyes felt glued shut, and I was certain I had bags under them.

"I'm too young to have bags," I groaned and turned onto my side. The Chihuahua stared at me with its sleek front piece and cool blue numbers. "You can't possibly understand."

It *was* time to get up. The day needed a jump start. Wasn't an active lifestyle supposed to keep a girl alert and stave off senility?

And, I thought as I slipped out from under the covers and slid my feet into my waiting slippers, *a date wouldn't hurt*. Half my queen-sized bed remained pristine and untouched after my night's sleep. I pulled my side taut, tucking the sheets exactly six inches from the headboard and covering that with my favorite Supima cotton blanket, then the down comforter, which had cost me dearly but had retained its shape and gave me four seasons of perfect temperatures. I tugged one of the throw pillows toward the center of the bed and felt the familiar thrill of perfect symmetry. I padded over to my dresser for my first costume change of the day.

I opened the top drawer and scanned through the drawer separators left to right before selecting one item from each section: sports bra, tank, running capris, and socks. My mother's voice intruded my thoughts as I dressed and laced my shoes.

"You need to worry less about perfection and more about your future. Let's talk about your eggs, honey," she'd said on the phone recently. "I'm concerned about your eggs."

"My eggs? I prefer organic, large, free-range, thanks. And I have at least a week until they expire."

She'd scoffed. "The eggs in your ovaries, sweetheart. You're thirty-two, and that is a dangerous age in terms of fertility."

"Mom," I tried again, "things are different in New York. I know Amber Murphy just had her fourth—"

"Eight pounds, two ounces. Beautiful baby girl. White-blond hair, just like James."

"Fantastic, but I don't live in Minnesota. I live in Manhattan."

"Well, la-di-da and congratulations," she said, still completely unimpressed a decade after her daughter had defected from the Midwest to an unknowable and sprawling city with high rent and a rat problem. "I'm just trying to warn you, Charlie, that's all. I heard a report on Dr. Oz, and I think your eggs are getting crusty."

I straddled my treadmill and pulled my hair into a pony while waiting for the machine to power up. "Crusty eggs," I said aloud and then louder, to the Chihuahua, "I have crusty eggs!"

I started running at a faster pace than normal, irritated with the world. I should not have started the day with a pity party. After years of toil and self-denial, my career was finally gaining momentum. Executive Chef Alain had started talking me up to the other cooks. When Chef Andersen from Aqua had visited a week ago, Alain had introduced me as "the formidable and brilliant Charlie Garrett." Over coffee the previous week, he'd assured me again that Felix was on the cusp of retirement, and that his long-ago promise to me that I would take over as head pastry chef at L'Ombre was just around the bend. Of course, after last night's debacle with the knife, I might have fallen a notch, but, in general, work was good.

Most days, I could reconcile the fact that I was ticking along in my thirties, nary a man or family in sight, but enjoying the passion and thrill of a job I loved. Of *course*, there had been sacrifices, I acknowledged as I took a grade 8 hill for a two-minute interval. I gripped the heart rate monitor, noted an excellent anaerobic number, and kept running. One had to sacrifice things like romance and dating and marriage proposals if one was going to go anywhere in the restaurant world.

"It's totally been worth it," I panted to the heart monitor, which rewarded me with an increase in beats per minute.

With each stride, I glimpsed the top half of my face in the mirror by the front door as I bobbed up and down. I was going to need a serious Estée Lauder intervention before heading back to the restaurant at noon. Circles under the eyes, sallow complexion, eyebrows in need of disciplinary action—and that was only the top half of my face. I ran faster, watching the numbers on the display pad arch upward and feeling a lovely layer of smugness descend over my foul mood.

"Can a woman with elderly girl parts do this?" I puffed, feeling sweat run between my shoulder blades and down my back. My abs contracted and I felt another swell of victory. Women with supple, baby-making eggs had shitty abs. And they had to work twice as hard for legs that looked good in a miniskirt, right? Of course I was right. I had my abs and my legs, and one day soon I would wear something other than chef's whites in public and then show off those legs and abs. Maybe I'd put my crusty eggs to work after all.

"Gross," I said aloud.

I slowed to a jog for a three-minute cooldown and walked on jelly legs to the rug in front of my couch and sat down on my yoga mat. I tucked my feet under the linen fabric of the couch and started crunching. *There! See!* I exclaimed as I exhaled with each crunch. The couch was one tailored and Scotch-guarded example of what a little sacrifice can garner a girl. While my job at L'Ombre was not about to afford me a house in the Hamptons, I did fairly well. Well enough to be able to buy a linen couch and six accent pillows with real down inserts. I noted all this as I completed my forty-fifth crunch. And, I also had a complementary, but not matchy-matchy, set of armchairs in a midnight blue chevron, thank you very much. Not to mention a spot in a neighborhood that was still up-and-coming. I had shed the woes of my closet-sized studio three years prior, and my linen couch and I were doing very well with the adjustment to spacious clean lines and exposed brick.

One hundred. I lay back on the yoga mat, listening to my heavy breathing. My hands rested on my midsection, and I was pleased to feel how flat things remained after taste-testing fourteen variations of our new éclair a few days prior. I rolled onto my stomach and pushed up into plank, then started in on my push-up regimen. I watched the timer on my iPhone count down as I started my first set of twenty in thirty seconds. I couldn't imagine this was doing me any favors in the bust department as I glimpsed my schoolgirl offerings flattened by my sports bra. I was deliberating over the relative advantages of having Michelle Obama arms over breasts that would need something more than a training bra when my phone rang. I startled, dropping to the floor and fumbling for the phone. I picked up when I saw the ID.

"Hey," I said, turning on speakerphone and going back to plank position. "I'm doing push-ups."

"Dang," Manda said. "I was hoping you were having sex."

"I don't do that anymore. Plus, I would never answer the phone under such conditions, not even for you." Fifteen, set two, sixteen, set two . . .

"You're panting. Stop panting and talk to your best friend."

"No," I said. "Twenty-four push-ups to go."

"How about stopping early just this once?" She was quiet while I ignored that ridiculous suggestion. "Okay, then. Well, I won't keep you, but I thought I'd call before the day ran off its tracks, as it most certainly will . . ." I could hear commotion in the background and then heard Manda again. "Wait—hold on—Zara, no! Rubber cement is toxic. No! . . . Dane, honey, keep your diaper on until Mommy can help you. Clean hands are happy hands. Come on, ruffians, let's have breakfast."

I made a face when I considered exactly what was on Dane's little hands. If the past was any indication, they were things that might eventually start to sprout or mold. I stared at the phone, momentarily worried that such virile germs could pass through a telecommunication system like little, super-smart terrorists.

"Wait." I let myself drop to the mat and glanced at the clock. "Why are you calling me so early? Isn't it like 5:30 a.m. in Seattle?"

Manda sighed. "Oh, to be young and frivolous with time once again."

"We're the same age."

"But you are single and childless. And frivolous with time. Nevertheless, you have to make time for a very special phone call today." Her voice had taken on the sing-song quality all humans adopted when getting ready to set up their lonely single friends with other lonely single friends.

"Who is it? Bald? Divorced? Yoga instructor?"

"None of the above, thank you very much." I heard one of Manda's three progeny scream bloody murder in the background. "Oops. I have to go. Might be blood. I'll call you later. He said he'd call you after work tonight. Don't forget one word! Remember every part of the conversation."

I used the edge of the couch to do some tricep raises. "Who's going to call?"

I could hear the smile in Manda's voice. "Avery Malachowski."

"Whaaat? Why? How? Where did you see him?"

"He'll tell you all that." I was losing her, I could tell. The duration of an average phone conversation prior to Zara's birth five years before was two hours, twenty-one minutes. Since the onset of lactation, the average call was down to four minutes, thirty-four seconds. "Bye! Everyone say 'Bye, Auntie Char!'"

She clicked off in the middle of the kids' warbling, and I held the phone, still breathing hard from my workout. I hadn't thought about Avery Malachowski in nine years, though I'd thought plenty about him in the months leading up to those years. He and I had lost touch after finishing culinary school together—he disappearing into the shiny, happy restaurant scene of southern California and me diving into the shark tank of New York City. We'd toyed with the idea of continuing our relationship, one of us piggy-backing on the other's opportunity and looking for a job on the coast we didn't want. But we'd parted ways, not *too* sadly, as I recalled, as we were both fiercely ambitious and primed to conquer the culinary world.

I took a ferocious pull on my water bottle. *Avery Malachowski,* I thought as the water level dipped. The last I'd heard of Avery, he was working as a sous chef on a cruise ship. I wrinkled my nose, remembering all the news reports of cruise passengers being pummeled with stomach viruses. I untied my laces and walked barefoot into the kitchen to grind some fresh coffee beans. I put the fine grind into the waiting glass carafe, and, as I watched the coffee brew, it occurred to me that Avery might be in town. Maybe he was fishing for a date or a drink when his ship docked or whatever it was that cruise ships did. Did cruise ships even dock in Manhattan? That kind of behavior sounded distinctly New Jerseyish.

My phone vibrated to announce a text. Manda had taken a screen shot of her Facebook exchange with Avery and had typed above, "See! He's dying to see you! Yearning! I think the word is yearning!"

The Facebook conversation merely showed Avery's request for my number, nothing about a marriage proposal or running away together. Manda was not getting enough sleep if she seriously thought a few words on social media meant promises of undying love.

I did a double take as I looked at the clock. I cursed as I sprinted to the shower, leaving my French press to over-steep and my dirty socks on the kitchen floor, two transgressions that would bother me throughout my hasty shower.

By the time I had my hair swept into a work chignon and my workbag slung across my winter coat, I had only a second to scoop up my phone and tuck it into my pocket, where it would sit, neglected, until after midnight.

2

I pulled the last ramekins from the oven and inhaled deeply. I could be wrong, but I doubted it: no more perfect smell existed than that of beautifully baked chocolate cakes.

"Dang, lady, those look like love in a dish." Carlo tsked and shook his head.

I smiled at my little cakes. "Thank you. I've been tweaking this one for a while, and I think I finally have it. I added just three more grams of raw sugar per cake when greasing this time, and the cacao content is up from 68 percent to 70 percent—"

"Aaaand, I don't care, honey. Sorry." He took the tray from me and nodded toward the swinging door that led to the front of the house. "Me savory, you sweet. Plus, everybody's here for family meal, and Chef is itching to start. A hungry restaurant staff is an angry restaurant staff. You go first." He paused by the swinging door. "I'll follow you."

I stood before the chilled bowl of just-whipped cream. With my spine curved over the bowl, I sifted a fine dusting of Valrhona cocoa onto the tallest peaks of the cream, then stepped back to evaluate.

Carlo groaned. "Restless natives, Garrett. Restless *French* natives. Get a move on."

"Okay, fine." I had some tinkering left in me. (Maybe fresh mint for garnish? . . . No, too predictable. . . . A single, perfect raspberry?) With no time left, I stepped away from the sifter and armed myself with the huge bowl of cream. Walking at a clip, I pushed through to the dining room, Carlo right behind me.

When I'd started, family meal was one of my favorite parts of working at L'Ombre. We certainly did not eat off the menu. Truffles, fois gras, seafood, and caviar for forty-five people exceeded the restaurant's resources in both finances and prep time. The food at family meal was intended to be simple but tasty. We cooks took turns organizing and cooking for the restaurant staff before the first seating of the evening. In the early years, hand-stretched pizza had made regular appearances, as did roasted chicken, spaghetti and meatballs, and vats of chicken noodle soup. Recently, though, some newer recruits in the kitchen had turned family meal into more of a family feud. Eager to show Alain their individual style and prowess, the newbies had whipped up ten square feet of vegetarian lasagna with made-from-scratch ribbons of pasta, individual Beef Wellingtons with flaky pastry crusts, pillowy gnocchi dunked in decadent Bleu d'Auvergne with a finish of nutmeg grated tableside. Irritatingly good but, in my opinion, completely missing the point. Much preferring the days of yore, I'd rushed to the restaurant that morning, determined to take my turn at family meal dessert with camaraderie and comfort, not flash, in mind.

"Lava cakes?" Carlo had whistled when I'd told him of my plan. "You've got moxie, Charlie. The whippersnappers are going to eat you alive, presenting a dish that's also on the menu at Applebee's."

I rolled my eyes. "I'm being ironic. You know, taking back the obvious and making it sublime?"

Carlo's brow had knit together in worry. "I don't get it."

I sighed. "They'll just need to eat first, speak later," I had assured him, and now I felt eyes and whispers follow me as Carlo and I made our way through the dining room. We stopped first at the four-top where Felix sat with Alain and the house manager, Richard.

Felix's bulbous lips pursed when I placed his ramekin on the square white plate in front of him. "Well, this is an interesting choice." He drew out the words to let me know just how in-ter-est-ing it was.

"Indeed," Richard agreed, picking up his dessertspoon and pushing gingerly at the crust of the cake. "A humble choice for *Savor* magazine's 'rising star.'" He made air quotations with one hand but kept his other hand busy scooping up a first, dainty bite.

Felix narrowed his eyes at the mention of the *Savor* piece. He'd been so unimpressed with my first write-up in the press that he'd gone out of his way to make sure I saw his copy of the issue smeared with egg yolks at the bottom of the trash bin next to our station.

I watched as he pushed his spoon through the buttery crust and into the cake, and waited as the lava spilled out of the center, a perfectly slow puddle of chocolate, sugar, eggs, and deliciousness.

I allowed a small smile when I saw Alain close his eyes briefly during his first bite.

"Enjoy, gentlemen," I said, demure and maybe a teeny tiny bit smug. If Alain's table could be persuaded, the whippersnappers didn't stand a chance. As I moved to the next table, Felix stopped me with one hand on my arm. He raised his voice to be heard across the room.

"A humble preparation, Chef Garrett. And I must admit, your little cakes are charming." He paused, making certain everyone could hear his next words. "But don't press your luck, my dear. What's next: Twinkies and Oreos?"

The room erupted in laughter, and I maintained a forced smile as I served up the remaining cakes, table by table. *Oh, to be the top dog*, I thought for the umpteenth time since signing on at L'Ombre. *Oh, to escape the daily hostility of Felix, the rampages of Alain, the snarky comments from the army of egocentric, narcissistic, self-absorbed males in this kitchen.* I could feel my neck muscles tighten, and I took a moment to do a shoulder roll.

"Chef Garrett, this is nothing short of perfection." Danny's nose was inches from a tuft of whipped cream. I could see his bandages peeking out from the sleeve of his white coat. "Seriously. Ignore those bastards. This cake should be on the menu. Here and every other place where people want to forget their troubles."

I smiled. This time it was genuine. "Thanks. I'm happy that you, at least, like it."

He frowned, pausing with his spoon midair. "Look around, Chef. I'm not the only one."

Sure enough, the staff—the chefs, the porter, the servers, the reservationist, even the line cooks—were attacking their cakes. I smirked when I saw Marshall, the newest and most opinionated of the haters, actually lick the side of his empty ramekin.

"Give me this over a *flan parisien* any day of any week," Danny mumbled to his spoon, but then he looked up at me with a panicked expression. "No offense, if the flan was your recipe. I just don't like custard. Or apricots. Or fussy crap." He winced. "Not that you're fussy or crappy or—"

"That's enough, Danny," I said. "Stop talking." I left the empty sheet pan at a serving table and sat next to Carlo, who waited with two plates of paella.

I swooned quietly with my first bite. The dish sang with the flavors of Spain and was packed with chunks of browned rabbit, chorizo, and mussels. It was spectacular and camaraderie crushing. "Who made this? Who possibly had time for this?" I was talking through a mouthful of Arborio rice. "I made this once in culinary school and it took an entire day of my life that I'll never get back."

"Reza made it." Carlo used an empty mussel shell to pluck the meat out of another shell. "He said he cooked it over an open fire with orange and pine branches for kindling." Carlo grinned at me, a dribble of olive oil snaking its way down his chin. "According to Reza, it's the pine cones, though, that really do the trick. I'm sure you discovered that yourself when you made it on the day you'll never get back."

I nibbled on a cut of caramelized chorizo but didn't have the chance to reply. Alain was clearing his throat to begin the preservice meeting and had taken his position by The Urinal. Staff members were discouraged from using our colloquial term for the water sculpture that was one of L'Ombre's signature images. A Very Famous Dead Artist, whose name was whispered but never confirmed, had created the piece that stretched from ceiling to floor and undulated a steady stream of water that changed color under multi-hued spotlights. The curves along each side were supposed to evoke the silhouette of a woman, but a smart aleck hostess had named it The Urinal years ago, and the name had sticking power.

Felix joined Alain in front of the group. Both men were impeccably clean, their white coats starched and tailored. Alain stood with a soldier's posture, his hands behind his back, chin uplifted. The room quieted as servers took out their notepads and got ready for the artillery.

From an outsider's perspective, the serving staff sat prettiest in the restaurant hierarchy. They worked far fewer hours than the kitchen staff. They earned beautiful money in comparison to the pittance paid to the cooks, many of whom were still working to pay off loans from culinary school. Servers were the cute younger sisters of the restaurant, bubbly and fresh and still wearing bronzer at the end of a double shift. But the serving staff knew who buttered their bread, literally and figuratively. Without the cooperation and blessing of the cooks, especially Chef Alain, a server could be left with a section of hungry diners seated along with two-weeks' notice.

"All right, folks," Alain said. "First, we have a few changes to tonight's menu. The Oak Forest mushrooms for the langoustine didn't arrive in time, so we've substituted with enoki mushrooms from Champagne Farms. Also, we are adding an entrée to the menu tonight. It's lemon pine-nut-encrusted sea scallops with a celery mousse and my signature vinaigrette. It took three months to get it right, and the end result is phenomenal. So sell it." Alain paused while the servers took notes. "In wines, we're out of the Napa Valley El Molino, the Talenti, and the Chateau Margeaux '86."

Alain paused and, while the servers wrote furiously in their pads, my thoughts wandered. I tried picturing the customers who might have opinions about Oak Forest mushrooms compared to those from Champagne Farms. Did they wear tweed and bifocals? Or were they übermodern with sculptured haircuts and electronic cigarettes? I shook my head, annoyed with myself and my train of thought. *Let the mushroom people be mushroom people*, I chastised myself. *You signed up for this gig, Charlie, remember? You're living your dream, remember?*

Alain changed gears for a second and threw out a quiz question, one of his more sadistic rituals during family meal. "What are the six ingredients in the jalapeño emulsion we serve with the salmon?"

Silence. A blonde in the back ventured, "Jalapeño, olive oil, shallots . . . ?"
More silence.

"Fleur de sel, ground pepper, lemon juice," Alain finished for her, giving her an icy glance over his beakish nose. "Wake up, people. All right, here's an easy one. What's the difference between *jamón ibérico* and prosciutto?"

Four hands went up, and Wade got it right.

"*Jamón ibérico* is dry-cured from black Iberian pigs in Spain, not to be confused with *jamón serrano*, which comes from a less expensive white pig.

Prosciutto is also dry-cured, but it is from Italy. It is the common man's gourmet ham, which is why we don't serve it." Wade finished with a cock of the head and a high-five with another server.

Alain snorted. "Thank you for the editorial comment. Please keep it to yourself, however, when recommending the melon and *jamón ibérico* appetizer."

He spent the next five minutes grilling the staff on the origin of our rice vinegar, what dessert wine paired best with Felix's raspberry brûlée, and the correct serving temperature of the parsnip purée. An hour and a half before the first seating, he released us to finish our prep work and tend to our stations.

"Balls to the wall," Carlo said as we shuffled en masse into the kitchen. He gave me a once-over. "Hypothetically speaking."

"I'm going to assume you mean that as friendly workplace banter and not sexual harassment."

Carlo backed away and toward sauté, hands up in surrender. "Listen, I don't mean any harm. Certainly not to a pastry chef. You people make little boys go crying to their mamas."

Felix heard the last part of our exchange and barked, "Garrett! Enough idle chatter!"

"Yes, Chef!" I broke into a run on my way over to Felix and a long night of pursuing perfection.

3

SOMETIME between the first and second seatings that night, Felix turned into Satan. I became aware of his metamorphosis as I was readying a set of twelve crusts for the rhubarb tarts with toasted almond streusel. I had finished baking the streusel, turning it exactly every four minutes, until it was golden brown, dry, and nutty. It was cooling on a rack nearby, and I had turned my attention to rolling out the dough. I peered at one section that had a pocket of fat rippling the surface. I moved to trim it but didn't get there fast enough.

"Uniform pastry is classic pastry!" Felix pounced, one stubby finger poking the sky as he talked. "You filthy *Américains* and your desire for these . . . these fatty blobs in pastry dough! You have made pastry into a bastard child!"

I did not remember making pastry into any sort of child, much less one from an unmarried woman, but so be it. After years of servitude under Felix's absolute monarchy, I had learned to lie low and keep my mouth of braces-straightened teeth (another peeve of Felix's) shut until the storm blew over, which, likely as not, would not be until the following day. I trimmed the errant dough and slipped it into our rubbish bin, barely taking note of Felix's continuing tirade. Something about George W. Bush slipped through—a nice touch, I thought—and I must have missed my cue to give a response because Felix shouted through my meandering thoughts.

"Do you hear me, Charlie Garrett?"

"Yes, Chef!" I said, though, for all I knew, I might have just agreed to petitioning the WHO to annihilate vegetable shortening.

"Everything all right, Felix?" Alain called from his perch at the pass, the spot where he sat guard and performed inspection on every dish that left the kitchen. He tilted his chin downward and looked over his reading glasses toward our side of the kitchen.

Felix stood taller in his Crocs, red-faced and momentarily silenced. "Of course, Chef." His smile looked more like a grimace. "I am merely teaching young Garrett here how to improve her work. A lesson in craft, correct, Garrett?"

"Yes, Chef," I said, clenching my jaw in submission.

I filled each tart shell with raw rice and loaded them into the oven for the parbake. After wiping down the counter and going over it twice with clean, dry towels, I reached into the fridge for tubs of Dutch rhubarb. I lined them up on a marble cutting board, and Felix put his nose frightfully close to the fruit and inhaled deeply. He leered at the rhubarb, revealing rows of gold fillings in his back molars.

"Ah, the Dutch have it right," he said, stroking one stalk as if it were a newborn cat. "Crimson sceptres, so full of flavor, and such a short season. But we have them today, and we will let them dance for us."

It was difficult not to get creeped out by Felix.

I began peeling the stalks into delicate ribbons, to be placed gently atop a piped filling after the crusts had cooled. I'd only finished about half the pile when Alain's voice rang into our section and bounced off the tile walls.

"Fire one *palet d'or*! Fire one rhubarb tart!"

My eyes darted to the clock on the wall. The second seating wasn't supposed to begin for another fifteen minutes, and Felix was happy to direct his frustration at me.

"You are working like a snail, Garrett! Those tarts should be finished." He looked over my shoulder. When he continued speaking, loudly enough for the whole kitchen to hear, I could hear the sneer in his voice. "The rhubarb is too thick! No more than two centimeters in width! You must start again!"

I could feel my heart pound, and it took a small supernatural act on my part to keep my cool. My hands shook as I placed the cut rhubarb into a tub and under the counter, where I knew I would retrieve it later. Two centimeters wide, exactly. Felix had picked his first poison of the evening, but I knew from experience that if I could salvage the already-perfect "mistakes," I could use them later in the evening without a peep from him.

Alain called again. "I did not hear a response about the tart and the cake. Felix? Charlie?"

"*Oui, Chef!*" Felix shouted, already on his way to the pantry to gather the gold leaf garnish for the *palet d'or*. I reached into the cool storage and removed the only rhubarb tart that remained after the first seating and slid it onto a fresh plate. A minute later, after a very light garnish of powdered sugar on the tart and the gold flakes shimmering on the ganache of the *palet*, Felix delivered both desserts to the pass.

Alain arched over the plates and, after a cursory inspection, nodded. "Beautiful. Good and fast work, Felix."

Felix bowed slightly. "Thank you, Chef. It is a difficult work, teaching these chefs from another generation. They want all this glory, all the media, the interviews, but they lack the skills to be *parfait* in the kitchen." He was talking so loudly, his voice had no trouble cutting through the cacophony of pots and pans and the general chaos of the large kitchen. The man had a stage voice. "But I am happy to be able to guide young people through this laziness. It is a calling."

I caught Carlo's eye from the other side of the kitchen. He made a motion as if he were vomiting.

Felix was halfway to our station when Alain's call came again.

"Fire three rum walnut cakes and one brioche butter pudding!"

I veered to the refrigerator instead of continuing with the tarts. In my years of commercial cooking, I'd found that shouting a loud response to an order inspired confidence in a girl and temporarily distracted her superiors. So I pretty much hollered my reply.

"Yes! Chef!"

<hr/>

Four hours later, I sat on a small stool in the corner of the pastry kitchen. My feet throbbed, and my head was in my hands. I let my neck muscles relax and felt sure my head weighed at least sixty-five pounds. Maybe sixty-eight if I included my hair. I reached up to pull my ponytail out of its prison. My hair fell in a limp spray down my neck.

Carlo stood at the threshold to the pastry area, his apron slung over one shoulder.

"Char, you look a little rough."

"Shut up." My words seemed a bit slurred, though I was far too tired to think of drinking anything more dangerous than warm milk.

"Tough night?"

"Not particularly," I said, wiping away a spot of drool making an escape out of the corner of my mouth. "Felix was a little loopier than usual, but I got it all done."

"Report the douche to Alain," Carlo said in a hushed voice. "Why do you put up with him?"

I lifted my head. "Because Alain already knows, and, for now, that's enough. I'm putting in my time, just like you." I stood and rolled my head in a half-circle, willing the kinks out. "Alain has said from the day he hired me that I am to become the next head of pastry at L'Ombre." I felt my insides quivering, both from exhaustion and from the frustration that bubbled every time I remembered Alain's unfulfilled promises, now slipping into their sixth year of impotence.

Carlo clucked his disapproval, just like a disbelieving Latina grandma. "Felix has announced his retirement four times during the last two years. And he just keeps coming back. Like the resurrection nobody prayed for."

I shook my head. "Eventually Felix will retire or lose his mind entirely, and Alain will need a new head pastry chef. And just like that." I tried snapping for emphasis, but after trimming twenty-four tart shells, my fingers were Jell-O. "Just like that, I'll be executive pastry chef at one of Manhattan's premiere restaurants."

Carlo rolled his eyes. "Just like that, eh? You've got five years in already, sis, nine years out of culinary school, and not to be critical, but you're not looking any younger."

Felix rounded the corner, his Crocs squeaking on the newly mopped floor. His gaze passed briefly over Carlo and then narrowed at the juncture of countertop and stove. He pointed, wrinkling his nose in disgust.

"Charles, you have become soft in your cleaning. Look at this congealed butter. A clean workspace produces clean thinking, and clean thinking produces clean baking. You are aware of this, *non*?"

Carlo coughed and then retreated to the safer confines of the savory world.

I moved as quickly as I could to the offensive spot and had to squint to locate the offending droplet of hardened butter. I quickly scoured and scrubbed, far more than a transgression of that proportion required, and then stepped back for Felix to evaluate. He sniffed, which, in Felix vernacular, meant, "I will not kill you . . . this time."

"Chef Garrett, Chef Bouchard." Alain cleared his throat. He stood at the edge of the pastry section, rocking backward slightly on his heels as if our floor were made of quicksand and he feared being pulled under. "Nice job tonight."

Felix rustled up a smarmy smile.

I blinked and said, "Thank you, Chef."

"You have an admirer, it seems," Alain continued. "He is waiting at a two-top by the orchid wall. He has asked to meet the pastry chef."

Felix smoothed his hair and removed his apron. "I will come at once."

"Actually," Alain said, his hands clasped behind his back, "the gentleman has requested audience with Chef Garrett. He came to meet the woman who was featured in this month's *Savor*."

Felix sputtered a bit, but Alain was no fool and immediately pivoted backward toward his comfort zone at the pass. My eyes followed his departure, and I glimpsed an eavesdropping Carlo doing some sort of celebratory neck dance for my benefit.

"It appears you are on your own this time," Felix sneered. He stepped within my personal space, and I had to work not to cringe. "For some patrons, a shiny magazine photo and *les nichons* are enough to impress." His gaze roamed in a slimy insult over my chest.

I clenched my jaw. "Chef, I believe my work speaks more eloquently than my appearance."

He snorted. "There you are probably right." He walked away, pulling his coat off the hook as he left. His final jab ricocheted off the back wall. "You might want to pay attention to that disgusting nest on your head before you go meet your fanboy."

The door slammed behind Felix, and I spun to take a look at myself in the reflection of the convection oven.

"Holy sweet Moses," I said aloud. My hair was still just past my shoulders, still rimrod straight, and still dark brown and in bad need of highlights. But the *scope*. The *size*. The *breadth*. Had I been drinking heavily? Sleeping under bridges? Avoiding vitamin D? My arm plunged, elbow-deep, into my bag to retrieve a brush, a comb, a rake—anything to make sense of my tangled mop. *I should never have sat down*, I thought. "One should never sit down and let one's sixty-five-pound head drop into one's arms until one is home and in bed."

Carlo came to stand in front of me and put two beefy hands on my shoulders.

He shook. "You're talking to yourself. Crazy people talk to themselves, and you are not yet crazy."

I silenced.

"This is the exhaustion speaking," he said in his best Montessori teacher voice. "Comb the hair, do something girly to your face, and get out there. Just because Felix usually handles the fans doesn't mean you can't do it, too. The dude just liked his dessert. He's not going to propose marriage."

A sudden pierce of a laugh escaped me. "No danger there!" My arms felt weak as I pulled the nest into a neat bun and coaxed every stray hair into place. I looked at Carlo hopefully.

"Much better." He pulled on his coat. "I'll see you tomorrow, Garrett. Soak up the praise." He started out the door but stopped, his foot propping it open and letting in a chilly spring wind. "And don't do that *thing* you do. It's so annoying."

I made a face. "What? What thing?"

"Where you tell people how many times you had to change cacao producers and the differences between American and European butter and why measuring cups are the spawn of Hades."

"Those are all very, very intriguing topics of conversation, Carlo. Maybe you need to get out of your area of the kitchen more often and—"

"'Night!" He shouted and let the door slam behind him.

I huffed, patted the back of my hair, straightened the cuffs on my chef's whites, and pushed through the door to the dining room. Waiting for my eyes to adjust to the low light, I scanned the empty tables, all of them fresh, pressed, and set for the first service the following evening. Richard passed me on his way through the kitchen door. He carried a small mountain of crisp white napkins and peeked around the pile to catch my eye. He nodded discreetly at a table along the orchid wall. I squinted as I approached, finding something familiar about the man but not quite settling on it until I remembered my conversation with Manda that morning.

"Avery Malachowski." I offered my hand as I came to stand at his table.

"Charlie," he said with a full-wattage smile. I remembered him telling me his dad was a dentist in Ohio and how, if I wanted, he could score free bleaching trays for me any time. He pulled me into a bear hug, and I hastily ran my tongue over my teeth, searching for a miscellaneous almond skin or rhubarb thread. My dad was an accountant.

He continued to hold me, my rumpled whites pressing against an Italian suit and starched dress shirt. His hair was neatly trimmed, his neck warm against my cheek.

Avery stepped back, hands still around my waist, and appraised me. "You look fantastic," he said, his tone suddenly hushed. With a roguish grin, he added, "Even better than I remember. And I remember it all."

I felt my face get hot as a nervous laugh escaped me. "Yes, well, it's been a long time. Nine years or so?" I pulled away but not before patting his forearm as if I were his geriatric nurse and off to get an afghan. *Social skills! Social skills!* I reprimanded myself. *Pretend you remember how to talk to men! Pretend your best friend isn't your Hobart industrial mixer!*

Avery motioned to the open seat but paused to check his hair in a mirrored wall behind me. I narrowed my eyes, remembering suddenly this exact image of Avery admiring himself. I cleared my throat, and he snapped to attention once more. "Please sit. Do you have a moment?"

"No. I mean, yes. I do have a moment. But I shouldn't sit down." I gestured to my whites, then to the high-backed chair covered in navy blue Ukrainian linen. Alain had just started letting the staff sit on the chairs during family meals, but only because we were still clean at that time of day.

"Oh, come on," Avery said. "Just for a few minutes. With an old friend."

His eyes were still remarkably blue and remarkably persuasive. I considered, then unfolded a napkin from a nearby table and smoothed it over the chair. I sat gingerly, hoping no butter crumbs had adhered themselves to my butt and were now melting into Alain's precious fabric.

"How are you?" Avery said brightly. "Things are good, right? You look like you're doing just what you said you would." He swept the room with one open arm.

"I'm doing well, thanks." I nodded in time with my words. "I've been here at L'Ombre for five years now. I've learned a lot."

Avery rolled his eyes. "You've *crushed* it, Charlie. I read *Savor*. Congrats on the great press."

"Thanks," I said, sitting straighter. "It was nice to get that kind of affirmation after all the work."

"I totally hear you." He nodded, suddenly solemn. "This business does not suffer fools. It can thrash a person's soul, you know?" He searched my eyes with his, and I nodded, though any self-respecting New Yorker did not talk about souls and thrashing in the context of one's career. This man had definitely been living in Southern California.

"And listen," he said, pointing to where his plate had rested during the meal, "that puff pastry box filled with chocolate truffles and orange zest kicked my *ass*."

"Fantastic," I said, feeling a bit like a culinary student again, anxious for the full-throttled approval of her peers. "I struggled a bit with rolling the pastry for that recipe. You know, the humidity in spring is so inconsistent, and the moisture content of butter can be—"

Avery took my hand. "You have beautiful skin. And your eyes are absolutely fantastic. They really pop." He squeezed my hand on *pop*.

I stared, mouth open. "Thank you." It was all flooding back now, the reasons we hadn't worked out a decade ago: the flirting with other women, the inability to stay focused on any conversational topic that veered away from Avery himself, the time near the end when he missed a lunch date because he lost track of time at the self-tanner. Right. Manda would be bummed, but I was tired and this was going nowhere.

"I should go." I stood so abruptly, I hit my thigh on the edge of the table. Gritting my teeth against the bruise that was surely purpling, I winced. "Thanks for coming by, Avery. It's great to connect."

"Wait! Don't go!" Avery pulled on my hand with both of his. His eyes were big and intent on my face. "We have to talk. I need to ask you a very important question."

I looked around, relieved to find the dining room empty. *What's with Mr. Intense*, I wondered? I mean, if he wanted to ask me out, that was fine. I'd say no, but there was still no need to get hysterical. Avery tugged me gently toward my chair.

"Charlie," he began and then paused to fiddle with the open buttons on his shirt. "Charlie, I'm so, so glad I came by."

"Right," I said slowly. *We've covered this.*

"What I've seen, what I've tasted, how you look," he said, his glance taking in my face, "well. You're everything I was hoping to find."

I felt my eyes bug a little. "I am?"

"Yes. Charlie, I want to propose something to you."

"You do?" My voice had gone squeaky.

"Yes." Avery's jaw tightened, and his eyes shot Lasix-corrected laser beams into mine. "Charlie Garrett, I think you should quit your job and come work for me."

I opened and closed my mouth like one of the tuna Carlo had filleted a few hours prior.

"Now, before you shoot me down," Avery continued, one manicured hand held up in warning, "let me tell you why I'm right. First, you're sick of New York. Am I right?"

"Well, I don't—"

"You are. The nasty, urine smell on the subway, the constant noise even in your 'quiet' apartment, the pathetic lack of trees and grass—"

"We do have Central Park—"

"No. No, you don't, Charlie. You *think* the park belongs to all New Yorkers, but that's only if you go between the daylight hours of ten and six and you bring pepper spray."

He had a point.

"Second, you are sick of *this restaurant.*"

"Avery, I'm doing very well at L'Ombre."

"Ah!" He pointed at my nose, and I moved back an inch. "Notice you did not deny hating it here! I know you are doing well, but if you're honest, Charlie, and I hope you will be honest . . . " He lowered his voice and leaned toward me. "Felix is never going to retire. Or at least he won't before you're forty years old, maybe forty-five, and then, honestly, will you even want his job anymore?"

"How do you know about Felix?" I asked, feeling at once very provincial and very exposed.

Avery shrugged. "I've done my research. Third and most important," he ticked the number off on his hand, "you want a life. You need a life. You're here too much, Charlie. You work, what? Fourteen-, fifteen-hour shifts? Six days a week?"

I pursed my lips and refrained from commenting. The guy hadn't laid eyes on me for almost a decade, and suddenly he was my life coach?

"You have no life. You have no friends. You haven't had a date for two full years, Charlie."

"What kind of research do you do? Who are your sources?" I sat tall on that Ukrainian linen. "I *do* have friends and I *do* have a life. And, I might add, I'm a little bit offended by your comments!" I was trying to stand my ground, but my protests sounded pathetic, even to me.

"Look, I'm sure you do have friends and a wildly active social life." Avery's eye twinkled. "But, you have to admit, it's tough to see any of those friends when you work all the time." He moved forward in his chair so our knees were touching. "I'm the executive chef of a new restaurant in Seattle. I need a young, vibrant, inspired pastry chef at Thrill, and I. Want. You." He used one tan finger to Punctuate. His. Words.

We were quiet a moment. I could hear the insistent hum of traffic beyond the front door, and I was aware of a silenced vacuum cleaner, the final note of a maintenance crew that obviously wanted to close up for the night. After a pause, I cleared my throat.

"Avery, I'm flattered by your proposal."

"Good. You deserve to be flattered. You are completely undervalued here, Charlie. It's time you get the recognition and the responsibility you have earned. You should be head pastry chef, and you know it."

To my horror, I felt myself grow teary. Felix had never said such nice things to me. Felix thought I was *over*valued, that the *Savor* piece had been a fluke and that I had more years to put in before I worked my way out of the hole he had neatly dug for me. I hated to admit that Avery was right—I had been in indentured servitude for far too long.

But move? To Seattle?

I sobered. "Thank you for the kind words, Avery, but I have no interest in moving. Manhattan is the place I want to be and need to be. Seattle is out of the question."

"Why?" Avery demanded. "Your bestie, Manda, lives in Seattle, right?"

"Yes, but—"

"Mountains, oceans, fresh air, outdoor markets, hiking, skiing, culture, relaxed vibe, Starbucks . . . what's not to love?"

"Well, actually, Starbucks's bakery selections are abysmal and—"

"Charlie, you'll love the Pacific Northwest. All people who are smart and creative and driven *love* the Pacific Northwest. It's a law of the universe. Obey the law and come work for me. Here's the salary I can offer you to start. As the restaurant grows, this number goes up."

He scribbled a number on the back of a business card and slid it across the table. My breath caught in my throat, and I must have stopped breathing for a second because I began to cough.

Avery laughed as he stood. He slapped me on the back twice and said, "Now, *that's* the kind of reaction I was hoping for." His phone vibrated, and he slid a finger across the screen. "Vic, hi. Yes. She's here." He looked at me while I used the edge of a napkin to blot my eyes. "She's totally in. I'll call you back in a minute."

"Who was that?" I sipped some of Avery's water and tried regaining my sense of decorum.

"A friend. You'll meet him when you get out to Seattle." He leaned down and kissed me on the cheek.

"I'm not moving to Seattle," I said, tucking the business card into my pocket. I moved to stand, but Avery blocked my exit from the table.

He tucked one wayward strand of my hair behind my ear and then whispered, his lips brushing my earlobe. "I don't know if you remember this about me, but I'm used to getting what I want."

A parade of shivers marched down my spine. I sat very still as he walked away. When the front door closed behind him, I waited in the quiet and the dark, watching with wide eyes as the light shifted and the night fell.

4

A bone-shaking clap of thunder split the sky just as I emerged from underground. The man in front of me on the subway stairs screeched like a twelve-year-old girl and then cussed like a sailor at the sudden thunderstorm. And then he cussed at me because I accidentally jostled him from behind.

"Sorry," I muttered as I left him fumbling for a newspaper, presumably to protect his elaborate pompadour. Another rumble of thunder sent me and hundreds of morning commuters rushing along the sidewalk. I'd slept through three snooze cycles of my alarm and had missed the last express train that would have gotten me to work almost on time. Felix was going to be apoplectic.

I sidestepped a black puddle that looked as though it contained curdled milk and kept my nose pointed toward the pavement. I wore my backpack in front of me, tucked underneath my raincoat like a lumpy baby bump. I tightened the strings on the hood of my raincoat. Sadly, my umbrella sat neatly rolled and dry on my kitchen counter, another casualty of the morning.

Every mishap this morning could be attributed to Avery Malachowski. Our conversation last night had rattled me. I was in a foul mood as I walked to L'Ombre in the rain. I splashed through a small creek I'd never seen before on Broadway and remembered how certain I had been of a good night's sleep when I'd finally dragged my aching body through the door of my apartment the night before. I had barely stayed awake through all five steps of my skin care regimen. I'd scrubbed and exfoliated, cleansed and moisturized, and had nearly fallen asleep to the hum of my electronic toothbrush. Lights off and pajamas on, I'd climbed between the sheets, closed my eyes, and waited for deep slumber to descend.

And it had refused to come.

Instead, my head spun while all the things Avery had said looped on permanent repeat. Did I really hate New York? Was I sick of the traffic, the congestion, the noise? Or worse, had I gotten so used to the urine smell I didn't even notice it anymore? Was all this *my new normal*? The thought made me shudder. After an hour of rotating onto my side, onto my stomach, my side, my back, I was nearly hysterical. I felt like a rotisserie chicken. I could not sleep, and it wasn't only Avery's offer that had brought on insomnia. I also couldn't sleep because it was louder than a rock concert in my apartment. Clearly the new neighbors had a unique circadian cycle. I had never noticed it before now, but my entire apartment was in desperate need of soundproofing. We're talking big, fluffy foam strips on the walls and ceilings, like the ones in fancy recording studios. *How much did Coldplay pay for theirs?* I found myself worrying about these things around 4 a.m. and decided I would research foam and custom-made earplugs and white noise machines the very next day. As soon as I got a little sleep . . .

I sighed as the restaurant came into view. When I trudged up the back stairs and heaved open the kitchen door to L'Ombre, a sheet of rain followed me in.

"Hey, watch the drips!" Iveta, a bus girl, stood with one hand on her hip, the other balancing a mop. "I just finished this floor."

"Sorry," I said, aware that I'd said two words aloud that day and they had both been apologies. My rain boots squeaked on Iveta's clean floor as I hustled to the locker room. I hurried to hang up my coat, slipped into my clogs, smoothed my hair under a fresh chef's cap. Felix was nowhere in sight, and I breathed a cautious sigh of relief. *Maybe he's late, too*, I thought, hope welling within me. I was tying on my apron, walking to the fridge to start on the strawberry-champagne mousse, when I felt Felix tap me, hard, on my right shoulder.

"Nice of you to arrive at your place of employment today, Garrett," he said. His voice was gravelly, and I could hear the disdain in his words. "You will never run a kitchen on your own. You are too sloppy and too disorganized and too irresponsible."

I took a deep breath, bit the inside of my cheek. Arms full with a large bin of strawberries, I set the load down gently on one of the countertops I had scrubbed to perfection the evening before. *Sloppy? Disorganized? Irresponsible?* I tasted blood and stopped biting my cheek. *Head down, just do the work*, I told myself, shaking with blind fury.

"Garrett, did you hear what I said?" Felix was close enough to my face that I could feel the heat of his breath on my cheek. "In this kitchen, I require respect. I need a 'Yes, Chef.'"

"Yes, Chef," I said, my voice barely above a whisper.

"Louder!" he yelled.

I caught Carlo's eye from across the kitchen. Concern flickered in his gaze.

"Yes, Chef," I said, my voice unsteady but louder.

Felix mumbled to himself as he walked away. I was sure there was a nice peppering of French expletives in there, but I kept my eyes on the work of prepping the mousse. While the gelatin softened in a bath of champagne vinegar, I whisked egg whites and sugar to high, stiff peaks. *Irresponsible? Sloppy?* A teaspoon or so of egg white sprayed onto the backsplash, and I was nearly manic in my attack of the mess.

I'd folded the egg whites into the strawberry purée, incorporated the whipped cream, and was carefully spreading the mixture into twelve waiting pecan crusts when Felix reemerged from whatever vermin's hole he'd been inhabiting. I didn't look up from my work, just trained my eyes on the soft pink mounds of mousse, thinking words like *uniformity* and *precision* and *true revenge would equal prison time.*

I sure wasn't going to turn around and look, but it sounded as though Felix was getting started on some prep work, perhaps portioning the gold leaf or garnishing the first few rhubarb tarts. He was quiet, anyway, and when I'd filled the final crust, I straightened, feeling my spine resettle into an upright position. I picked up the baking sheet, nice and easy so as not to upset the perfectly formed crusts and quivering mousse, and I turned slowly to go to the fridge, but the tip of the tray bumped into Felix's girth. He had appeared out of nowhere.

He looked down his nose and over his glasses at the desserts.

I lifted my chin, daring him to say anything about the beauties before him.

To my horror, he stuck one fat finger right into the center of one crust. The finger emerged, cloaked in strawberry mousse, and then made its way to Felix's mouth. He rolled the filling around his mouth and then pursed his lips before spitting it out onto the floor.

"Needs more sugar," he said in a disconcertingly serene voice. Only his eyes betrayed his spite. "Do them all again." He wiped his finger on a clean towel and nodded to the puddle of his spit on the floor. "And clean that up."

Little stars floated at the edge of my vision, and I made a concerted effort to keep breathing. Felix was watching me with a bemused expression, and I saw Alain approach from the periphery, his countenance serious. I let my chin drop to look at the beautiful, photograph-worthy tarts I held before me. I looked up again, my eyes searching Alain's face, waiting for him to come to my defense, shred Felix for his behavior, say *anything*.

He set his mouth into a thin, straight line.

And he said nothing.

One by one, I released all ten of my fingers and watched a ribbon of pale mousse and silver metal go clattering to the floor. A wide arc of pink sprayed upward, but one tart remained pristine. From some part of my brain, I could hear Felix shouting about the mess on his shoes, but I told that part of my brain to just pipe down for a minute. I had one more thing to do. I crouched to the floor, cradled the only remaining, perfect tart, unfolded myself to my full height, and smiled at Felix.

"I quit," I said, pushing the tart into Felix's face, giving one extra turn of my wrist into his nose before the empty tart pan clattered to the floor.

Carlo and Danny were whooping it up around the corner while I shivered into my still-damp coat. I walked on unsteady legs to the back of the kitchen and stepped around Alain.

"Charlie," he said.

I shook my head once, hard. "Too late," I said and kept walking, pausing only to push open the door and venture back into the rain.

Halfway down the block, I noticed a smear of mousse sheltered on the inside of my thumb. I licked it off and shook my head.

Delicious.

And it most certainly did *not* need more sugar.

I slept the better part of two days after the Tart Incident. I have never loved Egyptian cotton like I loved it for those forty-eight hours. A few times, I stumbled to the kitchen and forced myself to eat a dollop of Greek yogurt or a slice of whole wheat toast, but my heart wasn't in it, so I just trudged back to my little slice of five-hundred-count heaven and went back to sleep. After two days of this, I lay in bed, willing my eyes to stay shut but feeling them pop open anyway. The Chihuahua said it was just after noon.

Sitting up on the side of my bed, I felt light-headed and ridiculously well rested. Was this how normal people began a day? Without the pounding headache and the feeling like one was swimming through molasses on the way to the coffee pot? I picked up my phone from the nightstand and turned it on for the first time since I'd given Felix's face a mousse mask.

I shoved a tart in Felix's face. Oh, dear Lord in heaven, what had I done? I swallowed hard and felt my pulse quicken. What had I been thinking? The weight of my five seconds of glorious retribution weighed heavily on me, and I let myself fall back again onto the bed.

I was unemployed. My rent was due in five days. I had made an enemy of a world-renowned pastry chef who held the keys to any recommendation for my next job.

My phone also awoke after a forty-eight-hour slumber, and I jumped when it began vibrating with a string of unread text messages. There were a few from Carlo, with sentiments like "You WHAAAAT?!" and "WHO'S FELIX'S DADDY?" I scrolled through two from my mother that read more like epistles, detailing a debacle with a failed sump pump and wet carpet in the basement. After checking twice to be sure, there was not one message from Alain, the jerk. Five years of my life devoted to his restaurant, and he didn't have the decency to come to my aid, or at least offer a fond farewell. Or a severance package. Or a boot for Felix's ample rear.

Just as I pulled up Manda's number and was about to make the call to begin my pity party in earnest, my door buzzer sounded. I scrambled out of bed and threw a sweatshirt and jeans over my sleep shirt. Raking fingers through my hair as I walked, I reached the door and peered through the peephole. A man I didn't recognize was holding a bulky package. The words on his cap read ABE'S MESSENGER SERVICE.

I unlocked the two deadbolts and undid the chain.

"Can I help you?" I said through the narrow slit that separated us.

"Delivery for a Mr. Charlie Garrett. Does he live here?" The man turned out to be a boy of maybe eighteen with a peppering of blackheads on his nose. He squinted through the opening in the door.

"I do," I said. "I mean, I am. I am Charlie Garrett. It's a Ms., not a Mr."

The kid considered this information and appeared to come to peace with it. "All right. I'll go with that," he said. He produced a phone and tapped in some numbers, then held it up to me through the crack in the door. "You have to talk to this dude first. Says here I can't give you the delivery until you talk to him. I'll put you on speaker."

I took the phone, confusion registering on my face. "Hello?" I said into the phone just as Avery Malachowski answered.

"Charlie! Sweet. Okay, tell the delivery guy you are cleared for Package One."

The kid could hear Avery's booming voice through the phone's speaker, so without waiting for a sign from me, he gestured for me to open the door, which I did. Then he handed me a tailored-looking white box tied with an orange and white polka-dot ribbon. I tugged at the ribbon and shimmied the top off the box. A beautiful strawberry mousse tart with a pecan crust was artfully nestled in yards of tissue paper. I couldn't help but laugh.

"How do you know about this?" I shook my head and pulled the tart box inside my apartment, aware that my stomach was rumbling with neglect.

"Oh, Danny the line cook and I go way back."

"You do?" I was incredulous. Danny and Avery?

"Nah, actually we don't. But a hundred bucks can buy a spy and a phone call when a certain pastry chef goes apeshit and gives her psycho boss a pie in the face."

"It was a tart. And I'm not apeshit."

"Of course you're not. Though you do have your quirks, as I remember. Package Two, delivery man," Avery said, still on speaker phone.

The kid produced a bigger box, wrapped in white and again tied with the orange polka-dot ribbon. I slipped a finger under the paper and unfolded one side without ripping. I must have been taking too long, because the delivery kid sighed and Avery said, "A little faster, Garrett. Not all of us are out of work."

The contents of Package Two made me giggle like the school girl I'd been when I'd first seen it.

"I can't believe you remembered this," I said, blushing at his thoughtfulness.

"The MegaPro Dynamic Action Label Maker with extra labeling tape. Remember how you used to drag me to office supplies stores and salivate over the organization sections? You are a weirdo, Charlie. But I thought the MegaPro might come in handy, Package Three, please."

The delivery boy was starting to look a little scared of me. Could have been the hair. Could have been the two days' worth of morning breath. Could have been my unfettered joy at opening a label maker (high speed and with a touch screen!).

I had to crack the door wider for the last package. It was tall, narrow, and awkward, and when I pulled down the brown packing paper, I saw a hefty shrink-wrapped bundle of moving boxes.

I stared, worrying my lower lip with my teeth, until the delivery boy spoke.

"SHE'S GONE MUTE, SIR." He spoke inappropriately loudly into the phone. "WHAT DO YOU WANT ME TO DO NOW?"

"Charlie," Avery said, "it's time for a fresh start. Fill those boxes, call a moving company, and send me the bill. Just get out of there."

"Avery, I'm flattered, but—"

"Oh, sorry! What was that? Hesitation? Reluctance? You've got to be kidding me!" I could picture Avery stomping around wherever he was, gesticulating with his hands. "There are no roadblocks here, Charlie. Only fear of the unknown, which, as I remember, used to be something we were excited about ten years ago. Remember?"

The delivery boy watched me. "SHE'S NODDING. SHE REMEMBERS."

35

"All right," I said, finding my voice underneath a healthy layer of inde-cision and worry. "I'm coming." I eased the moving boxes through the door. "Give me two weeks to wrap things up around here."

Avery whooped. "I'll give you one," he said, and I could imagine the victory in his grin. "One week, Charlie. We need our pastries out here, and you are the girl to do it."

"SHE IS SMILING," the boy shouted into the speaker. "MISSION TOTALLY ACCOMPLISHED. BUT SHE DIDN'T TIP ME," he called, seeing me turn away from the door.

I held a twenty through the door and saw his face light up.

"Thanks, miss. And bon voyage, or whatever."

Exactly, I thought as I let the door shut behind me. It was the *whatever* that might prove to be interesting.

5

As I descended the escalator into baggage claim at Seattle-Tacoma International, I saw Manda's orb of auburn curls before I could see her face. Her wild hair, her nemesis and the subject of many a late-night cry-it-out in junior high, had developed into a stunning and bountiful crop of shine and body in adulthood. The curls bounced and quivered along with baby Polly on her hip, and then she caught my eye.

"Woo hoo!" she squealed, much too loudly for my taste, as everyone within the vicinity began to seek out the woman at the end of Zara's pointing finger. When I reached the bottom step, Manda pulled me to her, both of us tripping over each other and the stroller lodged between us.

"You look fantastic!" Manda said, checking me out from north to south. Typically this kind of behavior would have made me painfully self-conscious, but Manda had been the person who stuck her nose into my armpit in seventh grade to verify that, yes, there was finally a hair growing in there. She was also the one to reassure me that I was absolutely, positively going to get my period before I graduated high school. She was correct on both counts, so the appraisal felt completely natural and safe.

"Thanks. You, too," I said, noting that underneath the graphic tee and jeans, Manda had reclaimed the pretty curves three pregnancies had distorted. I leaned over to kiss a babbling Polly and was struck by two things:

how soft her little cheek felt on my skin and how big she'd grown since the last time I'd visited. I stepped back quickly and ducked my head under the stroller umbrella to deposit a kiss on a sleeping Dane's forehead. His mouth was agape and long eyelashes feathered out above his smooth toddler cheeks, but he still gripped what was left of a slobbered-up granola bar in his pudgy hand.

"You're here, Auntie Charlie!" Five-year-old Zara buried her face into my hip until I crouched down and hugged her full on. Her hair smelled like lavender and vanilla, and I inhaled deeply.

"I'm here. Is that okay?" I pulled away to look into her face. "Can you share Seattle with me?"

"Certainly," she answered in a voice that reminded me of her attorney dad, Jack. "And you can sleep in my bed. It has Barbie sheets."

I raised an eyebrow at Manda, the former president of Edenton High School's Feminists for Change. "I love Barbie," I said to Zara and meant it.

Manda frowned as she herded our little group toward the baggage carrousel. "Jack's mother," she said in a low voice as we walked. "She sent not one but *three* Barbies for Christmas, *and* the pink house, *and* the damn convertible. I was completely ambushed." She looked around as though making sure no one was eavesdropping. "And then Zara started begging for the matching bedsheets for her birthday. I had to order them online. No self-respecting store in Seattle sells Barbie sheets, for the love of Pete. And I surely didn't want to have to go to Walmart. Might as well join the NRA."

I decided there was no emergent need to mention I'd looked into classes at the Westside Rifle and Pistol Range after the night Danny got slashed by Felix's favorite knife. Or that all the kids' presents I'd tucked into my luggage had come with free shipping from the thrifty folks at walmart.com. Instead, I hugged her around her waist as I walked, leaning down a bit in my heels. "I'm so happy to see you, and I won't judge you just because your daughter loves Barbie."

"I'm happy to see you, too." She grinned at me. "And before you know it," she pointed to my feet, "you'll forget all about crazy ideas like heels and black tailored jackets, and you'll feel comfortable in your own skin again."

I rolled my eyes. "I'm totally comfortable. These shoes have been begging to be worn since the day I purchased them four years ago." I reached down to smooth away a streak of dust that I'd missed and, in the process, nearly fell to my death.

Manda steadied me with one hand while maintaining a secure grip on Polly and stopping Dane's stroller with one foot. "You seem very controlled. And chic. And like you might break your ankle at any second."

"I love your pretty shoes, Auntie Char," Zara said, her nose near my new pedicure. "My Barbie has pretty shoes just like these."

"Have mercy," Manda muttered.

I spotted my red suitcase bumping down the conveyor belt and tottered forward to retrieve it, stumbling a bit to get past the wheels on Manda's double stroller. I hefted the bag up and off the carrousel and tugged it back to Manda and her entourage, concentrating fully on walking, not shuffling.

Manda looked triumphant. "Birkenstocks before the week's end!" she declared, and I sighed. While a pair of cork-bottomed soles did sound pretty glorious right then, I wasn't quite ready to go all earthy just because I was on the west coast. Somebody had to wear heels, and it might as well be me and Barbie.

We made our way to the car and onto the freeway before Manda began her pointed questioning, machine-gun style.

"How did you do this so fast? Are you exhausted? Are you nervous? What is Avery saying? What is your *mother* saying? Is she thrilled to have you out of Godless Gotham, or is she depressed you just flew over Minnesota without stopping? Hold on." She put a hand out to stop me before I could respond. "Zara Rose Henrick, you keep your hands to yourself. No poking your brother with colored pencils. I do not want Dane waking up yet. You know how cranky he is when he gets up before he should."

"But I'm boooooored," Zara said in an impressively anguished voice.

"Only boring people get bored," Manda responded cheerily. "Plus, I don't speak Whinese, so you'll need to choose a different tone of voice."

Zara didn't appear to want to dignify that statement with a reply, so Manda returned to our conversation. "Tell me everything. And maybe quickly because Polly is going to need to breast-feed soon. I'm hoping we can get to your apartment before she wigs out, but there's no insurance policy on that idea."

"Well," I said, with the shrug I had employed often throughout the last week, "Avery took care of everything. He got me out of my lease, he hired a moving company, he even found me the apartment here. I'm still in shock. I'm not used to making decisions so quickly."

Manda snorted. "Oh, really? Perhaps you are forgetting that I am the friend who waited with great patience while you deliberated *for forty-seven minutes* about whether to buy cherry red or cherry-*berry* red lip gloss for your first skating party in junior high."

"That was so fun!" I remembered. "We should go shopping again now that we're in the same city."

With one eye on the traffic and one eye on the rearview mirror, she said, "Fun? You thought that was *fun?*" She shook her head. "I love you. But it's never going to happen. These days, I'm lucky if I can get out of a store with only one or two of us in tears."

Polly began fussing, and Manda raised an eyebrow at me as if to say, "See what I mean?" She groped under her seat and came up with a Mason jar packed with pacifiers. She plucked one from the top of the heap. Contorting her arm into a pose any yogi would admire, she fumbled for Polly's mouth until she heard an appreciative suck. "Tell me about the apartment. Belltown is infinitely hipper and more chichi than I have ever been. I can't wait to see it. How did the photos look?" She signaled to pull off the freeway, and we merged into a pretty neighborhood with mature trees showing off the tender green of new spring leaves.

"He wouldn't send me any photos," I said, craning my neck to find a street number on one of the buildings. "Said he wanted to surprise me."

"Unbelievable." Manda shook her head. "I don't remember Avery Malachowski being such a romantic when you dated him. Or such a big spender, what with all the moving trucks and special deliveries. Jack and I drove by his new restaurant, and it looks swank-o. Very posh." She hit the steering wheel with her fist, appearing to tumble upon a distant memory. "Wait. Wasn't he the one who would divide the gas tab evenly down to the last cent?"

"Oh, wow. He was," I said, remembering ranting to Manda about that very issue right before Avery and I broke up. "I guess he's changed."

"Um, for the better." Manda's voice was awe-filled as we pulled up to the address I'd given her.

The building looked like brand-new construction, though that might have been the glass talking. Twenty stories, I guessed, and all sides of the building shimmered with reflections of the clouds and blue skies above us. I pushed open the passenger door and let my gaze travel over my new home.

I could glimpse the insides of a few apartments on the lower floors. Modern furnishings, lots of stainless steel, platinum finishes, colorful, abstract art against white walls.

Manda came to stand by me and handed off Zara's tugging hand.

"Can we go in, Aunt Charlie? Please? Can we go into your new mansion?"

My laugh sounded tinny and nervous. "For sure. Avery said the concierge would have my key."

"Oh, to have a concierge!" Manda moaned. "I need one of those so badly. And a cook. And a nanny. And a masseuse."

"How much do you think this place goes for?" I lowered my voice as we approached the front doors, Zara pulling us ahead. Manda pushed the stroller with a newly awake and irritated Dane and a hollering Polly.

"The real question is, when do you have to start picking up the tab?"

I held the door for Manda and the screamers and took a deep breath of the white tea fragrance that floated out from the foyer. "He said the first six months were on him. Until I feel completely settled."

Manda shook her head. "Love it and live it up, girl. Tomorrow has enough troubles of its own."

The concierge rose from his chair at an elongated desk. Two striking arrangements of cherry blossom branches arched upward from each corner of his workspace.

"Welcome," he said, nodding slowly. His trim goatee, clean-shaven head, and meticulous bow tie suggested two screaming little people and another punching the elevator buttons without pause might not be his typical social situation. "Ms. Garrett?"

I thought I saw a flicker of relief in his eyes when I reached out to shake his hand instead of Manda, who was starting to fumble for the clasp on her nursing bra.

"We are pleased to welcome you to Silverside Lofts. My name is Omar, and I am the head concierge at your service. Please do not hesitate to contact me with any questions, concerns, or needs."

"I'm Manda," she said, introducing herself and jostling Polly at the same time. "I'm Charlie's best friend. And I really, really, really appreciate all you do. Do you freelance?"

Manda was grinning, but Omar looked a little nervous. I took the key from his outstretched hand. "Thank you for the warm welcome, Omar." I looked toward the elevators, where Zara was now spinning cartwheels and singing a song from *Frozen*. "Can you tell me which apartment number is mine?"

"Of course, Ms. Garrett. You have the penthouse apartment. Our top floor, the twenty-fifth. Your key will also access the fitness center, the executive lounge, and the rooftop terrace. But perhaps the executive tour should wait for another time when you are a bit more, ahem, settled in?" Omar's eyes bounced from Dane's five-alarm tantrum to Zara's Idina Menzel imitation to Manda's muttering at her tangled bra strap. Omar was not built for this moment.

"Sounds great," I said, already striding toward the elevator. "Thank you," I called over my shoulder before pointing to the up button for Zara. After a stomach-dropping, rapid ascent, the elevator chimed for the top floor, and we stepped directly into the apartment.

"Holy catfish!" Zara squealed and took off at a run.

I let my bags drop with a thud onto the polished marble floor. Vaulted ceilings and walls of windows made me feel as if I was perched eye-level with Mount Rainier, which presided like a snowy watchman in the distance. A clear day in Seattle was money, and I felt like the girl with the Midas touch. I walked to a far window, past a gleaming kitchen with not one but two Dacor ovens, thank you very much, past a long, kitten-soft gray sectional, past a flat screen television that was sure to catch every nuance of Colin Firth's face when I curled up with him and *Pride and Prejudice* later that night. I kicked off the infernal high heels and stood before the window. A southern view of the city lay before me—water, sky, the Space Needle, Puget Sound—and I felt the exhaustion and worry seep out of my shoulders. *I did it,* I thought. *It might be crazy and I have to unpack and make lists and stock my kitchen and find Avery's restaurant and make supply lists and develop a menu and get to know my staff. . .* I sighed. *But I did it. And the view sure is lovely from up here.*

"I'm moving in." Manda's voice tugged me out of my reverie.

I turned and saw her curled in the corner of the sectional, Polly's little fist clutching the top of her shirt while she ate. Dane was sitting at one of the barstools by the kitchen counter, sucking applesauce out of some sort of vacuum pack and looking a bit less hostile.

"I'm moving in and leaving the kids with Jack."

"Mommy!" Zara rounded the corner, looking offended. "You can't leave us with Dad. He doesn't know how to braid!"

"You'll adjust," Manda said. "Braiding isn't that hard."

Zara narrowed her eyes for a moment until her face relaxed into a toothy grin. "You're joking, Mom. You won't leave us with Daddy. He's *tried* braiding, and he's super bad at it." She skipped back down the hallway to what looked like the master bedroom, outfitted with a tall, narrow mirror perfect for aspiring vocalists.

I lowered myself onto the couch, smoothing the fabric slowly with my hand, lining up my heels on the dense area rug. Closing my eyes and letting my head fall back on the cushion, I heard Manda thump Polly's back to burp her.

"You made it," Manda said. I could hear the smile in her voice without looking at her face. I knew she wasn't just talking about a cross-country move.

I felt a smile pulling at my lips. "Let the adventure begin."

6

I was starting to sense a theme. Since the last time I had seen him, Avery had made the leap from "cheapskate" to "indulgence king," and I wondered if he had had professional help to make the transition. Thrill's interior actually made me gasp when I entered the restaurant the next afternoon. I'd been up to my eyeballs in boxes, packing tape, and shopping lists, so by the time I entered the front of the house at Thrill, I was a walking, breathing target market for one of their famous *mojitos*. Omar had already recommended them to me twice.

The walls of the restaurant were inlaid with hundreds of planks of polished knotted wood, running the length of the dining room and only interrupted once by an enormous rectangular window. The paint colors were variants of white, and the floor was some kind of charcoal, veined slate. A long fireplace filled the better part of one wall. A tidy gas flame danced behind glass and bounced firelight off a sleek wood mantle. The low-lit chandeliers dotting the room gave off prisms of sparkle and glam. Tables were set for the evening, but I was alone in the room.

I picked up a menu, feeling the weight of the heavy cardstock, russet with faint white polka dots of different sizes sprinkled behind the white text. The savory menu made my mouth water with its emphasis on local seafood and innovative preparations of Northwest produce. The options for dessert, however, were yawnworthy. My mouth straightened into a line, and I stood taller. I could do better. I *would* do better.

Avery burst through the kitchen door, his shoulder cradling his cell phone, hands gesticulating wildly.

"We have gone over this before, Margot," he was saying. "Either you trust me or you don't. I need two weeks, and I'm not budging on that." He seemed surprised to see me, but he quickly recovered and came toward me with open arms. "Listen, I must run. We'll talk soon."

Phone still in his hand, he pulled me in for a hug. "You're here! What do you think?" He brandished a tanned forearm, gesturing to the restaurant.

"It's stunning," I said. "I love it." Members of the waitstaff were beginning to filter into the dining room in a wash of black shirts, black skinny ties, and black trousers. Some were tying on long black aprons with THRILL printed down one side in crisp white lettering.

"Come meet everyone. We've just finished eating and are about to start the preservice run-down." He slung an arm around my shoulder, and we walked somewhat awkwardly toward the group. They'd gathered by the picture window that overlooked a secluded, brick-paved courtyard on the cusp of a raucous springtime bloom. A flowering cherry tree stood in the middle of the space, knotty bark running down its trunk, its roots bumping up the brick pathway. Tiny purple flowers lined the branches heralding the shift toward warmth and longer days.

"What a tree," I said.

Avery waved at a tall, slender man with rimless glasses on the far side of the room. "Hmm?" He glanced where I was staring. "What tree?"

I looked at him, wondering if he had become blind since we last saw each other.

"Oh, right. That tree. Nice." Avery steered me toward the skinny dude with glasses and said, "I have someone I'd like you to meet. Vic Arteaga, meet our new pastry chef, fresh from Manhattan's L'Ombre, Ms. Charlie Garrett."

Vic's hand was baby-soft, but his handshake was firm. "The famous Charlie Garrett. This man has sung your praises for a long time. Welcome."

Avery just stood there, grinning and waiting for me to, what? Whip up a soufflé or something?

"It's a pleasure to meet you," I said. Vic was turned out in a starched purple-checked button-down and a tailored dove-gray suit. His attire stood in stark contrast to a room full of people clad entirely in black. "And what is it that you do here at Thrill?"

"I'm the—" he began but was cut short by Avery.

"Vic is new, too," he said, his eyes widening a bit. "He is working in our newest department. Marketing. Marketing and communications."

"Absolutely." Vic's voice was polished, relaxed. "I'm helping Thrill move into its next phase."

I cocked my head to one side. "A 'next phase' so soon? You've only been open a few months, and you're already changing pastry chefs. Surely that's enough change for the time being?"

"Well, no," Avery said. Then, "Yes. I mean, we are stretching and changing and growing all the time, Charlie. You know, all that dog-eat-dog stuff. It's a different world with social media and branding . . ." Avery trailed off and nodded at a man who stood with hands on his ample hips in front of the group of seated servers and cooks. "Looks like we'll have to continue this discussion another time. Chet is ready to begin."

I turned my attention to Chet. He folded his hands across an impressive belly and rocked slightly in bright blue Crocs. The group quieted.

"All right, everybody. Hope you're fat and happy after that meal. Thanks, Doug and Aldo, for hooking us up. Great meatballs, right?"

A smattering of applause and whoops rose from the group. Meatballs sounded fantastic and a deliciously far cry from fussy Beef Wellington. I felt my shoulders begin to relax.

"Let's get to logistics. First, I'm exec tonight. Chef Michaels is needed elsewhere."

I leaned closer to Avery while Chet went over menu changes. "Who is Chef Michaels?" I whispered. "I thought you were exec."

Avery kept his eyes on Chet. "I am. I go by Avery Michaels now. Didn't I tell you?" He flashed The Grin at me, but I wasn't distracted this time by the upper and lower arches.

"No, you did not," I exclaimed in a whisper. "What's wrong with 'Malachowski?'"

He looked at me like I was the only kid on the bus who didn't know what *vagina* really meant. "Michaels makes far better sense for what I'm trying to do here. You get one shot for the public to remember you, and I don't want them tripping over some Polish tongue twister." He turned his attention back to Chet but added in a more gentle tone, "And don't worry about me sharing duties with Chet. I'll be on the line when you start next week. I'll make sure you have everything you need."

I turned back to Chet as he enumerated the merits of Thrill's extensive wine list. "Remember, folks, no booze, no job. We keep the lights on around here because of your efforts to sell the fine people of Seattle a lot of alcohol. A silky risotto or an inspired asparagus salad can only do so much."

"So get 'em sloshed," a petite blonde server called from the periphery of the circle, teasing conspiratorial laughter from everyone but me. I was heartily in favor of a glass of wine or two with dinner. In fact, wine could often be the perfect accompaniment to enhance the flavors of a dish. But I didn't like the idea of pushing the wine list at the expense of the food. Call me a sentimentalist, but if diners were schnockered by the time the dessert menu arrived, who was to notice if I was sending out a perfect meringue or a Rice Krispie treat?

Avery nudged me. "Get the pissy look off your face. Chet's introducing you."

I came to attention and noticed all the faces in the group had turned toward mine.

" . . . top of her class at CIA in Hyde Park, and then to a restaurant you might have heard about in New York. Chef Michaels, what was that place again?" Chet winked at Avery.

"L'Ombre," Avery supplied, nearly bursting with pride. "I'm happy to note I completely and shamelessly stole her from Alain Janvier." An appreciative murmur vibrated through the room, and Avery clapped me on the back. "I've known this woman for many years, and let me just say that she will absolutely floor you with what she can do with a little butter and sugar."

"I'll probably use a few more ingredients than that," I added. I noticed Vic approved of my comment with a smile of his own.

Avery looked like a proud papa. *How long has he been building me up around here?* I wondered. *I hope I don't disappoint . . .* He didn't appear to want to say anything more, and the room was silent and staring, so I stepped forward.

"Thank you for the very kind introduction, Chet and Avery, and for the warm welcome, everybody. I look forward to making great food with all of you, and, as a side bonus, I will happily indulge anyone who wants to dish about how your esteemed Chef Avery went through an inappropriately long phase during culinary school that involved hair gel and a nose ring."

Avery groaned when the room erupted in laughter, but I could tell he was loving it.

Chet dismissed the staff, and many of them stopped to welcome me to the team before heading to their stations. Avery was keen to introduce me to a devastatingly beautiful young woman who walked as if her sternum were tied to a helium balloon. Shiny, thick black curls bounced halfway down her back as she walked, and her wide brown eyes and olive skin made more than one head turn as she passed through the dining room. When she reached our little group, she pulled me into a bony but strong embrace.

"Oh," I said into her slender neck. "Hi. Um. Hi."

"Charlie!" she said. "Or should I say, 'Boss'? I really should. Sorry." She looked at Avery, but her expression looked more like an excited puppy than a repentant one. "I'm Tova. So great to meet you."

"Tova is your second-in-command," Avery said. I thought a look passed between the two, but Avery continued quickly with his introduction. "One day Tova will be a fantastic pastry chef herself, but she's just starting out, aren't you, Tova?"

"Absolutely." She nodded earnestly. "You have my blessing to order me around and have me do your bidding. I will not be offended." She put up her hands as if to plead guilty.

"How long have you been at Thrill?" I asked. I liked the openness of Tova's face and the fact that she seemed to have parked her ego at the door. We were a long way from chefs inflicting knife wounds here at Thrill.

"Two weeks," she said. "Just moved here from L.A. And not missing the traffic *one bit*. Can I get an amen?"

Vic said a stilted "amen," but I just laughed. I liked this girl so far and hoped her pastry skills were up to par.

"Well, we should get going," Avery said, clapping his hands as he turned to face me. "I'll walk Charlie out."

I let Tova hug me again and reciprocated an air kiss with Vic. Avery steered my elbow toward the front door and handed me a sheath of papers waiting by the host's station.

"Here's your request for the last inventory of the pastry kitchen, but I can't vouch for its accuracy. You'll probably want to stop by and check it out yourself." His eyes sparked with mischief. "Bring your label maker."

"Oh, I surely will," I said, already flipping through the papers.

Avery stepped toward me and leaned in. I felt his breath when he whispered, "Thanks for being here. I'm, um, really glad you took the leap."

I nodded and should have been touched by the sentiment, but I could see Vic just past the window, squinting at us and nodding, his eyes narrowed and arms crossed. Something about the way he was watching us made me uneasy.

"I'll be back tomorrow," I said, stepping away. "Tell Tova to get ready to work."

Avery let out a sharp laugh. "She's ready and willing, I assure you." He walked toward the kitchen but said over his shoulder, "We've all been waiting for you, Charlie."

I took a deep breath and felt the warm rush of being wanted, wooed, appreciated. Only a few days in, and Seattle was turning out to be a lovely fit.

7

❧

THE following afternoon I decided to celebrate, having unpacked the final box in my apartment, with a walk to the Queen Anne Farmers' Market. I wiggled into a tank, my favorite cardigan, and, in a burst of springtime hopefulness, a new pair of shorts from the Gap. I hummed as I made my way across a handful of city streets. I passed dads toting children in backpacks, hipsters from Microsoft snort-laughing about someone's cerebral joke, and four women walking abreast, yoga mats slung over defined deltoids. My thoughts meandered as I recalled images from the last few days spent in my new apartment, and I found myself making a mental list of my favorite things about it:

- The walk-in closet, too large for the size of my wardrobe, but headily efficient and now color-coded with my shirts, dresses, sweaters, and pants all hanging perfectly.
- The kitchen. Oh, the kitchen. All of my tools, knives, pots, cutting boards, which had been so carefully puzzled together in my tiny New York galley kitchen, could not fill even a third of the available space in my new digs. Thinking of this particular perk made a giddy lump form in my throat.

- The soaking tub *and* standing shower with dual jets. I found myself wandering through the tall glass doors and into that sanctuary of tile and pristine grout even when fully clothed.
- The neat stack of broken-down cardboard waiting next to my door. All done, all done, and God bless America, all done.

A shiver of organizational victory pulsed through my fingers as I turned a corner and came to the entrance of the market. I was out of breath, and my ponytail was drooping after a walk that had turned out to be much longer than it had appeared on GoogleMaps. I stood for a moment, catching my breath and gathering my thoughts. Now that I'd tidied and established my personal space, all my attention and energy could focus like high-wattage spotlights on Thrill and the dessert menu there. I felt a shot of adrenaline just thinking about it: I was finally the head of pastry at a top-notch restaurant. It was finally *my* turn, my gig, my shot at making a name for myself as the best pastry chef in the city. No Felix, no broken promises, only the chance to prove what I could do. I took a deep breath and faced the market. Time to investigate what Seattle had to offer in the way of fresh, local, and inspiring.

I curled my toes in my new Merrells, a purchase strong-armed by Manda but one I'd been secretly thrilled to make, not only because I loved the deep blue, but also because I couldn't bear the thought of footbinding in those heels any more. I had to roll my eyes at my fickle, poser self: it had taken less than a week for me to trade in my New York chic for West Coast comfort.

The market stretched before me, a riot of sound, color, and delicious smells. Live music reached me where I stood, though I couldn't see where the sitar player was sitting. For being so early in the season, the tables on either side of the street were heavily laden with produce. I could see English peas, asparagus, arugula, several varieties of chard, kale, rhubarb, radishes . . . My mouth tingled as I walked slowly from booth to booth, drinking in the knowledge that the food I was checking out had not been trucked over the Jersey Turnpike or from a far-flung spot upstate, but from somewhere nearby, where people still felt dirt in their hands and not just in their nostrils after a day of walking in the city.

I paused at the end of a block, and my gaze zeroed in on a mountain of gorgeous strawberries a few stands down. Cutting in and out of the throng,

I reached the stand and stood under a banner that read FORSYTHIA FARMS. I crouched to be eye level with the berries, narrowing my eyes at their color, shape, and size. The red was deep, but still bright. Shape: irregular, as they should be, and still shooting delightful stems that poked out the tops like tiny berets. The berries weren't too small, and best of all, not too large. No Costco mutants, I was pleased to note.

"You're talking to the strawberries."

I stood abruptly and, in the process, bumped hard against the table. A mini-avalanche of strawberries bounced out of the crates and onto the concrete below. I scrambled for hand sanitizer in my bag and didn't even let the gel dry before pushing against the flow to contain the fall of more berries. The man behind the voice had run around the booth and was at my feet, picking up the smattering of berries that had fallen to the concrete. His thick mop of sun-touched blond hair was so close to my bare, pale, New-England-winter legs, the backs of my knees began to sweat.

He stood, holding a big silver bowl of retrieved berries. A slow smile spread over his handsome face. "Sorry. I think I startled you."

I cleared my throat and tried to look dignified. "You did. But I'm sorry about the berries. Let me buy the ones that fell." I opened my bag and pulled out a handful of crisp bills. "How much do I owe you?"

"Whoa, hold on there, sister," he said, hand up and eyes laughing. "We're talking berries, not gold." He squinted. "New around here?"

"Maybe," I said, the New York armor sprouting anew with impressive speed.

He seemed to be enjoying my discomfort. "New York?"

I sucked in a breath. "How did you know that?"

"The shape of the eyebrows." He nodded, suddenly solemn. "All New Yorkers have very well-manicured eyebrows."

My hand flew to my right eyebrow and swiped a shaky line along its curve. "Seriously? I've never really thought about that. I can't believe that's how you knew."

He laughed, a low rumble. "That, and the fact you're holding a bag from the Met." He nodded at my bag. "And your gargantuan sunglasses. People with big-ass sunglasses are typically from the East Coast."

I frowned. "Bigger frames mean better protection from sun damage." I took in his tan, ruddy cheeks, broad chest and shoulders. Sure, it looked great now—amazing, actually—but in thirty years, who would be wishing he'd worn some big-ass sunglasses during peak sun times?

He set the bowl of berries on the table and held out his hand. "I'm Kai Malloy."

His palm was rough and warm in mine. "Charlie Garrett," I said.

"Fantastic name," he said, the dark brown in his eyes trained on my face. "It suits you."

I turned my face away from his open assessment of me and went back to investigating the strawberries.

"What brings you to Seattle, Charlie?" Kai said. He walked around the booth to resume his post. "Business? Pleasure?"

"Oh, you know," I said airily. "A little of both." This man was far too friendly, I decided. And too beautiful. Two of my favorite red flags when it came to men. I was not going to give him the pleasure of thinking he had me all figured out. Big sunglasses indeed.

"Great," he said, a bit more subdued. "What's your line of work?"

"I work in food, actually," I said, pushing my sunglasses on top of my head.

"Really?" He smiled. "Are you a cook, then? Because if you are, I know of a new place over on Capitol Hill that's looking for—"

I wrinkled my nose. "I'm not a *cook*. I'm a *chef*," I said. "A classically trained pastry chef, actually. High-end dining. Michelin stars. That sort of thing."

"Wow," he said, eyebrows up. "Sounds impressive."

I paused, trying to gauge if there was a touch of irony in his tone. "Well," I said with a slight shrug, "the pressure is pretty intense. It's not for the faint of heart."

He nodded in greeting to a man who had approached the stand and was fingering berries before adding them to his reusable cloth bag. I must have been scowling because Kai whispered to me over the pile of berries, "What's wrong?" His lips matched the color of the strawberries.

I watched the man sniff a berry, centimeters from his nose. He squeezed the fruit, and then put it back. I looked at Kai, motioning for him to move farther down the table so we could talk more privately.

"That man is bruising your fruit. You should stop him." I shuddered involuntarily. "And judging by how close he's holding the berries to his nostrils, I'd have to assume his hands are full of bacteria." I shrugged. "Classic trifecta of gastrointestinal disasters: feces, fingers, food. I'd watch him or you might have a food poisoning incident here at Forsythia Farms. Blood on your hands."

Kai did exactly what I thought he would not do. He laughed.

"You are a piece of work, Ms. Garrett." He crossed his arms over his chest and nodded in appreciation. "I find you refreshing."

I huffed. "I'm not a glass of iced tea." Then I pointed at his chest with my index finger. "And I'm just trying to help you out. No farmer wants to be blamed for making the public sick."

He whistled. "Wow. Does it get windy up there on the pedestal?"

I blinked. "I'm not sure I understand your meaning." His cheekbones were utterly distracting, so I frowned at them.

His face remained serious, but he looked like he wanted to laugh again. "I thank you for your concern," he said, eyes big, "but I don't own Forsythia. I'm just helping out a friend. But I'll pass along your advice."

The snotty-sniffer held up his bag and caught Kai's eye, ready to pay. Kai turned toward the man, but I stopped him with my arm on his. I pushed two twenties into the pocket on his shirt.

"Sorry about the spill," I said and started back toward the entrance to the market.

"Wait a minute, New York," he called after me. "This is ridiculous. And way too much!"

"Keep the change," I said over my shoulder. I saw him shake his head, the bills still in his hand as I hurried away.

8

I sat on my living room floor, looking at a rainbow of Post-its, papers, recipe cards, and newly printed labels. Only two days remained until my first night on the line at Thrill, and I had mountains of work to complete. Unable to sleep past five, I had risen in the inky gray light and waited only for my French press to do its work before tackling mine.

I heard the concierge's buzzer sound, signaling a visitor. I looked at my watch to verify the time.

Yes, it really was six o'clock in the morning, and yes, there was really a human being leaning mercilessly on the elevator buzzer downstairs. Was Omar gagged and bound, or who was being so pushy?

I pushed myself up with my hands and walked to the concierge phone in fuzzy socks—absolute necessities, it turned out, on the stunning but chilly marble floor of my new apartment. I reached to answer, but my thoughts lingered on what I'd been needling moments before: the merits of a Linzer torte versus lemon crêpes with blackberry sauce.

"Hello?" I said.

"What took you so long? Let me in." It was Manda.

Less than a minute later, she stepped out of the elevator, her curls gathered into a hasty ponytail. The shoulders of her coat shimmered with the rain that had been falling since the previous night.

"Normal people answer their cell phones. Normal people are reachable by the outside world." She strode past me and into the apartment, dripping and sloshing and making wet footprints on a floor that I had not Swiffered yet that day. "I thought all New Yorkers were obsessed with their phones," she continued, progressing quickly to the kitchen and pouring out the last of the coffee in my carafe. "But then, you've always been contrary."

"Good morning, Manda," I said, my voice droll.

She ignored me. "Thank God that Omar person wasn't at the front desk. He never would have let me through. Some hipster who looked even more exhausted than I feel was there and didn't give a rip that I wanted to go up to the *penthouse*." Her voice resembled that of a insouciant British lord.

I leaned against the counter and felt its cold surface beneath my sweatshirt. "Lovely to see you at such an ungodly hour."

Manda's head snapped up after splashing her coffee with cream. "Did I wake you? Oh, honey, I'm sorry. I honestly forget that there are people in my age group who sleep late because they can." Her eyes took in a sweep of the apartment and landed on my work-rainbow on the living room floor. "You were not sleeping. You were working."

"True. I can't sleep. I start at Thrill the day after tomorrow." I walked back to the heap of papers. "There are so many decisions to make. Like this, for example." I brandished an updated printout of my spreadsheet and pointed to the column I had labeled SUMMER: FILLED DESSERT/BERRIES/ INDIGENOUS PRODUCE. "A Linzer torte would present nicely, and the nutty crumb of the pastry would be a perfect pairing with Washington strawberry preserves, but lemon crêpes with a blackberry sauce seems to just scream 'summer,' don't you think? I'm very particular about berries, though, and I worry that I couldn't get enough that were organic and local, as well as precisely ripe—definitely not *under-ripe,* so disgusting—each evening."

Manda was not often quiet, which was why I noticed.

She stared at me a moment and said. "Step away from the spreadsheet. We're going to breakfast."

I groaned. "No, no, no, we are not. I have so much work to do, and I don't feel like it, and I haven't showered for two days, and no."

"We're going to a diner, not the Four Seasons." She sipped her coffee and watched for my reaction.

"Absolutely not." I shook my head so fast I felt a twinge in a still-sleepy neck muscle. "Diner food is almost always disappointing . . . and greasy and sad and flavorless."

"At least you're not an elitist."

I ignored that. "I already have steel-cut oats in my Japanese rice and porridge cooker. And I bought a local thick-sliced bacon I've been waiting to try." My voice had taken on a bit of a whimper.

"Diners have bacon. And you can heat up your precious fancy oatmeal later." Manda raised one eyebrow and gave me the same look that caused her children to wilt. "Charlie, you have to rest every now and then, even when you're working under a deadline. I used to have a job that paid me money, remember? I used to read books about life-work balance." She tossed me my new apple green rain parka that had hung on a silver hook by the door. "Hurry. I left Jack alone with the kids in the car. He hasn't had his coffee, so we need to pray for their safety."

I gave her my best withering glare.

She didn't even blink.

"Nice coat," she said. "A girl needs some color when living in a soaked-out city." The elevator began a wail of protest as Manda continued to hold the door ajar for too long.

"I'm getting concealer and lip gloss, and you can't stop me!" I called as I jogged to the bathroom.

"Meet you downstairs in two. Not joking, Char!" Manda called as the elevator door began to close. "This is not prom '99. It's only breakfast!"

By the time we pulled up to Howie's Diner, I had some kind of organic Oreo sludge stuck in my hair. Polly and I had shared the middle row of seats in the Henrick minivan, and I had made an absolute fool of myself blowing raspberries on her plump cheeks to keep her entertained. I didn't remember her eating anything during the car ride, but somehow I had dark brown, slimy crumbs woven into the right side of my hair when Zara rescued me and showed me how to open the sliding door.

I gagged and tried to think of nonslimy things as I pulled out as much as possible. "What is this stuff, anyway?" I grumbled, still peeved at getting kidnapped against my will. I sniffed my finger and recoiled. "Carob? Carob, Manda? You should be ashamed of yourself."

Manda adjusted Polly on her hip and placed a hand on Dane's head. "Dane, honey, will you please hold Aunt Charlie's hand? She's very cranky, and she's only going to get crankier when she realizes I have someone for her to meet."

I stopped in the middle of the street, ignoring Dane's pull on my arm. "You did not."

Jack scooped Dane into his arms and nudged me toward the sidewalk. "Argue safely, please. Cars drive down streets."

I stared at Manda. "You are setting me up over breakfast at a diner? Surely you have not stooped to this level."

"There is no stooping." She circled an arm around my shoulders and shepherded me toward the door to the restaurant. "He might not even be here. And he doesn't know we're coming, so it's not like we'll share a table or anything."

I blew out a frustrated sigh. "Manda, we've talked about this. I can't date anyone right now. Men are difficult and moody and needy, and they don't understand my life."

Manda shushed me. I hated getting shushed. "Trust me," she said. "This one is at least worth a glance over maple syrup."

"Probably imitation maple," I muttered, but the door was open and a waft of butter and cinnamon escaped. I marched to my sentence in begrudging obedience. Jack held the door for us, and we stepped over the threshold. While jostling next to another large group in the minuscule hosting area, I took stock, trying not to look too eager in case Mystery Man was watching for us. Oh, for a stroke of good luck and a Mystery Man who was currently changing a flat tire on the side of I-5 and (darn it!) couldn't meet us after all! I sniffed and tried to look disinterested as I scanned the room.

Buttercream yellow on the walls, a nice counterpoint to the white wood trim around big windows and tall baseboards. Old, pocked tin ceiling painted turquoise. The room was short and narrow with booths down one side and a smattering of two- and four-tops down the center. A counter with spinning barstools ran the length of the restaurant and faced an expansive ledge separating the dining room from the kitchen. I could only see one cook manning the grill, and I wanted to roll my eyes in anticipation of what could come from this kind of chaos. The restaurant was cozy—I allowed that much—but one cook?

"Auntie Charlie, do you have to go poopy?" Zara's voice rang out as a summons.

I shook my head. "Definitely not. But thanks for checking." I could feel the color rising in my cheeks, a sensation I had come to dread since I first noticed it in fifth grade.

"Oh, Char, The Splotch lives on," Manda said, her eyes just as empathetic as they'd been in elementary school. "I still think it's endearing."

"And a lot like having a quick bout of scarlet fever every time I'm embarrassed." My voice sounded harsher than I'd intended.

"Char, you look great," Jack said, pulling me into a shoulder hug. "And we're all stoked to have you in Seattle so we can pick you up for breakfast, right, kids?"

Zara did a fist pump and started jumping, which inspired Dane to do the same.

I let Jack smush my face into his flannel shirt and caught Manda's smiling glance. Jack Henrick had been a camp counselor for a long slew of summers, and while at times I had found his optimism to be a bit like an a cappella Disney medley sung during a funeral, even then, I loved the man. Not only because he made me feel like a treasured younger sister, but also for the way he loved my best friend.

"Don't worry about the dude," Jack said into my ear. "This one is not nearly as creepy as the last one. I promise."

I groaned into his chest.

"Zara and Dane, party of six?" One of the three servers on the floor held a stack of menus and searched the crowd. She had piles of toffee-hued dreadlocks pulled into a ridiculously thick braid that gathered to one side of her head and down the front of her turquoise HOWIE'S DINER T-shirt.

"I'm Zara!" Zara said, too loudly and hopping now on one foot. "We are ready to eat! And don't worry because Aunt Charlie does *not* have to go poopy!"

And just as The Splotch was beginning to recede, it reappeared with a vengeance.

The server laughed. Her eyes were large and playful, a mix of grays and greens. "Well, we do have a restroom if she changes her mind."

Jack followed the server first, all three kids touching at least one of his limbs. Manda and I fell in single file behind them and navigated the tight spots between tables. I read the back of the server's t-shirt. In red lettering it proclaimed, HOWIE'S DINER. LIFE IS TOO SHORT TO EAT WHEATGRASS.

"Ooh, he's here. I'm so excited." Manda's voice had gone up an octave in pitch. She poked me too hard in the side. "Nine o'clock, beautiful specimen working the griddle."

I rubbed my sore skin and looked through the peek-a-boo window to the kitchen. The cook caught my eye and lifted his chin in greeting. I felt my insides flip.

"You've got to be kidding me," I said in a low, strangled voice. I scooted into the booth next to Zara and Jack.

Manda must not have heard my anguish because she was practically high-fiving the waitress with glee. "Please give Kai a warm hello from us and tell him to stop by when he has a chance." Manda pried Polly's hands off her earrings as she talked. "How nice you get to work with such a lovely view," she added, eyebrows wiggling.

Our server followed Manda's gaze and then turned to me with a wicked grin. "He *is* a looker, isn't he? I'll let him know you girls were appreciative of God's handiwork."

She and Manda laughed together, while I sputtered my protest. I didn't remember saying anything about God or His handiwork! I just wanted to eat my steel-cut oats and thick-sliced bacon!

The server set down a galvanized tin bucket full of crayons, and the kids squealed in appreciation. "The good news is that there's actually a decent guy underneath all that exterior." She smiled toward the kitchen, her gaze lingering and affectionate. "Makes it even harder to hate him."

I wondered if I detected more than affection in her eyes, but she turned back to our table and pushed her heavy braid off her shoulder.

"My name is Sunshine, folks, and I'd love to bring you something to drink. Fresh-squeezed orange juice? Costa Rican coffee? Peach-mango tea?"

I squinted at Sunshine's nose stud. No Tang? Folgers? Lipton? What kind of diner was this, anyway?

When Sunshine had left to retrieve juices for the kids and hot java for the adults, I narrowed my eyes at Manda.

"How do you know him?" I said, sneaking a menu off the pile Sunshine had left at the end of the table.

Manda remained unruffled in the face of my sneering. "He lives on our block. Cute little bungalow, two doors down."

"Really nice paint job," Jack said. "And a killer front porch, though he had to strip the thing down to its studs when he moved in. The floor was all cattywampus, but nothing a little jack-up job couldn't fix."

Manda put her hand on Jack's arm, and he seemed to realize the issue was not a sagging porch floor.

"So he's handy," Jack said in summary.

Manda continued. "I scouted him out months ago but you weren't here, and now you are. Plus, he likes food and so do you."

"Just hold on," I said, defeating Zara in tic-tac-toe with a vicious diagonal line. I redrew for another game before she could notice. "Saying we both like food is like saying we both enjoy breathing oxygen. It is no basis for a love connection. And what's his boss Howie up to here, anyway, at this 'diner'?" I made quotation marks with clenched claws. "Is this some kind of cult-y diner? Everything is vegan? Are we talking meat-substitutes here, because I *told* you about my bacon waiting for me in my brand new, stainless steel fridge. Seitan is just what it sounds like. Lucifer—" I took a breath to open the menu and felt my salivary glands kicking in.

"I love that girl's name!" Zara said. "I'm going to name my Barbie Sunshine Ruby Mae Henrick right when we get home."

"Barbeeeeee!" Dane said. He was gripping an oversized crayon over his kids' menu and coloring an oversized drawing of French toast.

"Charlie," Jack said, one arm holding Polly, the other spinning some kind of psychedelic rainbow mobile in front of her face. "You know you're in the Pacific Northwest when your waitress's name is Sunshine." He shook his head and went back to getting his baby stoned with a toy.

Zara paused in her coloring. "I have a girl in my class named Begonia. And a boy named Cloud."

Manda shrugged under my gaze. "People are allowed to make their own decisions, Charlie. You might surprise yourself. When your own little one is looking up at you one day, your entire body heavy and tired after you've pushed out the placenta—"

"Eww." I shuddered. "Please don't mention any more birthing details before breakfast."

"You might, in that moment, think, 'This child is *called* to have the name Maple.' You will feel it in the depths of your bones."

I scowled, turning my shoulders more deeply to one side so my back was to the kitchen. "Maple is not a real name."

"Totally is," she said, nodding thanks to Sunshine, who had delivered her tea. "And androgynous. Works for boy or girl."

"What's wrong with Sam?" Jack said with sudden vehemence. "Or Jane? Or John?" He handed Polly across the table and into Manda's arms. "Why must we wonder if it's a girl or a boy when we see the kid's name on the class list for his *or her* whole life?"

This sparked a spirited dialogue between Manda and Jack, during which I played roughly eighty-seven games of tic-tac-toe with Zara and eighty-seven games of pretend tic-tac-toe with Dane. I loved hearing Jack push Manda's buttons and watching her erupt, curls bouncing. I also loved the way Jack laughed in exasperation at his prickly wife, and the way she watched him with smitten eyes. I nearly forgot how cruel and unusual they were to conspire against me for a breakfast blind date. All in the name of fun, but, inevitably, these meetings left me feeling more empty-hearted than when I'd walked in.

Buttermilk pancakes weren't typically equipped to fill gaping holes in one's heart, but the ones I ate that day at Howie's came pretty darn close. My first bite of Wilma's Cakes made my mouth water *while* eating. They were spongy and light but still had some gumption. The buttermilk seemed to be paired with something fantastic—sour cream? Crème fraîche? Not here, certainly . . . There were subtle notes of nutmeg and cinnamon, just the right touch without the pancake turning into a spice fest.

I moaned when I bit into a raspberry muffin.

"Exactly," Manda said, her eyes closed around the joy of a pecan roll. "Better than you-know-what."

"Watch it, now," Jack said, but without heart. His bacon, asparagus, and goat cheese omelet was nearly gone, but he ate with one protective arm curled around his plate in defense anyway.

"Everything tasting all right?"

I looked up, startled from my happy pancake moment. Kai stood at the head of our table, but the diner was so packed, he had to lean forward slightly to allow room behind him. I tried not to notice how close he was to me.

Jack reached above Zara's head to offer Kai a hand. "Wow. We heard about your restaurant from the Harpers, but honestly, we thought they were exaggerating. Dude, they were not."

Kai ducked his chin to receive the compliment. "Thanks a lot. I'm happy we didn't disappoint." He turned to the junior members at the table for a round of fist bumps. "Everybody like their food?"

Zara fulfilled her duties as spokeschild as Dane was occupied with finger-painting circles in a puddle of leftover syrup. "The waffles were perfect, but next time, can I have chocolate chips in them? But not carob because carob is revolting."

"Absolutely." Kai nodded a military assent. "And carob *is* revolting."

I couldn't hold it in any longer. "Why didn't you tell me you were a chef?" I snipped. If I could have wedged a hand onto my hip in defiance, I would have.

He looked at me, amused. "Well, for one thing, I'm not a chef. I'm a cook. At a diner. Not exactly Michelin stars and all that."

I winced to remember how *that* must have sounded. "You misled me. You said nothing about this." I gestured to the bustling room, my empty plate.

"I don't remember you asking much about me," he said, a bemused smile settling in. "Also, are you always this intense? You know, some people just have conversations instead of interrogations."

Manda cleared her throat. "So, apparently you two have met. No need for the whole 'Kai, Charlie, Charlie, Kai' thing. And yes, Kai, she's always this intense. But very likeable. And a fantastic baker. And athletic!"

"And I have a strong 401K!" I erupted, my cheeks *en fuego*. "Enough!"

Kai laughed with his eyes and his mouth. I wanted to hear him do it again as soon as possible. "Listen," he said. He leaned both arms on the table and settled his gaze on me.

I swallowed.

"I'm a cook at Howie's Diner. I hope this doesn't freak you out, but I actually *own* the diner, which may or may not be a good thing in your world. We've only been open a year, but I think we're doing okay. Howie was my grandpa's name and I named the pancakes after my grandma. My 401K is pathetic, but I hope you can get over that. Because even though Manda appears to have been right about your control issues and your food snobbery, you do have a great smile."

I bit my lower lip, my heart pounding into my shirt.

"And you look much prettier without the scowl."

Manda sighed. "I've been telling her that since she moved to New York. Thank you for agreeing with me. She *totally* looks prettier without it."

Kai kept his eyes on mine. "Totally."

"Pretty sure an insult with a compliment equals an insult," I said.

He ignored my words. In fact, he appeared to be ignoring everyone in the room but me. "Are you free for dinner tonight? I'll cook."

I made a face. "Or *I* can cook. I do know how."

"So that's a yes, Intensity Freak?" He had delightful lips, this one. They were distracting.

"Yes," I said. "But no. No, I can't tonight." My thoughts returned to the pile of papers on my floor, the pastry kitchen at Thrill, the email from the management team asking for my final notes on Tuesday's opening menu.

"Okay," Kai shrugged. "Tomorrow."

"No." I shook my head. "I can't tomorrow. Or this week. I'm sorry, but I'm starting as the new head pastry chef at a restaurant downtown, and I can't even think about anything but that right now."

Manda vouched for me. "She's not brushing you off. I had to kidnap her for breakfast."

Kai ran a hand through his hair. His eyes traveled back to the kitchen and a stack of order slips piling up on the metal wheel. "I get it." He thought for a moment, then turned back to me. "Your next day off, then. Meet me here at lunch. I'll feed you, and then we'll see what happens." He was already backing up, answering the call of the bell Sunshine kept ringing to get his attention. She glanced at me, then Kai, then rang it again for emphasis.

"Great to catch up with you guys," Kai called back over the din of the room. "And really good to see you again, Chef." He winked before letting the kitchen door swing to a close.

I shook my head slowly when I pulled my attention back to our table. "Now what?" I demanded of Manda and Jack, my eyes two question marks.

"Boom!" Jack said with a fist pump. "I'm not usually one for subtext, but even I could see the chemistry there. See, Char? Totally not creepy."

I sighed. "And just how does *he* fit into a sixty-hour work week, a cross-country move, a commercial kitchen, and an ex-boyfriend boss?"

Manda ate the final bite of her pecan roll. "When a man can cook like this, look like that, and give you the sass you desperately need," she said, locking eyes with Jack, "I think you'll figure it out."

9

TOVA handed me a wicked sharp twelve-inch, and I poised the point of the blade above the tart's center, ready to puncture its perfect surface. I was about to portion out the last of the evening's caramel nut tarts, one of my two new desserts on the menu and the second night in a row to sell out before closing. I bit both of my lips between my teeth as I made a careful cut to connect the tart's center to the lines I'd marked with a ruler on parchment paper below. Tova hovered over one shoulder. I could hear her breathing.

"Like that," I said, straightening slightly and examining my work. The symmetry was perfect, each triangle a perfect replica of its neighbor. Cashews, hazelnuts, and blanched almonds peeked out of their baptism in caramel jam, a sea of creamy browns punctuated by green pistachios. The tart shell formed a precise circle of pastry around the caramel and nuts.

"So cool," Tova breathed. "I want to eat it all, right now."

I smiled, surprised again at what a difference a move made. Four days on the line at Thrill had brought me ten times the accolades and strokes than six years at L'Ombre. Avery had taken to stuttering in my presence: his excitement over the increased dessert orders and sell-outs of my two new additions had clearly messed with his mind. The tart and my lemon crêpes had both been big hits. During the preservice meeting that night, Avery had read aloud from five new Trip Advisor reviews, four of five waxing eloquent about one of my desserts. I had three more new ideas percolating, and I couldn't wait to rid the menu of an anemic apricot flan that remained from before my time, but I was trying to be patient with the process. Nearing the end of my first week, I was happy with the progress that had been made.

I felt Tova's eyes on me, and I turned to face her.

"Charlie."

I had asked Tova to call me by my first name, so eager was I to rid my kitchen from the old-world politics that had smothered me in New York. I had to admit, however, that this new level of familiarity also took some getting used to.

"Charlie," she said, her mouth pulling down into a frown, "I am concerned. You have dark circles under your eyes and your skin is sallow, a far cry from the girl I met a week ago. Are you sleeping okay?"

I answered on my way to the oven to remove a sheet pan of flourless chocolate cake. "When I do sleep, I sleep very well. This week has been long on work, short on sleep." I set the pan carefully on the counter and pushed gently into the surface of the cake to test its doneness. "But this is normal for me, actually. I'm used to working fourteen-hour days."

I watched her adjust her chef's cap in the reflection of the oven door and thought, *I might sleep more if you were a teeny bit less clueless.* The kid had excess in the way of charm and enthusiasm, but Chef Alain would have fed her to the wolves after twenty minutes at L'Ombre. I kept meaning to ask Avery where he had found Tova, and what her previous supervising chef had said by way of recommendation, but I'd been running at top speed for days and hadn't had the chance to ask.

"Tova," I said in my most professional tone, hoping she'd catch on and I wouldn't have to actually say the words "Stop touching your hair."

"Hmm?" she said, fussing with some strays by her ears.

I opened my mouth to say something about the time and place for pomade, but Avery came into our workspace at a jog. His eyes looked wild, out of place with his tailored chef's whites, sharp lines, and clean apron. He wasn't wearing a cap, and his dark hair was sculpted into a neat tousle.

"Char." His words came out in a rush. "You need to come with me. Now." He grabbed my hand and started walking toward the back of the restaurant where the doors to his office and a small conference room stood open.

I skidded to a stop before we had made it past the double broiler. "Hold on, Speedy. I'm still working, remember? We have at least fifteen minutes until close. And there are three tables who haven't finished their entrées."

"No problem," Avery shrugged. "Tova can finish it out. Right, Tova?"

The two exchanged a look and with a slow smile, Tova said, "Absolutely. I'm on it. Don't worry a nanosecond."

I paused, considering this option to delegate. I had no confidence in Tova's ability to bake, form, roll out, fill, or cut. But I had seen the woman garnish, and it seemed to come naturally to her. All the desserts were prepared, so all she would need to do would be to prettify.

"All right," I said slowly. "You can do it. But—" I said with a cautionary hand raised. "Don't do one single thing I haven't seen you do before. This is not the time for artistic freedom. And leave the flourless chocolate cakes on the counter to cool. They're for tomorrow's service, and I will prep them for storage when I get back."

By the time I finished speaking, I needed to shout because Avery had pulled me halfway down the hall.

"What is going on?" My Crocs were squeaking on the scrubbed tile outside Avery's office.

"Okay." Avery stopped outside the conference room and lowered his voice. "Just roll with me on this one. I know it sounds odd, but trust me. It will all make sense pretty soon. All right?" His eyes searched mine with an urgency I hadn't seen from him.

I nodded and shook my head in one gesture. "All right. I'll trust you."

"Great," he exhaled, gripping my hands in his. "Awesome. After you." He gestured to the conference room, and I stepped inside.

The room was darkened but was still plenty bright because of a large, portable lighting set-up on metal stands. While my eyes adjusted to the dark, an attractive woman in skinnies, a cropped jacket, and an infinity scarf stepped forward into the light. Vic stood beside her.

Avery cleared his throat. "Charlie, this is Margot Rubin. I think you may have seen her around the kitchen yesterday and today."

"Of course." I reached out to shake her hand. "Avery told me about your work as a public television producer."

"He did, did he?" she said, her face inscrutable.

I nodded. "I have been a long-time supporter of PBS and NPR. I hate television, as a rule, but PBS is so important, so essential as a break from today's consumerist, low-minded entertainment culture. I *loved* the series on Eleanor Roosevelt last year. Did you work on that project?" I didn't even try to rein in my fangirl moment. I hoped she had met Rick Steves . . .

Margot raised one half of her mouth and looked at Avery before responding. "I'm afraid not. Avery might have been misinformed. I don't work for PBS. I'm a producer at Surge."

My face must have betrayed my complete ignorance.

Margot filled me in. "The lifestyle network? *Last Stop: Juvey? Confessions of a Cabana Boy?*"

I shook my head slowly, trying in vain to remember the last time I watched a TV show that didn't have to do with food, world history, or British people.

Vic cleared his throat. "Charlie, why don't you sit here, and Avery, you'll be beside her."

I followed his direction to two chairs placed in front of an imposing camera. A man with a mullet and a Slayer T-shirt nodded at me from behind the lens.

"Hold on a second," I said. "Why is he here? And what's with the lights?"

Vic and Margot both appeared ready to answer, but Avery jumped in.

"We're just looking into some marketing options for the restaurant." He spoke quickly. "Advertising, maybe a commercial. Vic brought Margot in because she's the expert."

"I wouldn't say that," Margot demurred, unconvincingly, I thought.

"So, Charlie," Vic said from where he stood in the dark. I could see a tiny reflection of light on his clean-shaven bald top. "Tell us about when you and Avery met."

I made a face. "I'm not sure what that has to do with—"

Avery nudged my leg with his knee. "Roll with it," he whispered. He was clasping his hands together so tightly I could see his knuckles turning white.

I turned to Vic. "I met Avery when he was going through a very intense cologne phase." I turned my gaze to the ceiling, searching for the name. "Obsession by Calvin Klein. Am I right, Don Juan?"

Avery laughed, his knuckles officially white. "That stuff was awesome."

I turned back to Vic, but he pointed to the camera. "That's great. Keep talking, but just look at the camera."

I paused a beat but obliged and looked down the lens. "It was hideous. He must have bathed in it before class at culinary school. He smelled like repressed adolescence. Or a smarmy grandfather."

"Who uses words like *smarmy*?" Avery looked at Margot for help, but she just stood, arms crossed around the many zippers on her jacket.

"You probably miss that smell," Avery said to me. He pulled me into a side hug and held me long enough for me to notice a different kind of cologne. Expensive-smelling, and the kind that you couldn't get at the mall. "I could bring a little Calvin K back, you know."

I laughed, surprised to be genuinely enjoying this rush of memories. "You probably wanted to smell like anything other than a culinary student who spent insane amounts of time with spices and oils and raw meat. And that was just the first class of the day."

Avery cocked his head to one side. "Charlie was the most beautiful girl I'd ever seen."

I groaned and he looked surprised, maybe hurt.

"It's true. You had this great smile and eyes that were sometimes green, sometimes blue, depending on how tired you were and what you were wearing." He became animated. "And she was a beast in the kitchen. She outscored everyone on every test, not just pastry. She was so intense, I was terrified of her. So," he grinned at me, "I decided the only way to conquer my fear of her was to ask her out."

I watched his face.

"She said yes," he said by way of finishing his story.

I turned my body to face him. "You never told me you were intimidated by me."

He shrugged slightly, eyes still on me. "I suppose there are a few things I've never mentioned."

Vic spoke from behind the camera. "Perfect." He motioned for the cameraman to stop filming and let a silence fall. His gaze rested on Margot, who was watching the little screen on a device the camera guy held out for her.

Finally she spoke. "She's the one."

Avery let out a cheer that could have originated in the prehistoric era, and Vic clapped his hands, once and loudly.

I felt my eyebrows knitting together in confusion. "I'm the one?" Then, my voice lowered, I leaned into Avery. "Am I still rolling with it?"

He shook his head and then turned to Vic, Margot, and the Mullet Man. "Can we have a moment?"

The three of them left the room, leaving Avery and me alone under the harsh glare of the lights. He moved his chair so that we faced each other.

He took a deep breath and let it out slowly. "Charlie, I didn't bring you out here just to be my pastry chef."

"You didn't." I said it as a declarative fact, wondering where in the world this conversation was going.

"I brought you out here because I knew you'd be perfect. You're beautiful, you're smart, you know how to express yourself, *and* you're a great chef." His mouth turned slightly upward into what looked like self-congratulation. "I totally called it."

"More info, please." I could feel my heart starting to pound, my 'Roll With It' threshold officially surpassed.

"Right." Avery leaned forward and balanced his elbows on his knees. He reached forward to grasp my hands in his. "Next week, we are going to start filming a show right here at Thrill. And you, my dear, are going to be my much-searched-for female costar."

The pistons in my brain began to fire away. "Wait. What? A TV show? Here?"

Avery stood, his excitement building. "I know! It's unbelievable! I met Vic at a Food in the Media networking event in L.A. about a year ago, and he's been agenting for me ever since. I had no idea he would make it happen so fast, but once he convinced Margot to take a look, things really steamrolled. We did have a few bumps with the pilot and finding the right costar, but now that you're here—"

"Whoa. So you knew all along that you wanted me to be on a TV show and not just revamp your menu?" The wrinkles in my forehead were beginning to hurt.

"Yes. Sorry I couldn't tell you the whole story," he said, coming to sit by me again. "But I thought you might not come. I remembered how much you hated TV, and I thought I couldn't chance it without you setting up shop here first."

I narrowed my eyes. "You lied to me."

Avery bounced one leg up and down, up and down. "I know. And I'm sorry. It won't happen again."

"You got me to move," I said, my voice rising in pitch and volume, "leave everything behind, including the restaurant capital of the country, and all of this under false pretences?"

"I'm sorry you didn't know the whole story right away," he said hurriedly. "But just think for a second. You *do* like it here. Right?"

I shoved my chair back with surprising force and stood up. "You lied to me," I said again and left the room, letting the door swing hard into the wall. One glance at Margot and Vic told me I was the only one who had been unprepared for our little meeting. I hurried down the hall, ignoring Avery's pleas as I walked back to my work, back to the reason I was there. I rounded the corner of the pastry kitchen and shook my head at Tova's inquisitive gaze. I'd wasted enough time in mindless banter for one shift.

I'm sure it killed him, but Avery had the decency to wait eight full hours before his text barrage began. I puttered around my apartment feeling like a kept woman and trying to ignore the ping of each incoming text. When the pings became so frequent they sounded like a video game from the eighties, I sighed and flopped angrily on the huge couch Avery was paying for. There were twenty-eight unread messages.

8:02 a.m. How much do you hate me?

8:02 a.m. Too passive-aggressive? Sorry. Try again. You have every right to hate me. Honestly. No pun intended!

8:05 a.m. I'm sorry.

8:06 a.m. I just want you to know I'm sorry. I really wanted you to like it here before I told you everything but now I see I was wrong. I'm sorry.

9:00 a.m. I'm trying to give you space. But any time you want to talk, I'm here.

9:01 a.m. Not really good at giving space. Listen, you should absolutely know that you are the only and first choice. Well, not the first, but the first girl totally BIT on camera, which I could have predicted but Margot wanted to give her a shot because she knows the girl's dad. She was horrible, this girl. None of the spice, flair, humor, beauty that you have.

10:24 a.m. I wasn't even piling on the b.s. with those last compliments. In fact, I'll raise you those compliments and tell you that you also look HOT on camera. I've been watching the footage from last night for the last two hours and while that shows how pathetic my life really is, I hope it also proves to you that I am IN THIS. I want and need for this to WORK. YOU ARE THE ONLY ONE FOR THIS JOB.

10:30 a.m. Am I coming on too strong? Do you want me to just let you think?

10:35 a.m. Can you think a little faster?

10:39 a.m. OK. Think about this: Your own pastry kitchen FOR REAL as soon as we're done shooting the season. In fact, your own pastry kitchen TODAY, just as it has been, only with a few extra people and cameras and mics peeking at your work.

10:40 a.m. And think about this: The publicity. Good publicity is good publicity, Charlie. And good publicity turns into good reviews, higher volume, more opportunities.

10:42 a.m. Don't TELL me you aren't thinking what I'm thinking. Cookbooks with your name and face on the cover. Speaking gigs that pay for that house on the beach you've always wanted. YOUR OWN PRODUCT LINE.

10:50 a.m. All you have to do is say yes.

I stared at the phone, not bothering to scroll down through the rest of Avery's messages. I was fairly confident I had the gist of his argument.

The clock on the living room wall ticked toward noon. Typically, I would be arriving at work, taking inventory, discussing the menu with Avery or

Chet, trying to keep Tova from destroying anything. I flung my legs off the side of the couch and stood, stretching kinks out of my neck and shoulders.

Pacing from one length of the room to the other, I tried to clear my head. Be reasonable, I told myself, walking a straight line along the wall of windows. Think this thing through. I thought of the beautiful kitchen at Thrill, the easy camaraderie of the staff, the willingness of Tova to listen to everything I said. I thought of the early accolades. I thought of my new digs and how quickly I'd become smitten with Seattle. I stopped pacing, taking in the view of the mountains and the Sound from my window. I thought about my career, what I'd achieved and what remained on my long list of what I wanted to do as a chef.

I thought of Manda, Jack, and the kids, our breakfast at Howie's.

I thought of Kai. I thought about how I liked thinking about Kai.

I said one naughty word and then jogged to my bedroom for a change of clothes and my bag. I could still make it in time for the first seating.

Avery's face lit up like an illegal fireworks display when I pushed into his office without knocking.

"To answer your question," I said, dumping my bag on his desk, "Yes. I do like it here."

"Exactly!" Avery said, triumphant. "So you'll do it?"

I stopped in front of him, nose to nose. "I won't put up with dishonesty, Avery. This cannot, will not, work if I can't trust you." My eyes were locked on his. "One more lie, and I'm gone."

He nodded quickly. "I totally understand. I promise. Total truth from now on." He held up four fingers in what, I assumed, was supposed to be the Boy Scout's honor and not a Trekkie salute. "You have my word."

"I'll give you one month."

He started to protest, but I put up my hand to stop him.

"One month working alongside all those people who know nothing about running a kitchen and everything about how to make people watch adolescent blather for hours on end. At the end of the trial period, I'll let you know my decision."

"Fine. Fine. I'm sure Vic and Margot will be okay with that. Don't worry," he said reassuringly, though I thought he was the one who looked worried. He hugged me, too hard. "Thank you, Charlie. This has been such a dream of mine, to be on TV, to share my restaurant with the world, and you are making it happen. Thank you."

"You're welcome, but I wouldn't go that far. I still don't understand why *I* have to be involved, and I'm only doing this as a favor. I'm serious, Avery. Don't mess with me." I pulled away and turned to the door. Avery opened it for me, and we were both startled to see Margot and Vic waiting outside. I looked at Vic, then Margot. She was looking at me like a petite feline that was allowing curiosity to get the better of her.

"You haven't even *seen* the Eleanor Roosevelt documentary, have you?" My mouth upturned in a wry smile.

She threw her head back slightly as she laughed. "I'm afraid not. But if it makes you feel any better, I have been pitching a show called *Presidential Kids Gone Wild* for the last three years." She winked at me. "No bites yet. But someday it will sell." She narrowed her gaze. "Well, Ms. Garrett, are you in?"

I nodded. "For now."

Avery looked victorious. "It's never too early in the day for a glass of champagne. Who's in?"

We all fell into step behind Avery, who strode ahead of us in search of four champagne flutes and our finest Perrier-Jouët. I would take part in the theatrics, I decided, and I would clink my glass and toast to our success. As long as I still had control of my kitchen and could create my desserts on my own terms, this could work. Maybe, I allowed, it would work even better than my original plan when I'd hopped the flight to Seattle.

I watched Avery uncork a bottle from behind the bar, and I met his hopeful glance with a smile. On my way to join in the revelry, I quickened my pace and, in no time, found I had closed the distance between us.

10

THE towering glass door to my apartment building seemed to grow heavier each night when I returned home from Thrill. Or perhaps it was my bone-weary self, dragging home at a ridiculous 2 a.m. or 3 a.m., that made it feel heavier and more cumbersome.

Tonight, I had been able to cut out "early" at midnight, but it made little difference to my brain and feet while I struggled with the stubborn door to my apartment building. I wedged my shoulder into the opening, and, at last, it gave an inch. I slipped through and stepped into the brightly lit lobby. Omar was laughing behind his desk, clearly charmed by a man who stood with his back to me.

As Omar greeted me, the man turned around.

I felt a slow smile peek through and thoughts of a long soak in the tub were momentarily forgotten.

"Hey," Kai said.

"Hi," I said to Kai. A flicker of electricity passed between us.

"I hope you don't mind that I tracked you down," Kai said, sweeping the lobby with his gaze. "Nice place, by the way." Kai was leaning against Omar's desk, an infraction I had previously assumed was punishable with death by concierge. But Omar only watched Kai with bright eyes, not even reaching for the fly swatter I knew he kept behind his desk. One side of his mouth pulled up slightly, and I had to drag my eyes north to his eyes.

"Thanks." I cleared my throat in an attempt to clear my head. "And how *did* you find me, exactly? We've already discovered you aren't, in fact, a strawberry farmer. Do you really own a diner, or are you going to tell me you're a private investigator posing as a cook?"

Omar laughed heartily. "Oh, Ms. Garrett. You have such a delightful wit." He looked at Kai and nodded approvingly. "One can see why you would go to so much trouble."

"What trouble?" I walked toward the two of them. I struggled under the weight of my bag and its burgeoning stacks of paperwork, recipe reworkings, Thrill's most recent numbers, and shooting schedules from Margot and Vic.

Kai gently lifted the bag off my shoulder and let it find the floor with a soft thud. "It was no trouble. Manda stopped by the diner today with a fairly evangelistic plea to surprise you tonight. She said you loved surprises, especially after a long day of work."

The look on my face must have clued Kai in. He raised an eyebrow. "You hate surprises."

I winced. "They make me panicky. I prefer to be in control of the world."

Omar tsked from his position at his desk.

Kai shook his head. "I had a feeling I should disobey Manda and text you a warning shot." Still shaking his head, he reached into the back pocket of his jeans and produced an index card filled with Manda's scrawl. "You might want to talk with her about how free she was with your personal information."

I took it from him and read aloud: "'Loves artisanal bread, Portuguese wines, overpriced cheese. Don't be worried if she's prickly at first. You'll do great!!'" I rolled my eyes. "Sorry. She is desperate for me to have a life."

"Well, I can't promise I can deliver that big an order, but we could start with dinner." Kai nodded to an umbrella stand by the front door. Next to it sat a large wicker basket with a green-and-white-checked liner. "Midnight picnic?"

I shushed all of those inner ninnies that were busy trying to convince me I was too tired, every muscle was too sore, and that my hair was a mess.

I knew, with every part of me, that what I really wanted in that moment was to share a meal with this man.

Omar must have seen the answer on my face. "Ms. Garrett, I will be happy to keep safe your bag while you are out."

I nodded my thanks, aware of the favor Omar was offering me. He was not one to tolerate being mistaken for a coat check.

"I'd love to," I said to Kai.

"Great, let's go," he said, offering his hand to me, collecting the picnic basket on the way out.

I took it, feeling its strong, warm pull as we moved into the soft night air of Seattle.

We walked in silence, making our way across the leafy patterns cast onto the pavement by the streetlights above. Kai continued to hold my hand, and I continued to let him. His arm brushed up against me as we walked, and he adjusted his long-legged pace to accommodate mine. We rounded a corner and arrived at a neighborhood garden bursting with rows of trumpeting tulips. I snuck a glance at Kai and saw him stifling a yawn.

"Oh, no," I said, embarrassed I'd only just thought of it. "You must be exhausted. When did you get up this morning?"

He smiled, his eyes on a spot in front of us where the sidewalk ended. "I've been up a while." Using his foot to push it down, he held a flimsy wire fence out of my way and gestured for me to climb over and onto the wooded path. "But I decided I was done waiting for you to stop by the diner again. Sometimes a man has to make a move."

I felt a jolt of happiness pass through me, so glad to be the girl Kai considered worthy of such a move. "Um," I said, turning to more prosaic thoughts, "where are we going?" The path was utterly dark, and the only light was that cast by a nearly full moon. I walked with my hands in front of me to prevent an errant branch from poking me in the eye. Kai took me gently by the shoulders and passed by so he could lead the way.

"I mean," I continued, trying not to sound rattled, "you're not posing as a beautiful man who makes buttermilk pancakes and muffins that make me moan, when really you're a serial killer. Or a kidnapper. Or a—"

"Don't worry," Kai said, but I could hear the smile in his voice. "Be patient. We're almost there."

"I have virtues." My breathing had become ragged during our upward climb. "But patience is not one of them."

I stopped short when we entered a clearing. It took a beat for me to realize I was standing with my mouth open.

"Wow," I said, and the word was carried by the breeze and out to the expanse beyond us. Kai had led us to a grassy oval clearing perched on the side of a cliff. The Pacific Ocean unfolded like a handful of diamonds below us. A teasing, warm breeze tugged at my hair, sending shivers along my scalp and bringing with it the perfect and ancient smell of sand and sea. I drank in the panorama, the moving silver ribbons of water, the regal moon, the stars playing hide-and-seek with wispy clouds.

Kai said nothing and set the picnic basket down onto the grass.

We watched in silence as the moonlight danced on the slow waves, winking and gasping with each crest before tumbling onto the rocky beach below. I must have stood there longer than I realized because when I turned, Kai had lit three small lanterns and had shelved them among the rocks that formed a curve around the picnic spot. He was shaking out a blanket, and I stepped forward to help. We let it fall onto the grass, and I smoothed the fabric with one hand, making sure the front was parallel with the edge of the cliff.

I looked up. Kai had stopped moving and was standing still with several covered dishes in his arms. He looked as though he were trying very hard not to laugh.

"What?" I kept both hands on the blanket, pulling it taut to keep it wrinkle-free.

"Blanket okay? Should I go get a level?"

I pursed my lips but kept my hands on the ground. "I like symmetry. And clean lines. And, um, perfect stuff."

His laugh rolled like an undulating wave. Dropping to his knees, he set the dishes carefully on the blanket. "The world must be a rough place for you, then, Miss Garrett. I'm sure it doesn't always follow your rules."

"Oh, with enough persistence, things usually work out in my favor," I said, distracted by the smells coming up from the plates he was uncovering.

He shook his head and handed me a package wrapped in foil. "I'm pretty sure my asymmetrical knife work will offend your moral sensibilities, but try not to think too much about it. We have fresh mozz, heirloom tomatoes, basil, and a sprinkling of goat cheese on your panini. It was warm at one point this evening, but the flavors only get better as you let them moosh."

"Moosh?" My stomach rumbled as I unwrapped the sandwich. "Sounds technical." I stopped talking because my first bite demanded a respectful silence. The crunch of crispy exterior gave way to an extroverted, summery flavor: notes of salt and a splash of bright tomato, still-warm mozzarella . . . I heard a sigh escape my lips and saw Kai thoroughly enjoying my enjoyment. "This," I said, mouth still full, "is perfect."

His eyes widened around his own bite of panini. Blotting his chin with a napkin, he said, "Good. That's what I was aiming for." He pointed to a collection of plastic containers. "After you've regained your composure, we also have my grandmother's famous new potato salad with bacon and cider vinaigrette, sliced mango and strawberries, and a triple-layer chocolate cake for dessert."

"All right, what's the catch?" I speared a slice of mango with my fork. "Do you live with your mother?"

"Not for the last sixteen years."

"Have you ever filed for bankruptcy?"

"Nope."

"All right, then," I said, undeterred. "Then you have a fetish. Something bizarre and off-putting that has frightened off all sorts of well-fed women before me. What is it?" I pointed my plastic fork at his chest. "Feet? Power tools? Chipmunks?"

Kai had stopped chewing and stared at a point just above my head. When he finally spoke, I could tell he had to make an effort to piece together his thoughts. "You know, I have heard the dating scene in New York is rough, but what kind of men have you had to wade through, Charlie?"

I giggled into my potato salad. "The chipmunks were only rumors, but feet and power tools showed up on my online dating suggestion feed." I stopped talking, horrified. What was with all the honesty? I just met this man, and he had me confessing to online dating profiles? Where is your dignity, woman?

Kai tore a bite of his panini with his hands. "I'm going to forego the chance to mock you mercilessly about online dating and just move on to asking you the same question. What gives? You're smart, funny, attractive, and while you appear to have nearly debilitating perfectionist tendencies, you know your way around the kitchen. According to the law of averages, you could have been married to an eager Mormon dude by the age of nineteen, and any other red-blooded American male by twenty-five."

I screwed up my face. "Am I to respond in gratitude for those words or should I shove you off the cliff? I'm really at war with myself on those two options."

Kai lobbed a generous piece of chocolate cake onto my plate and handed me a fresh fork. "Even we lowly short-order cooks know to offer a clean fork for dessert. Be nice." He nodded to my plate, and I saw a ripple of tension in his jaw. *He wants me to like the cake.* Damn. It was going so well, and now I was going to have to lie.

I smiled at him, steeling myself for my most impressive falsehood. Manda always said I was an abysmal liar, and I hoped to heaven the darkness of the night would at least salvage a bit of the man's pride.

I pushed my fork through the top layer of creamy frosting, then all three layers of the cake. Keeping my eyes down, I put the fork to my mouth. He'd used good chocolate, I knew, and after a moment, I picked up a note of coffee, which only intensified the flavor of the chocolate. The frosting was decadent and smooth, but not cloying. In fact, the entire bite struck the precise balance of sass and sweet.

I looked up at Kai, who was trying to look busy cleaning up our dishes. "This cake is so, so good. It's just the right kind of good." I took another bite and Kai waited, his hands still now. "I know what it is," I said after another swallow. "This cake reminds me of something. Not even something specific, but something . . . homey. And real. And *good.*"

I stopped talking, hit with a sudden and unwelcome embarrassment. I was pretty sure I'd crossed the line from *compliment giver* to *creepy gusher.* "Sorry," I muttered. "I think I overused the word *good* a bit there. Not the most helpful adjective."

Kai shook his head slowly, his attention solely on my face. "I think goodness is entirely underrated." The lamplight from the lanterns danced in his eyes. "Glad you like my cake. I have to tell you there was some pressure trying to make a cake that would impress a fancy pastry chef."

I smiled, feeling myself lean slightly toward him. "Thank you for baking it for me. And for making me dinner." I cocked my head to one side. "I've eaten some pretty amazing meals in the last few years, but I don't remember ever being this . . . satisfied." I was speaking quietly now, trying very hard to remember not to stare at Kai's lips. "Your food satisfies. It's like a visit to a small town park. Or a knockout sunset. Or the feeling after going for a run in a summer rainstorm. Or—"

"Charlie." Kai interrupted me, apparently feeling no such compulsion to avoid looking at people's lips. "Very poetic. But please stop talking."

His kiss, I was pleased to note, was a lot like his chocolate cake. Sweet with a little sass, and absolutely the best reason I'd ever had to shut up.

11

I inhaled, breathing in the piquant scents of salt and earth and pine trees. I was momentarily confused. Where was I? Reality set in when I felt a pinecone tangled up in my hair. Cool, damp air had settled into the space around me, and I could feel my clothes clinging to me in a decidedly not-indoor way. I bolted upright and saw Kai to my right, rustling but still asleep. At first glance, a passerby would think we were formerly wealthy homeless people, maybe victims of the dot-com bust. I still wore the cropped jacket, embroidered tank, and tailored jeans from the night before, though I'd shed my Toms at some point, probably after the chocolate cake and before the milky gray dawn arrived. Kai lay on his side, sandy curls running amok on his forehead, one arm cradling his head as a makeshift pillow. The lanterns had sputtered out long ago, and because of the clouds above and the quiet around us, I had no earthly idea of the actual time.

Trying not to wake Kai, I fumbled under the picnic blanket for my phone, wishing I hadn't scoffed at that beeping locator keychain my mother had given me one Christmas. Just before I went into full-blown panic, I found the phone, nestled right where the small of my back had just rested. The tender ache now explained, I opened the home screen and gasped in horror: 8:16. I had planned on starting my morning inventory at Thrill no later than 7:00.

I scrambled to a seated position, my mind racing. My shoes were damp with dew, making it hard to get them on. I was pointing my toes and wiggling in a bizarre lower body shimmy when I realized Kai was propped on one elbow and staring at me. An impressive cowlick spiked a curl above his left eyebrow.

"Headed out?" he asked, amusement in his eyes.

"It's so late," I said, breathless but finally victorious with the shoes. "I should have been at work over an hour ago. You, too!" I said, my anxiety suddenly doubling. "It's after eight! People are probably lined up outside Howie's, and you're not there!"

"Hold on there, tiger," Kai said, covering a yawn. "Sunshine is opening up this morning with my sub cook, Hugh. They'll be fine."

I was incredulous. "You have a sub cook? But you own the restaurant. How do you know he'll do things right? What does he know about your grandma's pancakes?"

Kai watched me as I circled our little clearing to gather our mess. "Hugh is a very capable cook. I trust him. And my grandma's pancakes aren't exactly rocket science." He reached over to still my hands as I started to stack our dishes from the night before. "Hey, take a deep breath. It's still early in the day, right? You've got plenty of time to make up for a late start."

I stopped and considered his advice. He might be right—in fact he probably *was* right, but nope, I couldn't go there. I tried taking a few deep breaths, but it felt like cheating. I quickly resumed my real-life shallow breathing.

"So, we must have fallen asleep," Kai said, his eyes sparking with mischief.

I shook my head, a smile creeping into my voice. "I guess so. The last thing I remember is laughing at your lame Trivial Pursuit story—"

"*That* is a very interesting story," he said, all seriousness.

"Please never, ever tell it again. Apparently it induces a deep, coma-like sleep in hapless victims." I leaned over and kissed him lightly on the mouth, but he tugged me toward him and made me linger for more.

"I *have* to go," I said in my kitchen voice when I pulled away.

He laughed, typically a response I did not receive when I used The Kitchen Voice. "So you've said. Just five more minutes? I'll sprint with you back to your apartment."

I shook my head and flicked a series of leaves off my jeans. "Sorry. I can't. I'm freaking out right now and I have to go."

"Hey, they can wait." He tried pulling me to him, but I pushed back, feeling a chip descend on my shoulder.

"No, I can't. I'm the new girl. Remember? I still have a lot to prove, and I don't want to set a bad example." *And what I do is a little more complicated than frying eggs and flipping burgers*, I thought, but did not say.

"Got it." He stood and gathered the corners of the blanket. "How about dinner on your next night off? Indoors, with plumbing and everything."

"I would love to," I said, already backing away. "But I feel like I'm forgetting something. Now that we have the TV deal at Thrill—"

"Whoa, what?" Kai sounded fully awake. "What TV deal? You're doing a TV gig at work? How did you not mention this last night?"

"I probably tried but I couldn't bear to interrupt you when you got to the part about the Genus IV edition, and whether or not the geography questions are truly worthy of Trivial Pursuit." I laughed when I saw him roll his eyes. "Call me," I called as I grabbed my bag and booked it up the hill toward a quick hot shower before a day in the kitchen.

"Soon!" I added and smiled in spite of myself.

⁂

I arrived, wet-haired but tidy, at half past nine, a perfectly respectable start time for a pastry chef, but not close to my ideal. Barely pausing to hang my coat, I plunged into the walk-in refrigerator, clipboard at the ready. The chill felt good after all my rushing around, and I noted with pleasure all the neat rows of clear containers, each emblazoned with a stripe of yellow painter's tape. Most of the handwriting was my own, indicating the ingredient, the amount, and the date and time it was stored. I noticed some loopy cursive in there, however, and I dropped to my knees to inspect Tova's work. My nose wrinkled at an illegible weight of rendered lard, not because of the idea of pig fat but because Tova's handwriting was cute and messy. If she started dotting her i's with little hearts . . .

The sealed door of the walk-in broke open with a flourish and I jumped, juggling with both hands to avoid dropping the lard. Avery strode in, took the container out of my hands, and placed it onto the wrong shelf.

He faced me. "Are you ready?" The drama in his voice sounded like something on a luxury car commercial.

"Probably," I said, not in the mood for games. "What are you talking about?" I tried turning back to my clipboard, but he held me by the shoulders.

"I just talked with Production," he said in a hushed, reverent tone. "Today is the day. They're going to film you during service."

"What?" I said, immediately panicked. "No! I mean, they can't. Margot said my first taping wouldn't be until next week at the earliest."

Avery shook his head slowly and tightened the grip on my shoulders. "Not anymore. We are flexible. We are going with the flow. We are totally chill."

I wriggled out of his grasp. "Actually, I am very *inflexible*, as a rule. I hate going with flows." I started to pace, which was markedly unsatisfying in such a cramped space. "I'm already late with my prep for tonight's service, and plus, I need *time* before I'm being filmed. Time to figure out how to be on camera, how to act, what to say, how to do all the fake smiling stuff and cook at the same time. I need to make index cards, Avery. I need to watch Rachael Ray. I need more time!"

His nod turned quickly into a shake of the head. "Right. And no. You don't need any time. You're going to be great. Don't worry." He took me by the hand and steered us toward the door. "The crew is waiting."

I tugged my clipboard off the shelf as he bullied me toward the door. "I have to finish inventory."

"Someone else will do that. Tova!" Avery called, hustling us out of the walk-in and toward the front of the house.

I caught a glimpse of my reflection in the stainless steel of a cook top. "My hair's wet! And I have no makeup on today!" The whole sleep-under-the-stars thing was turning out to be less and less of a brilliant idea, though I felt my skin prickle with the thought of Kai's mouth on mine.

I had no time to linger on that thought, because Avery swept me into the main house. We stopped to take in the transformation. A swarm of people in artsy glasses and variations of black V-necks scurried around the room, setting up lighting, cameras, and backdrops. Vic and Margot noticed our arrival and nodded, but continued in what appeared to be a very focused conversation.

A curvy young woman in cropped hair dyed an unnatural, spiky white approached with an inquisitive stare. "Charlie?" she said. When I nodded, she held out her hand. "I'm Lolo. I'll be taking care of your hair and makeup."

"See?" Avery nudged me in the side. He appeared to be trying on a seductive voice for size. "Lolo here is a *master*, I'm sure of it. Charlie will be in great hands, right, Lo?"

Lolo looked at Avery for a moment, not unlike a zoo patron would take in the curiosities of the komodo dragon exhibit. Without a word, she turned and made her way to a makeup chair and mirror while dodging a crew of men taping cords onto the floor.

Avery nudged me, and I tripped over my Crocs as I followed. I sat gingerly in Lolo's chair. She put both hands on my shoulders and locked eyes with me in the mirror.

"You're freaking out, aren't you?"

I sighed. "I hate TV. I thought I was going to have this weekend to prepare, watch a few episodes of some horrible reality show, and go over the shooting schedule. I have severe stomach cramps right now, which can only mean loose stools, and this is happening when I should be prepping for tonight's service." Seeing the look on Lolo's face, I added, "Sorry. Too much information."

Lolo nodded. "Probably."

I continued my rant. "Exactly! I don't know how to do this. I'm talking about my bowels and we just met. I should never, ever have my words recorded. And I don't know how to smile and cook and be nice to people when I'm working. And . . ." I pointed to my head, "I don't have time to worry about hair and bronzers and eyeliner when I have to get ready to serve dessert to hundreds of people. And no matter what—this is non-negotiable—I will *not* show my naked body on camera."

Lolo had listened to my tirade without interrupting. When I finished, she reached for a comb and started pulling it through my hair. "Here's what you need to know about this whole thing. First, bronzer is so four years ago. Second, no one wants to see your groceries. It's just not that kind of show. So you can take a sigh of relief on that one."

I pulled my chef's coat more tightly around my chest and let out that sigh without shame.

"Third, that schmooze you were just talking to? What's his name?"

"Avery."

"Right. Maybe *Avery* gave you some bad intel. You're not supposed to be an actress. This is a *reality* show." She sprayed some misty stuff on her hands and massaged it into my hair. "That means you can't practice, and you can't try it out first, and you can't worry about doing it right. Because whatever you rehearse beforehand will look forced and bizarre on camera."

I felt my shoulders relax a smidge. The head massage wasn't hurting.

"So whatever *Avery* said, I would ignore." She lowered her voice. "This is the eighth time I've worked on a show with Vic and Margot. Some shows have been winners; some have been losers. I don't suppose you saw the first episode of *Nailed*? About the blind carpenter who owned a nudist ballet studio?"

I shook my head, dumbstruck.

"Ghastly. Only lasted two episodes past the pilot. Took them a long time to get over the scars of that one. So there definitely have been losers. But the winners all have one thing in common, other than perfect styling." She stood back to inspect a sleek twist she'd just pinned at the nape of my neck. "The winners," her eyes on mine, "were the real deal. No faking, no positioning, no begging people to like them. Just themselves—the good, bad, and woefully unattractive." She spun me around in the chair and handed me a mirror so I could see the back of my head. "Lucky for you, you're gorgeous and you have great bone structure. But beyond that, just be yourself. Try to forget anyone is even watching."

She shrugged.

I clenched both arms of her styling chair, waiting as her disciple for any other bits of sage advice. She offered just one more.

"And listen: no matter how bad you're feeling, never ever cry in front of Margot. On-camera crying is a gold mine for ratings. But off camera, she will stop listening and won't respect you again. She sees tears as weakness."

"That won't be an issue," I thought, relieved I could check one thing off my list. I hadn't cried in public since watching *Where the Red Fern Grows* during Mrs. Hoffman's end-of-year party in fourth grade. I'd been horrified then, and I remained horrified at the thought of letting all that emotion and control seep out of my eyeballs. If Margot wanted no tears, no tears would I provide.

I held back a coughing fit as Lolo sprayed my hair with industrial-strength shellac. *Just be yourself*, I thought, as a man with remarkably neat eyebrows tsked and then attacked my face with a tackle box full of makeup.

Forget anyone is watching, I thought, as I reentered the pastry kitchen and watched the Hobart mixer work an oversized whisk into coffee buttercream frosting.

"Forget anyone is watching," I muttered as I piped a border of whipped cream along the edge of a Key lime tart.

"No way," Tova said, and I looked up to see her directing a feline smile at one of the cameramen. Her black curls fell prettily under her chef's cap and shone under the lights. I noticed a carefully drawn bright red lip, jarringly glamorous against her plain white chef's coat. "Forget they're watching?" She batted curly eyelashes. "The watching is the best part."

I pushed a stack of dirty sheet pans into her muscled abdomen. "These need to be scrubbed, and the dishwashers are backed up. Go to it, sis."

She pushed her lips out in a sultry pout, eyes still on the cameraman. "What if I miss something good?"

Ignoring that concern, I narrowed my eyes at her. "Tova, where did you go to school? And where did you work before coming to Thrill?"

"Indian Paintbrush Community College. It was awesome and super cheap. And I worked at Spago before this."

I stood still, a sharp pulse of awe pushing aside the community college issue. "Spago? Wow. So you worked with Sherry Yard?"

She smiled at the cameraman as she dunked the sheet pans under the running faucet in our deep sink. "Oh, the dessert lady? Absolutely not. She'd never let a hostess anywhere near her part of the kitchen."

I realized the camera dude had trained his lens on my face, and I quickly pulled my mouth shut from its gaping position. A Spago hostess! A very pretty, well-endowed, lusciously lipped Spago hostess! An Avery hire, and blessed, I was sure, by Margot and Vic. *Oh, well*, I thought. *She's all I have.* She cried out from her spot by the sink and then showed the cameraman her fingers, scalded red from the hot water. If she had been paying attention to her job and not the cameraman—and that was a big if—she would not have sustained first-degree burns. My first day in front of the cameras, and my B-Team sidekick was whimpering about her acrylic nails.

This was going to be a very long day.

I glanced at the clock and saw we were ten minutes into the start of service. I ran through a mental checklist, knowing the first orders were only minutes away. My late start had followed me all day to this point, and I worried that my double-checking would not be enough, considering how distracted I'd been. The hair, the makeup, the lights, the noise, and the movement were foreign and irritating. Adding to the mayhem, Margot and Vic had come back to the kitchen every five minutes to pepper me with questions about which angle would be best to film garnishing (the east wall), and if I had any objections to opening my coat a few buttons (I did), and if I could "pop out" to the main house a few times each hour to interact with the clientele (give me a break). So when Avery rounded the corner midway through the first hour of service followed by a gaggle of lights and microphones, I had to force my face into a semblance of sanity.

"How can I help you, Chef?" I asked in the most polite voice I could muster, doing my best to ignore the artificial light glaring off the surface of my counters. I had five desserts going out to the pass, four of which still needed my attention that very moment. I gritted my teeth and looked questioningly at Avery.

"Heeyy, Char." His voice sounded absolutely bizarre, like cotton had taken up the space between his vocal chords and his tongue. "How's it going back here?"

I raised one eyebrow. "Just fine. I have five desserts coming your way." This was my hint. *Go away.* He did not take it.

"Sweet. That's really great. You're really great at your job."

I nodded slowly, a trace of concern poking through my annoyance. "Thanks, Avery. You don't sound, um, like yourself."

His eyes widened, pleading. Mouth still stuck in that trembling smile, he looked like a fish with really great hair. I glanced over at Margot, who stood next to the cameraman. She had both hands on her diminutive hips, or where her hips might have been if she'd had any. She looked highly irritated. Vic stood next to her, biting his lower lip with his teeth, his eyes bulging slightly behind his glasses.

I returned my gaze to Avery. He looked utterly lost. *He's tanking,* I thought. The poor guy was absolutely crashing and burning. He wanted this so badly, but he was crumbling under his own expectations.

I leaned up against the counter and wiped a fine layer of perspiration from my forehead. Locking eyes with Avery, I smiled. "Being an executive chef is stressful, right?" I hoped my voice was calming, like those people in the movies who try to talk the terrorists into letting the hostages go. "Remember how we used to deal with stress in culinary school?" I walked toward him, grabbing two rubber spatulas off the counter as I moved. "Remember Julian Lennon? That one song of his we always sang?"

Avery smiled, a slow and cautious smile. "His *only* song, as I recall. But I could never remember how it started."

"Well, it's much too late for goodbye," I sang, tugging his arms into a corny dance posture, forcing him to join me in a clumsy two-step. He laughed, nerves still making his vocal chords strike a higher pitch than normal. I mimicked his white-man's overbite, and I felt his arms relax a bit when he laughed again. He sang a line with me, totally off-key, but he did appear to be regaining control of his faculties.

"You okay?" I said into his ear when he remembered our signature and only real dance move, a low dip with jazz hands.

"Thank you," he whispered, his lips lingering by my cheek.

I waited for him to pull me into a standing position, and when he didn't, I cleared my throat. "All right, then. Back to work," I said, scrambling as I pulled myself up.

"Back to work," Avery said, his voice now rid of the cotton strangle, but moving into some sort of dream sequence. The sappy expression on his face was a perfect match.

I heard Tova sigh behind me. I whipped my head in her direction. She looked like I probably looked after watching any film involving Meg Ryan and Tom Hanks. I retrieved a baking sheet from storage and let it clang unceremoniously on the countertop. "Final garnishes on the rhubarb and the Key lime, Tova. I'll take the other three plates."

Turning back to my work, I hunched over the desserts, hearing the shuffle of the film crew as they moved to another part of the kitchen. Avery hung back a few steps, and I looked up to meet his glance.

"Perfect!" he mouthed and gave me an effusive thumbs-up. "Charlie to the rescue!"

I shrugged and looked again at the plates below me, unsure whose script we were all so busy following.

12

Even the patient, lingering daylight hours of spring were giving up on me by the time I jogged up the walk in front of Jack and Manda's house later that week. I looked again at my watch and sucked in my breath. I was late. Very, *very* late. After much discussion and calendar checking, we'd finally found a dinner date that would work for the Henricks, Kai, and me, but even after all our efforts, I was the kink in a great plan. And I was late.

Reaching the wraparound porch, I tiptoed through an obstacle course of toys and bikes, jump ropes, sidewalk chalk, and a line of dolls, several with at least one eye poked out, perched in a line leading to the wide porch swing. I heard laughter from inside, and I pushed open the screen door. The squeaky hinges announced my arrival, and Manda came around the corner with a glass of red wine in her hand.

"She lives! Those text messages were not from some other Charlie Garrett," she called over her shoulder. I could hear Jack and Kai echo her surprise.

"I'm so sorry," I gushed and dropped my bag on a comfy velvet armchair before leaning into Manda's ready hug. "I kept trying to leave for the last two hours, but Avery had a mile-long list of things we needed to discuss and the TV people had their own lists and, well." I forced a tired smile. "I'm here now."

"No worries," Manda said, though I could tell by the eyes I had known since the years of N'Sync that she was disappointed I had missed dinner.

"Your roasted buttermilk chicken and garlic mashed potatoes are keeping warm in the oven."

"Mmm," I said in concert with my rumbling stomach. I tried keeping the disbelief out of my voice. "It smells amazing."

Manda narrowed her eyes at me. "You sound surprised." She pursed her lips. "Okay, fine. The chicken and the potatoes are from Whole Foods, but!" She lifted one finger in triumph. "I made, with my own hands, a spaghetti squash casserole with kale and edamame. It's delicious. Even Jack liked it."

We'd entered the Henricks' cozy dining room. Manda had painted one wall a deep, oceanic blue, and it pulled the space together like a cozy blanket. The long oak farm table where the men sat had been her grandmother's. Jack had Zara and Dane on each of his knees, Kai was across from them, and Polly sat in queen position at the head of the table. She appeared to be trying to kill something on the tray of her high chair.

"I did like that casserole. She's right," Jack said.

I watched to see if his face would betray the sure and utter lie, but the man was a professional. He'd been married to Manda and her cooking for a very long time. "But, babe, please don't start in about going alkaline," he said, a hint of desperation creeping into his voice. "Or paleo. Or flavor-free. Or whatever nonsense that woman at the co-op keeps proselytizing about."

"Baby steps," Manda said quietly to me as she went to retrieve my plate from the oven.

Kai stood from the table and pulled me into a hug. I felt myself relax into his arms, and I took a deep breath of his clean smell: soap, fresh air, maybe a touch of cinnamon from his day in the kitchen. He kissed me quickly on the cheek. A growth of new whiskers brushed my skin.

"Hi," he said, his smile reaching me from his lips and his eyes. "It's good to see you."

"You, too," I said, lingering with his arms around my waist. "Sorry I've been texting more than calling."

It was true. My communication efforts had been repeatedly thwarted as the show and the restaurant absorbed all my time. Since our starry night three weeks ago, Kai and I had met each other for a single rushed coffee date at a spot just down the street from Thrill. He had met me between takes and had been patient and gracious about several other failed attempts to get together since then. Our texts had been sweet and sassy, but I felt a rush of adrenaline to finally be in the same room with him again.

Jack snorted. "Texting is to modern couples what love letters were to previous generations, don't you know that, Char?" I could hear him ramping up for one of his favorite topics: how technology depletes the human spirit. "The thing about technology," he said, bouncing Dane and Zara on his knees and making them laugh hysterically, "is that it saps all the human out of the human being."

"I'm okay with the texts," Kai said into my ear. "As long as I can see your actual face as much as possible. You're much more beautiful than emoticons. Except for maybe the flamenco dancer."

I laughed, but I really wanted to purr. "That flamenco dancer *is* a looker," I said, feeling lovely even after twelve hours spent in the company of lights, heat, and grease.

"Sit." Manda returned with my food and ordered me to the empty chair and the only untouched spot at the table. "Kai, please, if you would, pour Charlie some wine and enjoy adult conversation while we put our offspring into the baths they desperately need. Who's stinky?"

"I am!" Dane announced with a sense of pride that many men never relinquish.

"I am *not*," Zara said. "But can I go first? And use bubbles?"

"Perhaps," Jack said as he stood. He carried both the older kids like sacks of potatoes while Manda followed behind with a sleepy Polly. Before hitting the stairs, Manda stopped by the table and lowered Polly's head to my level. I kissed her repeatedly on top of her fine blond hair, behind the ears, on the one spot of her plump cheek that had escaped puréed carrots.

"Love you, Pol," I said as Manda ferried her away. "Can I read the other two some stories before they go to sleep?"

"Hallelujah and yes, you may," Manda called. "I'll call down when it's time."

I turned to Kai and speared my first bite of buttermilk chicken. "You in for story-time?"

"Absolutely," he said. "But I don't want to embarrass you when they like my voices better than yours."

I made a face. "Your *voices*? What is this, a Disney movie?"

He shrugged, feigning disinterest. "Go ahead. Talk your trash. But if this is a competition, and for men, everything is, just know you're about to get crushed."

I nodded, pulled daintily on my wine. "And why are you so confident of your magical ways with children? Do you have some I've never met?" I regretted the words immediately, noting at once that I didn't know him *that* well and he could easily be hiding progeny somewhere.

He smiled and tore a chunk off the round of rock-hard spelt bread sitting in the middle of the table. "One in every state of the Union. I had a wild youth."

I stopped chewing and stared at his face.

He rolled his eyes. "No kids, Char. But I do have nephews and nieces. And they think I'm amazing."

I finished my first drumstick and proceeded to the second. "How many siblings do you have?"

"Two sisters," Kai said. "Both older, both a little bossy, both fantastic people. Gemma lives in Portland with her husband and baby girl. Dahlia lives in central Washington with her family. I'm going to go visit them and their orchard sometime soon. Maybe you can come." He bumped me gently with his knees and watched my face for my reaction.

"I'd really like that," I said, meaning it. "I'd like to meet the women who know best how to boss you around."

He laughed. "I didn't say they were any good at it. Just that they do it."

I scooted my chair closer to his and kissed him on his mouth. "You taste good," I murmured.

"That chicken is wicked good with buttermilk, paprika, and a little garlic."

"Paprika!" I cried. "Smoked, right? But what in the name of heaven is in that squash thing? Did she actually stoop to tapioca?"

"Quite possibly," Kai said, shushing me with another kiss. "Also, you are inappropriately loud right now."

"I love smoked paprika," I said and then jumped a foot in the air when I felt a small, cold finger poke into my armpit.

Dane erupted into a cackle, and Zara giggled into her hand.

"Aunt Charlie is tick-wish!" Dane said, falling on the floor in spasms of laughter.

I willed my heart rate to slow. "Yes," I said. "Very."

Kai lowered to the floor and went into full-on tickle attack on Dane.

Zara spoke to me in an oversized stage whisper. "Aunt Charlie, you were *kissing* Mr. Malloy. That is *super nasty* because he is a *boy*."

I pulled her toward me and hefted her over my shoulder. I was happy her shrieks drowned out my panting. When did the girl get so heavy?

"He *is* a boy," I said. "And he definitely has cooties, which is why we all need to go upstairs and wash our hands before story-time."

"We just had a bath!" Dane protested from his upside-down perch behind us. Kai was carrying him by the ankles up the stairs.

"But you never know if you accidentally picked a booger between now and then," I said, depositing Zara in front of the bathroom sink.

"You do realize you're neurotic about cleanliness," Kai said into my ear. His closeness made me shiver.

"Just looking out for our collective health," I said, hoping Kai would stay close and that the kids would take at least fifteen minutes to scrub.

"Are you going to be one of those moms who goes in for a kamikaze hit at the playground, wielding hand sanitizer and preventing your children from forming any real friendships?"

I balked. "Of *course* I will bring hand sanitizer to the playground. Those places are cesspools for bacteria." I shuddered.

Kai shook his head as we followed Zara and Dane into the room they shared. "You are a total weirdo. You're hot," he added, thoughtfully, "which does buy you some time, but you are still a weirdo."

We piled onto Zara's twin bed, legs and arms everywhere. After much deliberation and negotiation, the kids picked out two books each, two more than typically sanctioned, but approved by Jack and Manda on this special occasion. I suspected they were doing little cartwheels of joy downstairs having a few extra minutes of peace and canoodling.

As promised, Kai was irritatingly fantastic as a storyteller. The voices were spot on, especially some German nursemaid action he employed for the witch in Hansel and Gretel.

When Kai had finished with the breadcrumbs and the baked children, a story I had always found terrifying, I gathered my reserves and all the dramatic flair I could muster and started in. "'Once upon a time,'" I read, "'there lived a sweet and lovely girl named Cinderella.'"

Dane groaned. "Princesses are yuck."

"They are not!" Zara said, the curves of her eyebrows rippling with concern. "And we read the scary witch one for you! It's my turn."

"She's right, dude," Kai said, his tone conciliatory. "Plus, it is pretty sweet when the fat lady makes the pumpkin turn into a car on wheels, right?"

"Pretty sure we can't say 'fat' in this day and age," I said under my breath to Kai.

"Calling a spade a spade," he said back and gestured to the open book.

I cleared my throat. "'Cinderella lived in a castle with her cruel stepmother and two ugly, mean stepsisters.'"

"Pretty sure we can't say 'ugly' in this day and age," Kai said quietly while the kids fought over who would get to turn the page.

"'One day, an invitation arrived from the palace,'" I continued, trying for "light and airy" to balance out all the devoured children and unkind adjectives we'd already encountered. Zara draped one leg across mine. Dane relaxed into Kai's side.

My phone chimed from the bedside table. I reached over and glanced at it.

> Avery Michaels: What about a melon dessert? Do you do melon?

I turned the phone to vibrate. "'All of the maidens of the kingdom were asked to join the prince for a royal ball,'" I said, reaching again for my phone when it vibrated another incoming text.

> Avery Michaels: Margot wants to know what time you're coming in tomorrow. And did you tell Vic your idea about filming family meal?

I cleared my throat and kept reading. "'*Surely, I may go as well*! Cinderella cried, but her evil stepmother had other plans.'" I was feeling really good about my Cinderella voice, sweet but not saccharine, just a touch of victim, because, come on. The girl had it rough. Before I could continue, the phone vibrated again, and Zara snatched it from my hand.

"A-ve-ry," she read. "Who's that? He has texted you lots of times." Her hazel eyes enlarged with the injustice of each interruption.

I plucked the phone from her hand and avoided eye contact with Kai. "Avery is my boss. He's asking me some questions about work."

A smidge of bitter bled into Kai's tone. "Avery is a boss who doesn't seem to know his employees can't pitch tents at his restaurant. They do have lives."

"He sounds like a mean and evil step-boss," Zara said, very serious. "Maybe you should get another boss."

"Avery is not mean and evil," I snapped, instantly softening when I saw the hurt on Zara's face. "He's just doing his best," I said more gently. "We are all trying to do good work, and that can take a lot of time."

I saw Kai's jaw tighten, but his eyes remained neutrally focused on Cinderella and her plight.

"Shall we keep reading?" I said brightly. I adopted a particularly cranky voice for the stepmother that had a giggle-inducing effect on the kids, and though my phone registered nine more texts from Avery by the time the ball was over and the slipper found, the kids and I quickly became proficient at ignoring it. So much so that I looked up, surprised, when Kai took Zara's pink unicorn pillow and smooshed it down, none too lightly, right on top of the next vibration.

When the Buzz Lightyear and Rapunzel nightlights were emanating a cheery glow in the room and I had kissed both children's cheeks six times each, Kai pulled shut their bedroom door with a quiet click. I wrapped my arms around him in the semidarkness. He held me close, and I let my head rest on his chest. Manda's laugh floated up the stairs as Jack's voice became animated with some story.

Perhaps I shouldn't have, but I couldn't let go of the texts and the irritation on Kai's face.

"Listen," I said, pulling away so I could see his eyes. "My work is really important to me," I said, sounding more tentative than I'd have liked. I cleared my throat. "Sometimes I'm going to have to be in touch with Thrill even when I'm with you."

Kai waited so long to answer, I wondered if I should repeat myself. Finally, he spoke. "I totally get it," he said. I wondered if the brightness of his tone was authentic or a tad forced.

"You do?" I said, then backpedaled quickly. "Of course you do. You work in the same industry."

Kai suppressed a smile. "Technically. I mean, we both serve food, but if this were a feudal system, for example, you would be a member of the nobility and I would be a peasant."

"But a very good-looking one," I said, moving in for a kiss. A shiver ran up my spine. "And one that smelled remarkably good for all the mucking of stalls and milking of cows that you did."

"I think you're mixing metaphors," he said between kisses.

"Shh," I said, "or I'll have you imprisoned for treason to the queen."

"You're not doing this right," he said, but within a few moments, I'm pretty sure he changed his mind.

13

TOVA'S nose—empty of the piercing she'd gotten on Monday, her most recent day off, and that I'd insisted she remove before we started work—hovered only inches above the mixing bowl. We'd finished the early morning prep and had the sublime gift of extra time before plunging into the next round of tasks, so I was taking the opportunity to teach her how to make a piecrust.

"So, this is a miniversion of what we will make on a larger scale later today," I said, pointing to the bowl. "We've whisked our flour and salt, and we are ready to incorporate our fats. Now, people feel very strongly about the butter-lard issue, but I like a mix of both. More butter than lard, but a combo of both makes for a very flaky and flavorful crust."

Tova nodded. "Whatever you say, Charlie, I will do. I grew up on frozen Pillsbury, so anything homemade is an improvement."

I smiled, feeling magnanimous. "I'm sure the Pillsbury ones were made with love, too."

Tova snorted. "Probably not. My mom was more interested in her revolving door of boyfriends than in making piecrust."

"Ouch," Mike, the cameraman said quietly from behind his mammoth lens, and I realized how accustomed I had become to having my every move and conversation filmed.

"So even though we make this in bigger batches, the same principles apply," I said. I pointed to my precise, tiny cubes of butter and lard. "Chilling is essential. Pastry dough is very temperamental and really only shines when you respect its need to remain cold and as untouched as possible. I remember—"

"You're so insensitive!" Tova's exclamation was sudden and loud.

"Excuse me?" I asked, genuinely baffled. My hands hovered above the metal bowl.

"I'm trying to talk to you about my alcoholic mom who had issues with promiscuity, Charlie." Her eyes were brimming, but no tears fell. "I lived in a shack. With no running water. And lots of bugs." Her chin dropped indignantly.

I stared, unblinking. "I'm sorry," I said. "I had no idea."

"Of course you didn't." She flipped her hair as she continued. "You're so absorbed with yourself and your career and your rise to the top." She punctuated this last sentence with a poke by one righteous fingernail to the ceiling. "I'm a woman, too, Charlie. I would think you'd want to help another female chef in this *male-dominated profession*."

Why did I get the feeling she'd had to practice saying those words together?

"Listen," I said, hands still clumpy with lard and flour, "I *have been* helping you. In fact . . ." I moved one step in her direction. "I have been ignoring the fact that you are eons behind where you should be to have your position here and have, instead, taken you under my wing."

"Your wing is rigid and uncaring!" she cried, one single tear rolling down her cheek.

"All right," I said, flipping the faucet knob and pumping three vigorous slams on the soap dispenser. "I need a break and so do you. We can do pie crust another time."

The light on the camera dimmed, and Margot stepped around the crew. "Excellent. Perfect, Tova."

I looked at Tova, who looked extraordinarily pleased with herself. "Wow," she said. "That was intense." She met my confused expression. "Thanks for going with that, Charlie. I really felt the freedom to *become* the scene."

"What the—" I began.

Margot put her hand on my arm. I could feel its icy temp through my shirt. "You were fantastic."

My brows knitted together. "I wasn't *fantastic*. I was offended. Can someone please tell me what on earth just happened here?"

Margot pointed to a spot on the clipboard she carried. "We were working on a story line for Tova in this episode and thought we could address the issue of women in the professional kitchen. This scene will be a part of a montage that will highlight the struggles she's had, the injustices, the victimization, the victories she's scored in such a male-dominated profession."

There was that phrase again, clearly outlined for Tova during a previous tutorial.

"So," Margot finished, "Tova did an excellent job of drawing out the delicate war between feminine strength and relationship building."

"Was any of that real?" I asked, my mind whirling.

Margot looked bemused. "That, my sweet girl, is the question we must always ask and to which none of us has a good answer. Hence the enduring success of reality television." She smiled, and I saw a line of crooked lower teeth I'd never noticed before. "But to ease your mind, yes, Tova was speaking from the heart. Right, Tova?"

"Wow," Tova said, basking in Margot's attention. "I'm so glad you liked it, Ms. Rubin. It's really such a huge honor to be working with you." She must have felt me staring hard at her because she turned and wilted a bit. "Just so you know, Charlie, my mom really did sleep around."

"The shack without running water?" I was doing all I could to remain civil.

She shrugged, suddenly sheepish. "A split-level in Las Vegas. But sometimes my mom forgot to pay the water bill and they shut it off! For, like, two days!"

I shook my head and took a deep breath before addressing Margot. "I don't think I'm meant for this." My eyes took in the entire kitchen, most parts of it clicking along at a normal pace, but my area crowded with people and cameras and boom mics and forced emotional scenes. "I told Avery from the beginning that I wouldn't tolerate dishonesty."

I saw a flicker of hardness flash through Margot's eyes, but it was gone before it settled into anything tangible. "I understand," she said, her voice crisp and professional. "You need a break—you've been working every day since we started filming. I'm going to suggest to Avery that you take the next two days off. It's midweek, so he can manage fine here without you until the weekend. Go somewhere, relax, and we can resume filming of the pastry segments when you return."

More than anything, I wanted to let my head roll in a slow half-circle in an attempt to get rid of the kinks and strain that had gathered into a huge orb of tension at the top of my shoulders, but I was not about to show Margot how tired I was. "All right, I'll think about it," I agreed. "A couple days off does sound good."

Margot nodded quickly, then motioned for the crew to move out. "Rest well. You deserve it."

I returned to the bowl of piecrust, deciding to finish it off with cinnamon-dusted apples and an inch-high streusel. I knew just the man who would appreciate a homemade pie.

"Sorry about the outburst, Charlie," Tova said quietly when she stood again by my side. "And I do want you to know I totally listened to what you said about lard and butter. It made perfect, awesome sense."

I raised my eyebrows in her direction. "I'm on to you now, Tova. And I'm willing to guess that compliment wasn't exactly genuine."

She started to speak and then stopped, her pretty painted lips parting in a smile. "Okay, fine. But I do like pie. That much is true."

I shook my head but found myself giving Tova a pass. "You fit in around here way better than I do."

"Thanks!" she said, effusive. "You're so sweet. And Charlie!" She beamed. "I think we'll have a super emotional reconciliation on screen, don't you?"

I closed my eyes and took my time counting to three. Then I texted Kai. I was hoping it wasn't too late to get in on the day trip to sun and orchards and a bossy sister or two.

Kai picked me up the next morning after the breakfast rush at Howie's, and we were on our way out of the city by ten.

"Hey," he said, holding the car door ajar for me. He leaned in to kiss me softly on the cheek. "Mmm," he murmured into my hair, "you smell delicious."

"You too," I said, my nose in his warm neck, still damp from a shower. "How do you scrub all the kitchen smell out of your skin? I always feel like it's a losing battle."

He pulled back and took me in with his eyes, making me feel a little exposed and a lot happy. "I use a very special soap made only here in Washington. And Tibet. Washington and Tibet. The secret is sandalwood."

"Seriously?" I said, all ears. "Can I have some?"

He shut my door and jogged around to the driver's side. "You know," he said while turning the ignition, "for such a city girl, you believe lots of things told to you by nervous men on all-day dates. I use Dial soap. And you can certainly have some. I buy it in bulk at Target."

"See now," I said, shaking my head, "it's highly irritating that you set me up to feel like a total idiot and then you soften the blow by being humble and transparent. Shrewd, Malloy." I reached over and took his hand. "Why are you nervous?"

"Well, first, because you are breathtakingly pretty. The dress . . . " He stopped, took a deep breath, stole a look at me, even though we were in heavy traffic. "The hair, your face . . . you can be intimidating, Garrett."

I stifled a smile, secretly giving Manda props for convincing me to buy the dress. It was a maxi, insanely soft and comfortable while also feminine and beautifully cut along the bodice. The blue-gray on top slowly faded to a deeper blue by the time it brushed the tops of my new strappy sandals.

"I would think I'd be more intimidating in my chef's whites, my gelled-back bun, and my I'm-a-girl-and-I'm-angry kitchen face."

He sniffed. "No way. I could totally take you down in the kitchen."

I raised one eyebrow. Then I cleared my throat. He ignored me and kept his eyes on the road.

"But," he added, "hit me with wavy, day-off hair, freckles, and a feisty smile, and I'm a goner."

I let my spine sink into the seat, willing my back to relax and my mind to stay far, far away from Thrill and Margot and Avery and TV shows. Much of Seattle was hurtling through a weekday, sidewalks full of people walking with purpose, talking on cell phones, trying to dodge the light rain that had developed in the clouds overhead. I watched the city fall away as we moved first past traffic, concrete, and metal, then neighborhoods, trees, and driveways.

Kai and I laughed and talked as we felt the miles and our normal lives drop behind us. I recoiled when he picked the radio station (eighties punk), and he mocked me mercilessly when it was my turn to choose (seventies funk with an unrepentant helping of disco). We agreed to let Paul Simon sing us through the Cascades and so listened to him tell stories about diamonds on the soles of her shoes and Rene and Georgette Magritte as we climbed and then descended in the greens and blacks and purples of the mountains.

"So, tell me about the orchard. And how about a crash course on family names, please." I reached for my bag and took out a memo pad and a mechanical pencil. I'd drawn a neat line down the middle of a page, with "orchard" on one side and "family" on the other when I felt Kai's eyes on me. I met his stare and surmised he wasn't going to compliment my dress and hair this time.

"You're taking notes." He said it as a statement of fact, and I nodded, forsaking my impulse to say, "Duh."

"Family details can get confusing," I reasoned. "I don't want to accidentally call your niece the name of a nephew. I'm guessing that in a family where the children are named Kai, Gemma, and Dahlia, the kid names might be some hair-raisers."

Kai shook his head. "You are, um, quirky, Garrett. Scratch that. You're a head case."

I was rummaging in my bag for the little container of extra graphite I kept with me at all times. My pencil was running low, and I would not suffer a dull point.

Kai was still talking when I emerged victorious. He was starting to mutter. "This from the woman who shares her name with millions of American *men*." He pointed at my list. "But just to fly in the face of your prejudices, I'll have you know that Gemma and Kory's little girl is named Lucy. And Dahlia and Ruben have two kids, Ted and Anna. Mainstream, Fourth of July, all-American top-100 names, all the way."

I grunted and wrote the names under the proper heading. I quizzed him about the kids' ages (Lucy was a toddler, Ted and Anna were fourteen and eleven, respectively), and the ways in which his sisters met their husbands. I had just moved into work experience and pet/food allergies when Kai strong-armed me across the front seat, not unlike the way my mom used to hold me back at stop signs.

"What?" I asked, scanning the road for oncoming vehicles.

At that, Kai swerved, pulling onto a wide shoulder and next to some sort of farm stand. He put the car in park and turned to me, eyes bright. "I love the CIA. I do. I think they play a pivotal role in national security. But you," he said as he took my notepad out of my hands and tossed it roughly into the back seat, "are a chef, not a CIA operative. And we are in central Washington during the summer. So you can ask Gemma all about the time she got hives at summer camp when she was eight when you actually *meet* Gemma. But for now, can we please stop with the talking points? There's someone I want you to meet."

Before I could respond, Kai bounded out of the car and was reaching for a handshake with an elderly man. A light breeze lifted the canopy above the baskets of apricots, blueberries, and cherries. I opened my car door and lifted my chin to the movement of warm air and the cloudless sky, amazed at how much a climate could change when a girl crossed a mountain or two.

"Charlie," Kai said as I approached the stand, "I want you to meet an old friend of mine. Tom Breyon, this is Charlie Garrett." I thought I saw Kai's ears pinking but felt Tom's hand in mine before Kai finished speaking.

"Well, I'll be," Mr. Breyon said, his blue eyes crinkling with mischief. "I thought I might not make it to this auspicious day." He tried, unsuccessfully, to repress a grin. His hand was as rough as a swath of sandpaper between my two palms. I held on, taking an immediate liking to this man in worn Levis and Velcro tennis shoes.

"What makes this day auspicious?" I asked.

Kai said, "Tom, I really don't think—"

"Well, for one thing, I don't often have the pleasure of seeing women around here, see."

Kai rolled his eyes and looked as though he might have heard this line before.

"My wife was the most beautiful woman in the world, God rest her soul. After she died ten years ago, the only people who kept hanging around were my male field hands and an occasional tomboy." He frowned for dramatic effect. "*Tomboy* is actually cutting those girls some slack. They rarely shave their armpits and seem to think *organic* means 'don't bathe.'"

I drank this man in, my laughter only appearing to egg him on. Kai wandered among the baskets of fruit, dipping his nose, feeling the apricots for firmness.

"So," Mr. Breyon continued, "this day is auspicious because I have a lovely city girl here and I can already tell, she took a shower today."

I grinned. "Well, this *is* a red-letter day."

"Secondly, this day is one for the books because Kai Malloy has had the good fortune to nab a girl and dupe her into visiting his hometown. I believe this is the same man who said at the end of his high school years that he would shake the dust off his feet as he left and not worry about ever coming back."

"That was Jesus who said that," Kai called from over by the blackberries. "I just said I thought Wenatchee was a waste of space and that I was sick of everybody knowing all my business."

Tom nodded slowly, the wrinkles around his eyes deepening. "Auspicious, I tell you."

"That's probably enough of this conversational topic," Kai called from the end of the row of baskets. His ears, I noticed, were still pink. "If you can take a moment away from harassing your customers, I'd like to purchase some fruit."

Before attending to Kai, Mr. Breyon winked at me. "Welcome to Wenatchee, Miss Garrett. You got yourself a good man here, even if he is a bit of a pain."

I watched Kai negotiate a price with his friend, neither of them looking one bit interested in the money exchanged once the banter had concluded. I watched him hug Tom warmly and ask him to say hello to mutual friends. And I felt his arm loop around my waist as we walked back to the car, our bags full of apricots, berries, a box of crackers, and Mr. Breyon's house-made strawberry-rhubarb jam. Kai felt alive and warm and protective in all the right ways.

Yes, I thought, *a very good man.*

14

WE were still unfolding from Kai's car when the front door of the rambling white farmhouse flew open. A tall, slender woman wearing a flowing batik skirt, tank top, and headscarf came charging toward us, one finger pointed menacingly at Kai.

"Tom Breyon just called," she said, striding past a painted sign that stood in the yard, its careful lettering announcing Forsythia Farms. "You're here. With a real, live *girl*. And I have to hear this news from an elderly man at a highway stand? Have you not one considerate bone in your body, Kai Malloy?" By then end of this little monologue, she was laughing, her sinewy, muscular arms draped around her brother's neck.

"Good to see you, Dahls." Kai lifted her and spun her in a half circle, making her skirt ripple outward in a colorful arc. He set her down and turned her toward me.

"Charlie Garrett, this is my eldest and bossiest sister, Dahlia. Dahlia, meet Charlie. Famous pastry chef and a woman who alphabetizes her clothes according to label."

"What?" I sputtered, noting the way my heart had started to thump loudly in my chest, suddenly eager to impress this woman. "First of all, I'm not famous—"

"Oh, yes, you are!" she said, barreling toward me, arms outstretched. "You are famous in our family. You're a girl! And Kai let you come here with him! You're already a legend around here." Dahlia gathered me into a neck hug. My nose rested on her bony collarbone. "So lovely to meet you, Charlie," she said, eyes bright. "My dolt of a brother could have given me a little notice, and I would have at least cleaned the toilet. But you'll just have to take your chances. Come," she said, tugging on my hand. "You can freshen up while I get drinks. Ruben is out in the fields, Kai. I'll pack a lunch, and you and Charlie can take it to him."

"See?" Kai whispered into my ear. I was still not used to having him so close. The word *scrumptious* came to mind. "I told you she was bossy."

He held the screened door for me, and I stepped into the front hallway. My eyes swept over the rooms before me. A family lived here, I could see, and by the looks of it, one that was spirited and creative and lively and full of love. Creaky oak floors cushioned our steps, punctuated every now and then with colorful rugs. I loved the wide white baseboards and molding, the abundance of beautiful photography, family portraits, and children's artwork. I slipped into a tiny bathroom tucked under the stairs. The toilet, as it happens, was sparkly clean, making Dahlia out to be either a liar or a woman with very high standards of cleanliness. Either way, I felt relieved.

After I finished slapping my cheeks in an effort to pretend I had encountered the summer sun before that morning, I walked to the end of the hallway and was greeted with a large, open room flooded with light. An expansive family room sat to my right, full of comfortable furniture, stacks of board games, and bookshelves crammed with worn titles. To my left, a large, inviting kitchen beckoned, and Kai had already answered the call. He looked up from where he stood by the island, his hands busy with a bag of tortilla chips.

He smiled. "Salsa and chips okay?"

"Perfect," I said. "How can I help?" I hesitated, waiting for Dahlia to give me the high sign. One never wanted to presume in another person's kitchen.

She turned from her post at the kitchen sink and grinned. "Two professional chefs in my kitchen! I should go take a nap."

"You certainly can," I offered. "We'd be happy to give you a day off."

"Um, no," Kai said. "No, we would not."

Dahlia punched him in his side, not gently, I noted, and then pointed me to a cutting board.

"I'd love some help with the margaritas," she said, gesturing to a pile of limes waiting to be juiced. "This isn't exactly a lunch, but Kai said you guys ate lots of Tom's fruit and snacks on the way in." She rolled her eyes. "I'm so happy to hear that after meeting that anorexic woman Kai introduced us to at that swanky Seattle lunch spot a while back."

Kai stared at his sister. "She was not anorexic. She was genetically pre-disposed to terrifying thinness. Also," he pointed the tip of his knife at her as he spoke, "that meeting occurred about three years ago, so have I finished serving my sentence yet?"

Dahlia shook her head at me conspiratorially. "She was a train wreck. Too eager to please. And she didn't eat her salad. It was a *salad*." She huffed at the memory. "*That* woman," she added, eyebrows raised, "never made the cut to a farm visit."

I felt my cheeks getting warm and decided my safest response would be to get to business with the juicing. I cut and squeezed, content to listen to the easy banter between Kai and his sister. They caught up on local gossip, discussed the weather and the season's harvest. When I brought the lime juice to Dahlia, she thanked me no fewer than five times, then went into full-throttle interrogation mode as she spun the rims of our glasses into a mound of kosher salt.

"So, Charlie, how long have you lived in Seattle?"

"Only a few months, actually. I moved this spring from New York."

"Ooh, I love New York. The city that never sleeps! Why did you move to sleepy little Washington?" she asked, unblinking eyes trained on my face.

I looked at Kai, who appeared to be enjoying watching someone else endure Dahlia's pointed questioning. "I came for the job at Thrill. I've been working toward being a head pastry chef for about ten years, so when the opportunity came, I took it."

A few moments of demure interest in that little tidbit and then she was locking and loading the real ammunition. "Kai told me your name on the phone a few weeks ago and I may have done just a quick Google search. I read all about you on the Thrill website. Great photo, by the way. Are your waves natural? And you work for an ex-boyfriend. How's that dynamic working out?"

I could feel The Splotch revving up along my neck. Dahlia turned and had her back to me for a moment. I took the opportunity to widen my eyes at Kai. She *Googled* me? "Well, yes. We do work together, but it's going fine. There's nothing between us. There really never was. Very much. And it was a long time ago." I stopped talking, because when a person resorts to sentence fragments, that person should be silent.

Kai let out a sound of younger-brother exasperation. "'K. So we're done with the skinny lunch girl and Charlie's working relationship with her ex. Any other items to cross off the list before you start the waterboarding?"

"Hmph." Dahila sniffed at her brother. "I'm not being too nosy, am I?"

"If you have to ask that question, the answer is yes," Kai muttered, scooping salsa into a bright ceramic bowl.

Dahlia turned to me. "Am I being too nosy, Charlie? I'm just doing due diligence. It's so *seldom* that we get *any* information at *all* about Brother Dear's social life—"

"I'll be on the porch," Kai said and scowled at our grins on his way out.

Dahlia and I followed Kai to the porch off the kitchen, an airy room that opened onto a long, green backyard dotted with gardens. Splashes of magenta, deep purple, and show-off yellows nodded in the breeze. The view within the room was just as charming. Under a beamed ceiling and suspended by thick ropes, two sofa-sized porch swings faced each other. A smattering of other comfy chairs circled the seating area. The collection of soft cushions everywhere practically begged for a slow and luxurious after-noon nap. Or a fantastic makeout session with a very good-looking man. My eyes darted to Kai, and my pulse instantly quickened with the idea that perhaps Dahlia could read my thoughts. She set the margaritas on a rough-hewn table between the swings and poured each of us a generous drink.

I sat and sipped. "This is delicious," I said, nose in the glass. "Citrusy, salty, made with very good tequila."

Kai nodded. "Sweet. Less fiber, more floral and herbal. Patrón Silver maybe?"

We looked at Dahlia, waiting for the answer. She burst out in delighted laughter. "You're both total nerds! This is perfect!"

"The salsa is Ruben's mother's recipe, right?" Kai asked, ignoring her outburst. "And I'm sure Charlie loves being ridiculed for her food analysis as much as I do."

I laughed. "I don't mind," I said. "At least you're making salsa from scratch. My family never ate tortilla chips without melted Velveeta and a heaping spoonful of ground beef. And beef not raised on a sustainable farm, mind you."

"That concoction sounds *delicious*," Dahlia said with a smile.

I smiled back because, truthfully, it really was.

"The recipe for the margaritas was in a cooking magazine," she said with a shrug, "and I did it exactly as written. And the salsa, chefs, is from a jar with a bar code."

Kai frowned, but I had to bite back a smile.

"I'm not very much of an experimentalist," Dahlia said. "Certainly not like Kai, who commandeered my Easy Bake Oven by the time he was six and who thinks of recipes as cheating."

Kai shook his head but had to wait to swallow a mammoth chip piled with salsa before he could speak. "Not true. I think recipes are great. For children."

My turn to punch him. "I use recipes all the time, and I'm not a child."

"Speaking of children," Dahlia interjected, her eyes lively, "Charlie, when do you see yourself getting married? Raising a family?"

"All right, then," Kai interrupted. "We can pick up this line of questioning again *never*. Thanks, Dahls, for the drinks and salsa." He stood and waited for me to join him.

"What?" Dahlia said, looking ornery as she pushed her swing gently back and forth. "These are perfectly logical questions, Kai. You take a girl home for the first time in a decade, you better believe I have some questions at the ready." She winked at me.

"Right," Kai said, his ears pinking again. He steered me by the elbow back to the kitchen. Grabbing a brown paper bag by the fridge, he pulled me by the hand and called behind his shoulder as we made our way to the front door. "We'll drop this off with Ruben. You said he was in the blueberries, right?"

"Yes," Dahlia said, not moving from her swing. "Tell him dinner is at six. You two will be here, I assume? I could use some help, fancy chef people."

"Sure!" I said, heartily.

Kai rolled his eyes at me. "We'll be here."

Three hours later, Kai and I took our time making our way back toward Dahlia and Ruben's house. My face and shoulders had taken on a deep pink, and my hair, piled into a messy bun, was hot to the touch. After meeting an effusive and jovial Ruben and handing off his lunch, we had toured the farm. Kai showed me rows of blueberry bushes, strawberry plants, and apple trees. We picked fruit as we walked, tasting, talking, bickering about the best way to use them at their prime. We sat on a sandy spot on the river's edge, letting our feet get tugged along with the gentle current. We stood against the trunk of an apple tree, crushed blossoms still littering the ground, and kissed each other like we meant it.

I watched Kai's face as he told me about how much he loved his family, even with their intrusive questions and constant advice. His eyes softened when he described his nieces and nephew. The lines around his mouth deepened as he laughed through a story of when he and Gemma had hung out the upstairs window to spy on Dahlia and a high school boyfriend, only to be found out when he slipped on the windowsill and fell to the lilac bushes below. A broken arm and Dahlia's weeks of merciless rebuke made him give up eavesdropping for good. Kai's face, I decided, was one I could imagine watching for many, many years and not ever tire of it.

We followed a wooden fence line, and as we topped a lush, green hill, we glimpsed the house in the distance. Grasshoppers flew up around the path we cut through the grass, and the sun continued its slow drop toward the horizon. The air was close and warm, dancing among the trees and the alive summertime light. I took Kai's arm, and he moved closer to me as we walked.

"So what's the deal with never taking a girl back here? I would think you'd be an easy sell once she saw this place."

I could hear the smile in his voice. "An obnoxious sister and an afternoon in the orchard is all it takes?"

"Pretty much."

"Well," he said, slowing his stride as we neared the house, "I came close once. The skinny lunch girl Dahlia was telling you about. You know her, actually."

"I do?" I scanned my mental images of Kai and another girl and, happily, came up empty.

"Sunshine. The server at Howie's."

I felt my heart drop. The girl was gorgeous. And she had dreads. This was horrible news.

"We dated for a while, and I think she wanted more, but I just didn't. I felt bad about it, really. She's a nice girl."

I nodded, going for nonchalance. "You never took her here. That's interesting."

He stopped and pulled me into him. "You're gloating." The corner of his mouth pulled up into a smile.

"Am not," I said, tipping my chin. "Sunshine is a lovely person. And a very good server."

"Ouch," Kai said, wincing. "Might have heard a little snobbery in there. A lowly *server*, not a *chef*. At least *she* could go on a date more than once a month." He still smiled, but I heard a quiet rumble of discontent underneath his words.

I kept my arms around him, forcing him to stay close to me. "I'm working on that," I said, starting to kiss his cheek, his neck, his lower lip. "This too shall pass. Maybe sooner than later."

"Mmm," he said, not appearing to be as interested in conversation as he had been moments prior. "That's nice."

"Kai! Kai! Stop lip-locking and get yourself over here! And bring *the girl*!"

Kai groaned into my hair. "You've got to be kidding me."

I giggled, peeking around his shoulders at the woman waving at us from the open kitchen window. "Is that Dahlia?"

"Nope," he said, dragging his feet and me behind him. "It's the other one. Apparently Gemma drove all the way from Portland to meet you."

"Portland's five hours away!"

"These women will stop at nothing to make me uncomfortable."

I laughed. "This day gets better and better," I said, dodging Kai as he tried to pull me back to the car and Seattle. I quickened my pace to match his determined stride. Still laughing, I said, "I'm so excited there are *two* of them." I waved to Gemma, who was bouncing on the top step of the porch.

"Let's do this," Kai said, begrudgingly. "The sooner we start, the sooner it's over. And in advance, I'll just apologize now for the stories about my acne in junior high, my indescretions at Homecoming sophomore year when I asked two girls to the dance but didn't tell them that, and, always a family favorite, the story of when I bet Morris Harper I could beat him in a cherry pie eating contest and I ended up on IV fluids."

I tried to tamp down my grin but wasn't entirely successful. "This is going to be fantastic."

Kai shook his head as we ascended the stairs and became enveloped in a three-person hug with Gemma.

"Charlie, we have so much to talk about!" Gemma said into my hair. I saw Kai raise one eyebrow in victory.

15

FRIDAY morning, back at Thrill and a world away from the laughter and comfort food of Forsythia Farms, I paced along the back hallway outside Avery's office. I'd arrived early for the meeting Margot had called in a late-night email, and I wanted to take the extra minutes to rehearse my lines. Not lines for an upcoming episode, but lines for my speech. I could hear a murmur of voices behind the door, and I knew Margot, Vic, and Avery were already inside. Turning my back to the door, I began walking again, deciding to wait a few more moments before knocking.

A thousand years prior, I had competed on the debate team for one semester in high school. What were the maxims of oral persuasion again? I tried to remember the acronym . . . PCPF? Posture, Clarity, Poise, Focus? Or were they Posture, Clarity, Purpose, and Finality? I knew posture had to be in there because we used to mock Trish Friars for her exceptional, nipple-noteworthy posture during her turn on the stand.

Turning back once I reached the end of the hallway, I rolled my shoulders and cleared my throat, the sound bouncing off the quiet walls of the kitchen. With one last deep breath, I came to stand in front of Avery's office door. I knocked a peppy rhythm with my knuckles, and the door swung open.

Vic clasped his hands. "There she is," he said in a radio announcer voice. We air kissed, and he opened one arm to allow me into the cramped room.

"A few days off can make all the difference, can't they? Doesn't she look refreshed and renewed, folks?"

Avery sat in one of three chairs gathered into a tight semi-circle. His expression was difficult to read. Chagrined, or maybe brooding? He turned to nod at me but didn't rise from his chair.

Margot leaned against Avery's desk. A half smile formed on her thin, painted lips. "You look great, Charlie. How was your vacation?"

It struck me as a bit ridiculous that we were calling thirty-six hours a "vacation," but I played along. "It was wonderful. Thank you." I sat down in the chair offered by Vic and tucked my ankles under the seat in an effort to avoid knee-knocking one of the men.

"Good," Margot said, voluminous gold hoops swinging when she directed a chin nod at Avery. "We were just chatting with Avery about the response from Network. We sent them some footage from the last few weeks, and they were very pleased, much more so than with the pilot we filmed before you arrived, Charlie."

I managed a weak smile. About that . . .

"They gave the green light to film the rest of the season." Margot beamed, a sudden shift that appeared to require some effort. "Perfect timing, then, for you to return rested and ready to go. The next few weeks are going to be intense, very time-consuming. You'll need all your strength, plus your sharp wit and perfect camera face, two attributes Network particularly loved."

I swallowed. "Actually, I'd like to talk to you about the schedule."

Vic tried crossing his legs but gave up in the limited space. Avery kept his eyes on the floor.

"We'll get to the schedule in a moment," Margot said. She positioned a pair of reading glasses onto her long nose and looked through them at a clipboard on the desk beside her. "First, I want to be clear about the contract."

"Actually, I want to talk with you about the contract." I swallowed, getting ready for the nitty-gritty. "You'll remember I have an escape clause I can invoke at any time."

"An oversight, I'm afraid," Margot said, looking at me over her glasses. "Every person on set has signed an airtight contract that commits them to all thirteen episodes but you, Charlie. We were willing to waive it for the first few weeks because Avery insisted you'd be more comfortable if we gave you some space. Less likely to be scared off, if you will." There was the tight smile again. "Now that we've gotten to know you, we know that you are certainly not a fearful woman."

Vic snorted.

"In fact," Margot continued, one eyebrow up, "I know now you are a woman who has worked a long time to get to this level and you're not about to throw it all away."

I reached for the much-rehearsed phrases I'd practiced that morning in the shower. Something about work-life balance? Or the bit about needing time and space for true creativity? Working only between the hours of noon and midnight, no more fifteen-hour shifts, or extra takes at the end of the night? My thoughts bounced and ricocheted too long because Vic chimed in.

"Charlie, I'll put this to you plainly. You are the star of this show, and Network wants to fast track what we're doing so publicity can get a solid jump on a fall release."

I felt Avery tense next to me.

"The success of the show going forward hinges on you. You drive the plot line, you interest the audience, and the camera loves you."

"Avery is fantastic, don't doubt it." Vic's tone was placating. "You're brilliant, Avery, really."

Avery gave me a wry smile.

"However," Margot interrupted, "Avery *plus* Charlie equals something altogether different. In fact, Network specified that shooting can continue only if you, Charlie, are on board and committed to staying there."

Avery slumped in his chair. I felt my breathing becoming shallow.

Margot removed her glasses and leaned toward me. "You have the potential to do something spectacular here, Charlie. This contract spells it all out." She pointed to the document topping the pile resting on her clipboard. "You agree to another month of filming and a selection of promotional events associated with marketing the show, and, in return, you receive a hefty check, an opportunity to renew for a second season depending on the ratings, and my personal favorite: an initial investment and licensing for a personal line of bakery products." She turned to Vic. "Wouldn't she be perfect on little cupcake liners or scone mixes? The earning potential is huge here."

"Hold on," I interrupted. "What about my job? Here, at Thrill? The work is what brought me to Seattle, not a TV show."

"Of course," Margot said with a shrug. "You can keep your job. You'll need it for the show. And," she said more carefully after seeing the set of my jaw, "after this contract expires, you are free to continue in your role as head pastry chef. You can think about a second season when the time comes, but you can work all the hours you want at Thrill when we are not filming. Correct, Avery?"

"Yes. Absolutely." His voice shook slightly before he cleared his throat. "Charlie, you know your job here is secure. It can be the beginning of something big, or the final piece. Whatever you want." Then, as an apparent afterthought, he added, "You and I are a team. A great team. No strings attached."

I let my eyes linger on him, troubled anew at his willingness to be a chameleon, to change according to whatever wind blew through the room.

"It's only a few weeks," Margot said more quietly. Her gaze locked onto mine. "A few weeks of hectic schedules, long hours, lots of hair and makeup, and hoops to jump through." She leaned toward me. "But think of where you've been, Charlie. Think of where this exposure will take you. If you sign this contract and play by our rules for just a short time, at the end of this tiny tunnel you'll be able to make choices you never could have faced otherwise. After all these years, Charlie." She paused, taking in my expression. "After all your sacrifices, you are standing on the brink of having it all be worthwhile."

I stared at the paper. Long days, long years felt heavy on my shoulders. I felt their cumulative weight and the passion with which I had pressed on, through exhaustion, sickness, Felix and his tirades, Alain and his empty promises. I thought of the dream I had so long nurtured and cherished, the hope that I could run my own kitchen in the way I wanted, the accolades that would come, the ability to set my own standard and my own pace.

And I thought of Kai. His face, his hands, his patient phone calls and texts. I thought of his easy laugh and the way he made me feel happy and cared for. I thought of the way he looked at me . . . and I knew he would be willing to wait.

I squared my shoulders to Margot's tiny frame. "I need a day to review the contract before I sign."

Avery let out a quick rush of air and Vic did a fist pump. Margot looked bemused, which I supposed was the closest she came to being pleased.

"You know what?" she said, cocking her head to one side. "I knew, Ms. Garrett, that you would. Fearless women finish first and finish best." She seemed not to care that half the people in the room couldn't possibly qualify in that grouping. Standing, she lowered the clipboard with a jolt onto my lap.

"You remember that," she said and turned to go.

16

THE following night, a Saturday, made every person working at Thrill feel as though we were moments away from self-destruction. We were stacked from the first minute of the first seating. Avery strode in and out of the kitchen, muttering about the reservationist being on crack and how could any sane person think we could cook for all those people out there? Apparently even he had a limit for the amount of exposure he could take in one evening.

The servers looked frazzled and totally spent by eight o'clock, which was a very bad sign since we weren't even halfway through the evening. One woman, Gigi, who had come on board with others in Tova's pretty brigade, began crying hysterically, her mascara running in chunky rivulets down her cheeks. The salmon was overdone, she cried, and she *really* needed that table's tip for her rent, due the following day. Six f-bombs and a hushed, back-rubbing conversation with Avery later, she touched up her makeup and soldiered back into the dining room with Salmon, Take Two.

Of course, the cameras caught the entire debacle, one of them coming so close to Gigi's head at one point that she pushed it out of her way with an impressive shove and naughty word (F-Bomb #4). I was neck-deep in my own troubles after one of the gas burners in the pastry kitchen quit working just as I was building the heat for a finicky caramel. So I heard Gigi's tirade loudly and clearly, but I didn't watch closely enough to decide whether she'd been put up to histrionics like Tova had. When things had returned to the noisy but familiar chaos of the kitchen, I did see Vic nod once at Margot. I looked away, determined to know as little as I could about what happened behind the lenses of the black cameras that loomed everywhere around us.

Minutes after the Gigi debacle, Avery flew into our area, his eyes bugging, chef's cap shoved to one side of his head.

"Charlie," he said, his voice barely controlled. "We have a situation."

I looked up from plating a slice of deep-dish peach blackberry pie, one hand over the dessert with a sifter of powdered sugar. "What kind of situation?"

Avery nodded, rhythmically, up and down, up and down. "We have in our dining room," he said, still nodding, "some very special guests." He paused, his gaze flickering to the camera above my head. "TiffanTosh is here."

Tova let out a squeal and dropped the ramekin she was holding, nicking an edge on the counter.

I scowled at her and then turned back to Avery. "I'm assuming this person is famous since her name is so ridiculous."

Avery's mouth opened slightly, clearly disturbed I wasn't dropping ceramics, too. "TiffanTosh is not a *person*. TiffanTosh is a *people*. The newest power couple in Hollywood."

"Tiffany Jacobs and Macintosh Rowe?" Tova was talking and applying lip gloss at the same time. Her eyes kept darting to the door to the dining room, as if any moment a celebrity might walk through and want to discuss lip plumping. "They are amazing. So, so talented. And both of them are so gorgeous, I couldn't possibly decide which one is prettier." She looked to be considering this dilemma when she swiveled in my direction. "Ooh! And Charlie! They give truckloads of money to poor people in Africa or Asia or something. You like that kind of thing, right?"

I didn't have the heart to say what I wanted to say in that moment, her puppy eyes were so hopeful. I settled for just staring while she went back to glossing.

"All right," I said, returning to the pie. "What have they ordered?"

"No, no, no, no," Avery said, shaking his head vigorously. "I just met them." He stopped and nudged Tova with his elbow. "I *met* them!"

She sighed.

"We chatted a while," he said, "and I did not *allow* them to order. Not off the menu." He made a face. "Those are all desserts that regular people have eaten. No. You have to make something new, something different and just for TiffanTosh."

I rolled my eyes. "That name is such a joke. Do they introduce themselves like that? And did they order in third person or something? Like, 'TiffanTosh does not care for Key lime squares with brown butter crust.' Or 'TiffanTosh will need low-dust-emitting toilet paper this evening.'" I snorted when I laughed.

Avery and Tova stared. She wrinkled her nose. "That's so disgusting. Why did you have to go there?"

"They ordered together," Avery said, clearly trying to rise above my gutter talk. "They want to share a dessert."

"That's so romantic." Tova shook her head and actually sounded choked up. I was in TMZ hell.

"What can you do?" Avery asked. He worried his lower lip with his teeth. "Oh, and I forgot to say they're both gluten-free."

I groaned.

"But not sugar-free or dairy-free." Avery sounded triumphant, as if it shouldn't bother me that I couldn't use flour, but milk and sugar were no problem.

"My best GF work is already on the menu," I said, looking to the ceiling and tapping my fingernails on the counter while I thought. "The panna cotta, the budino . . . "

"Both delicious options," Avery said. The ingratiating tone wasn't moving me.

"No crusts, no crumbles, no cakes, no cookies that are worth the effort," I thought aloud. I closed my eyes, rummaging around in my mind for what I could offer these TiffanTosh people. Unbidden, the thought came to me. I pictured Forsythia Farms and the day Kai and I spent there among all the fruit careening to the sweet peak of summer's bounty. I wanted to capture *that*—the warmth, the sun, the vibrant flavors that jumped off the plate.

I opened my eyes. "Got it." I looked at Avery. "Get them a nice Moscato and come back in thirty minutes."

Tova and I worked double-time to complete the orders from "regular people," which were already in and gathering dust before TiffanTosh's interruption. When we had things in relative order and the remaining garnishes were ones she couldn't foul up, I turned to my empty workspace. Moving slowly and carefully to avoid bruising the fruit, I combined handfuls of plump raspberries and deep purple blueberries, a healthy cup of sugar, and some spring water into a heavy saucepan. It climbed slowly to a gentle boil while I stirred and folded it carefully onto itself. I lowered the heat and let it form a syrup before adding another handful of raspberries and a splash of raspberry brandy.

Avery came back to hover as I was finishing the dish. I puddled the warm berries into the bottom of a bowl and added a scoop of my housemade vanilla bean ice cream. Nestling the bowl onto a white rectangular dish, I added two ceramic shot glasses and poured in the final piece.

"What is that?" Tova asked, her voice hushed.

"Something I've been tinkering with. It's kind of a hot chocolate meets a *pot de crème*. Silky, espresso-laced chocolate sauce with a touch of cream and a pinch of freshly grated cinnamon. They can sip it, like a mini-cocktail. I think it will go well with the berries." I stood back, evaluating the finished product.

"So brilliant," Avery said to interrupt my thoughts. "Simple and absolutely stunning on the plate."

"Yeah, but I want to eat it all right now." Tova reached over to me for a fist bump. "If they send it back, I want it."

Avery swallowed hard. "Let's hope they don't send it back." He lifted the plate carefully into his hands. "Let's hope they think simple is good."

My heart was beating faster than I wanted to admit. I watched Avery go through the swinging door to the dining room and stood with my arms crossed, settling in to wait for a verdict.

⁂

The clock on Thrill's kitchen wall was barreling toward two in the morning by the time I used my shoulder to heave open the door to the outside world. The arches of my feet were throbbing, and I swore I could feel each individual, aching bone in my body. And, I noted, my cheek muscles felt the tremble of fatigue after having smiled for the better part of the last few hours.

My impromptu dessert for TiffanTosh was a coup. They had asked to see me, regaled me with compliments, and then insisted I sit at their table for a chat.

My grin widened again to remember what they'd said.

As an exclamation point to my euphoria, I just wanted to hear Kai's voice. Fumbling for my phone in my bag, I stopped outside the restaurant and lowered myself to a bench nestled between two lush planters filled with mutant coleus and pink impatiens. I pulled up Kai's number but decided to text. No need to wake him with a phone call, especially since he was due to get up in a matter of hours to open Howie's. But I could text him that I was thinking about him and let that be the first thing he saw in the morning.

> Me: I know you're asleep and probably all warm and drooly right now, but I want you to know I'm thinking about you and the way you get superscratchy with whiskers by the end of a day. I like the whiskers. And you.

I paused, thumbs hovering above the phone. The cool, damp air made me shiver more deeply into my cardigan.

> Me: Sleep well. I'll try calling tomorrow?

I was still sitting on the bench, feeling regret that I had stopped moving and would therefore have to *resume* moving if I were to get home, when the phone rang and made me jump high enough to send my bag in an arc off my lap and onto the ground.

"Kai!" I said, breathless with adrenaline. "I'm so sorry. Did my text wake you?"

"It's fine," he said, his voice rumbling a few notes below normal. "It's good to hear from you, even at an ungodly hour. How are you?"

"Really, really great," I said, trying to tone down my very-awake state in the face of his interrupted sleep. "We had an unbelievable night at work."

"Hit me," he said, still yawning. "I mean, hit me gently. Not too many details. Don't want you to go to prison."

I groaned. "That blasted nondisclosure. I can't wait to be able to tell you everything. When I signed up, I didn't really think the life of a pastry chef would be one of secrecy. Not that I haven't harbored a teeny tiny aspiration that I could be a Navy SEAL, but that pretty much ended in seventh grade. I got the impression it would be much more wait-in-the-desert and less Nancy Drew. I loved Nancy Drew." I bit my lips together, abruptly aware I was rambling.

His voice was deep and rough with sleep. "How about you talk in really broad terms? Or in a sort of code? Like, 'Tonight I saw a red item and a blue item,' and then I'll know we're talking about purple."

I closed my eyes. "This is so pathetic. Why don't we just resort to haiku? 'The pastry rose high. I did not make anyone vomit.' Wait, that's too many syllables, isn't it?"

"Um, the last poem I read was by Shel Silverstein, and I'm positive it had something to do with a unicorn that never made it on to Noah's ark. So, no poetry. It depresses normally happy people."

"Okay," I said, laughing. "No haiku. But I think I am cleared to say that I had a celebrity sighting tonight."

"Oh, let's play that game." I could hear a jolt of enthusiasm as he woke up. "I'll guess who and you just stay silent until I hit on the right celebrity."

"Sounds good."

"Joan Rivers."

"Do I have to stay silent if the proposed celebrity is deceased?"

"Dang. I thought I heard something about that. Okay, what celebrity would be hanging out in Seattle? Here's where I have an advantage because I grew up in Washington and I know the famous people list." He paused, and I heard a door creak shut behind me. Avery waved with one hand as he locked up with the other.

"I'm assuming you wouldn't be wowed by Paul Allen, even though he founded Microsoft with Bill Gates. No, probably not. Okay, how about Rainn Wilson from *The Office*?"

"No, but that man was not born with that name." I nodded when Avery gestured a request to sit next to me on the bench. He sat heavily and with the same Cheshire grin I still sported.

"I have it," Kai said. "Stephen S. Oswald."

"Who?"

"You're supposed to be remaining silent. Stop breaking the rules."

"Sorry," I said.

"Shh. And Stephen S. Oswald happens to be a very famous astronaut. I'm surprised you haven't heard of him."

I snorted and got called out for nonverbal rule breaking.

Avery nudged me. When he spoke, his voice was lowered. "I'm so glad you're still here. I have news."

I raised my eyebrows and covered the phone with my hand. "What?" I whispered.

"Sir Mix-A-Lot!" Kai sounded triumphant.

Avery turned toward me, draping his arm around the back of the bench. "TiffanTosh loved you. I mean *really* loved you." His eyes, though bloodshot with fatigue, danced with excitement.

"I can't believe it," I whispered. "They said I was remarkable and just what the dessert world needed. They called me 'a revelation'!"

Kai made another guess. "Kenny G? And if it was him, can you please describe the hair?"

Avery moved closer. "They said they really appreciated how simple but killer their dessert was, and that they were totally into paring down their lives. Fewer ingredients definitely *spoke* to them."

"That's so amazing," I whispered. "I was worried I hadn't done enough."

Kai broke through. "Carol Channing. Or is she dead, too?"

"So, here's the thing," Avery said, and I leaned in to hear his lowered voice. "They are having a private party at their new house outside the city next week. And they want *us* to cook."

Kai kept guessing. "I can't believe I didn't say this before. Of course. Mario Batali."

I could hear Kai evaluating his most recent theory, but I was too distracted to respond. All I could think about were the promises I'd made myself on the plane from Seattle to New York; how I'd told everyone—Carlo, Manda, even my mother—my singular goal with this cross-country move was to put myself in the position to be a recognized pastry chef. Kai's voice seemed suddenly distant, our little game something that was charming and sweet but that would also have to wait. I cleared my throat and took my hand off the phone. "Kai, I'm sorry, but I think I'd better go."

"Too close to the truth?" he asked, sounding victorious. "Can't hold your tongue any longer, eh? I *knew* it was Batali. Wow, I can't imagine having him stop into my restaurant. Did you freak out?"

"No," I said, hurriedly. "I mean, yes. I'm a little freaked out. But it wasn't Batali. And I can't really say any more."

"Oh," he said, subdued. "All right. I get it. What happens at Thrill stays at Thrill, right?" The bitterness in his tone was unmistakable and sudden.

I bristled. "That's not fair. You know I'm in a tough spot here."

He exhaled long. "You are. That's true. We both are."

We were quiet a beat, and I saw Avery do a little twirl with his fingers, prodding me to wrap it up.

"Listen," Kai said, more gently, "maybe discussions like this aren't best on the phone and after midnight. Let's shelve it and talk tomorrow. Sound good?"

"Sounds really good," I said, already letting my finger creep around to end the call. "Sleep well," I said and hung up while Kai's goodnight still sounded in the quiet air.

"They want *us*?" I turned fully to Avery and felt my eyes widen at the thought of such a personal request. "Don't they have their own chef?"

Avery shrugged. "Probably. But when you're that rich and famous, you don't need to get bogged down by little details like loyalty. They are having about seventy people, they said. The party is at their house in Medina. The place was in *Architectural Digest* last month, Charlie! They play backyard bocce with their neighbors, *Bill and Melinda Gates*! This is huge!"

He didn't need to tell me that, of course. We'd had our fair share of celebrities popping into L'Ombre when I lived in New York, and they always received undivided attention and set Alain into a dither every time. But the end of the meal was always the end of the relationship. Nobody had ever asked Alain and Felix over for a playdate.

I felt a quickening in my pulse that pushed aside the clouds of my exhaustion.

"Well, come on, then. Let's talk menu." I grinned at him. "I'm never going to fall asleep now."

He grinned back. "Who says workaholics don't have any fun?"

17

MANDA waved to me from under a giant, red metal sculpture. Actually, she shimmied while jumping up and down in some conspicuously new running shoes. Her hair bounced with each return to earth.

"Isn't this fantastic?" she said as she gathered me into a quick hug. "What a beautiful day! The sun is so warm! The Sound looks amazing! I love my new shoes! And there are no children anywhere around here that have passed through my birth canal!"

I rubbed one clammy hand over my eyes. "I'm really trying to be awake right now, but last night was not my longest night of sleep. I'll just keep sipping and listening to you talk about this very large, very bright focal point of the Olympic Sculpture Park." I cupped my Grande Caffé Americano and let its caffeinated loveliness seep into my bloodstream. Manda could have launched into a dissertation on insects and worms, for all I cared. I was having trouble rousing myself after menu planning with Avery until four that morning.

Manda frowned. "Ten in the morning is not early. Your life is so bizarre."

"Agreed," I said gruffly into my coffee.

"This is called The Eagle. Iconic to this part of Seattle."

I squinted and gave it time but finally shook my head. "I don't see it. It looks nothing like an eagle to me. Not even remotely."

Manda nodded. "Me either. But I love the color and the shape. Plus, if you stand between his legs, you can get a great photo of the Space Needle. Let's do it!" She pulled me over to a space between two red supports.

"This is vaguely obcene," I muttered.

"Oh, stop being so difficult. Let's try a selfie. I've never done it but I know all the young people do these things." She held her iPhone out in front of her and started rotating it very slowly, smiling the whole time.

"We are the same age," I reminded her, snatching her phone out of her hand and pulling her head close to mine. It took us six tries, but we finally caught one that captured some red from The Eagle, our faces, and the Space Needle sprouting in a confident trajectory between us.

"Well, Miss Sophistication, you suck at selfies, too. So there." Manda zipped her phone into a small pocket on the back of her shorts. "Let's walk down to the water." She led the way down a path that angled toward Puget Sound.

"You would have been a good collie," I said when she put two sharp fingers on the small of my back to guide me around a sharp turn. "I feel very well herded."

"Sorry," she said with a short laugh. "I'm so used to accident prevention. I can't believe how easy this is! This walking without a stroller, without a diaper bag, without a bag of snacks, without extra changes of clothes for four people." She grinned at me and started pumping her arms. "It's so easy! Let's break a sweat!"

I groaned. "Let's not. Let's assume a leisurely pace." I tossed my empty coffee cup in a public bin.

Manda screwed up her face in disapproval, but she slowed down. "What happened to a-thousand-push-ups-a-day-or-the-day-is-wasted? You're the runner here, sis. I thought I'd be the one begging for mercy."

I shook my head. "I haven't gone running in weeks. In fact, I still haven't been on any of the trails I was so excited about when I read about them in New York. The closest I've come to an accelerated heart rate is when we have a packed house and I'm hustling between ovens and the walk-in."

"I wouldn't say that's the *only* time you've had a reason for your heart to race." I had to hand it to my best friend. She had waited an entire seven minutes to bring up the subject of my love life.

I felt my sullen mouth break into the start of a smile. "I'm so impressed with your restraint. I thought you'd holler, 'Does he use too much tongue?' when you saw me approaching The Eagle."

She laughed. "I don't even need to ask that question. Kai does not strike me as a sloppy kisser." She waited, and when I didn't rise to her bait, she said, "And this is the part when you tell me what kind of kisser he really is."

"He's perfect," I said, not even trying to hide the information because one of the many merits of best friendship is that there are no limits on honesty, tears, insecure lines of questioning, or bad karaoke.

"I'm not surprised," she said and did a little hop of joy. "He seems like he was made for you. I'm so excited!"

"He's smart, he's funny, he's incredibly good-looking, he loves his family, he loves good food . . ."

"He doesn't break up with you when you can't ever see him and when you call him in the middle of the night and wake him up." She arched an eyebrow in my direction.

"How do you know these things?" I demanded. "Are you two dishing about me?"

"We are totally dishing about you." Manda rolled her eyes. "And I absolutely saw him this morning when he was taking out his trash and I absolutely interrogated him until he was so uncomfortable, he pretended he had something burning in the oven." She made a face. "Amateur excuse. He left for work two minutes later, so there was definitely nothing in his oven."

"You are unstoppable," I said, starting to breathe heavily with all the exercise. "I hope he doesn't think I'm a total freak."

"Oh, I wouldn't worry about that. He seems to have jumped that hurdle and stuck around anyway."

I shoved her to the other side of the path. "I did wake him up. I really wanted to hear his voice. But the bummer is that I couldn't actually tell him anything."

Manda tsked. "I hope you appreciate how much I love you. Every fiber in my being wants to pepper you with questions about that show. We have never had secrets before, you know."

I sighed. "I really, really wish I could spill it all. It almost doesn't seem real since I can't talk about it with you."

Manda nudged us over to a bench that faced the water. We dropped onto the seat and watched in silence as a stately container ship moved seamlessly through the distant waves.

"Kai reminds me of Jack in some ways," Manda said, eyes still on the water.

I waited for her to elaborate.

"He knows himself," she said. "He's good. He's true. I'd be surprised if the boy could tell a lie without his head exploding."

I smiled, knowing she was right.

"Jack is like that," she said. "He loves me in a good, true way. He loves my quirks and my brokenness and even my big mouth, though I have to use that mouth often to apologize for what comes out of it." She laughed softly. "And he makes us get it right. When we were first married and we'd get into a fight, I just wanted to get in the car and drive to Tacoma. And he never let me, the stubborn mule. I remember he would say, 'Manda, I love you and you love me and we are in this forever. And neither of us is leaving. So we can keep arguing and being pissy with each other for the next four hours, or we can just make up now and get back to being together.'" She shook her head, laughing. "Such an accountant. Always looking for the most efficient way to get something done, even if it's an argument with his wife."

"You got a good one," I said. "Other than having to teach him not to wear athletic socks with sandals, you really had very little rewiring to do."

She snorted. "Well, he did have that phase with all oatmeal-colored clothing. Not a good choice for anyone, especially those with Nordic ancestry."

We watched as a young family walked by, the dad pulling a little girl in a wagon and the mom struggling to rein in a golden retriever who appeared to think the leash was a polite suggestion, not a commitment.

Manda turned suddenly to face me. "All right, listen. I don't mean to be bossy or put my nose where it shouldn't be."

I looked at her, confusion settling on my face. "Why not?"

She ignored me. "But I just have to say this: I think you need to work less. There. I said it." She threw up her hands as if relinquishing a burden.

I squinted at her. "No offense, Manda, but you are repeating yourself. You have always thought I work too much." I felt a heavy stone of self-defense settle in a familiar place in my gut.

"I know, I know," she said, shooing the thought away with one hand. "But this time I'm serious. It's not just that you need to work less so that you don't develop hypertension or drop dead of a heart attack at age forty."

I winced.

"It could happen." She pointed with one finger at my chest. "But this time it's different. I'm up-close and personal this time, Char. You're not a million miles away in New York. I'm *watching* you this time, and I'm worried you're just not getting it."

"Not getting what?" I said, feeling my ire poke its head out of its dormant state. "I'm *getting* exactly what I've worked for, Manda. After many, many years of sacrifice." I heard strains of Margot's voice in my words, but I pushed on. "Of course I'm working too hard. Of course it's a lot of hours."

Manda nodded. She spoke quickly, each word chasing the next. "I just wonder if you're going to miss out on the really, really great things in your life just because you are on this locomotive and you can't seem to slow it down, even for a potty break."

I looked up at the water view, which didn't seem to inspire the same sense of calm it had moments before. "I will not apologize for who I am."

"Oh, give me a break," Manda said, slapping the bench with one hand. "You are not your job, Charlie. You are a talented, bright, beautiful woman who is missing her whole life because of her job. But you are *not* your job."

"Not fair," I said, jumping up and starting down the path again. Manda jogged behind me to catch up.

"What's not fair?" she said, her voice creeping up in volume and pitch. "I'm trying to talk to you, Charlie. I think you're not being fair by not using your listening ears."

"Whatever," I said, upping my speed to a powerwalk. "You're allowed to identify yourself as a mom. That's *your* job, and you wear it like a badge. In fact, you complain about it all the time." I shifted my voice into a whine. "'It's so hard, it never ends, I can't get a break, I'm too tired to have sex, I never have time for me, I wish I could sleep for eight consecutive hours, my butt is huge, I love walking without a stroller and fruit snacks.'"

It took me a good five steps to realize Manda had stopped walking. I turned and saw her standing still on the path, face crumpled and eyes big.

"Wow," she said, voice small, almost childlike. She shook her head slowly. "Is that what I sound like?"

I inhaled deeply and forced all the air out of my lungs, feeling my frustration deflate with a healthy poke of repentance. "No," I said, walking toward her. "You don't. Manda, I'm sorry—"

"Don't worry about it," she said, hand up to stop my words. "I get it. I shouldn't have pushed so hard. You do what you need to do." Her lips made a thin line. "You're a big girl, Charlie. I know you can handle this."

My shoulders slumped. "I thought I was. Handling this."

Manda didn't say anything for a moment. "Just be fair. Be fair to you, be fair to Kai. That's my only bit of counsel." She cleared her throat, and I thought the smile she mustered looked like a brave one. "Advice session officially over."

I put my arm around her. "I'm sorry. I think my social skills are deteriorating with time."

She sniffed. "You've always been a bit rough around the edges."

I fumbled my way toward penance. "Can I take you out for lunch? I don't have to be at Thrill until three today."

She shook her head. "Thanks, but I think I'd better get home." She stopped abruptly, and I hated to think of her editing her comments about what the rest of her day held with Zara, Dane, and Polly, just so I wouldn't think she was complaining. I didn't think I had it in me to hanker for a story about breast pumps and spit-up, but there I was, hankering.

"Hey!" I said, inspired. "Isn't Zara's birthday next weekend?"

Manda nodded. "Princess party on Saturday at ten. Lots of girls wearing get-ups we certainly hope they mature out of. Clear heels are cute at age six, but they send an entirely different message at fifteen."

"Let me make the cupcakes," I said, getting excited. "I've always wanted to do that for your kids' birthdays, and I couldn't when I was in New York. How many do you need? Pink with pink frosting?"

Manda looked at me, hands on her hips. "I don't want to add more work to your schedule."

"Pshaw," I said, borrowing a word from my mother. "This is not work. This is fun. And," I said, playing my best card, "I'll call Kai and see if he'll help me. You'll be avoiding high fructose corn syrup *and* watching me have a life. Win-win. Come on. Let me."

She kissed me on the cheek. "God bless you. Yes, please." We turned on the path and headed up a ramp toward the sculpture park. "Thank you. And

Zara thanks you. And Jack definitely thanks you because he won't have to pretend that the carrot-zucchini ones I usually make are edible."

I opened my mouth in horror. "You did not. Not for a birthday."

She shrugged. "Just be glad you came when you did. I might well have resorted to a date-and-fig flatbread I just bookmarked on my favorite blog." She turned to me. "Do you ever read *Chemicals Kill, Kids Suffer*? You might find some good ideas. She has a whole section devoted to sweets."

I shook my head and made the extremely adult decision not to say anything. I'd probably said enough for one walk.

We were standing at The Eagle again when Manda turned to me. "Just so you know, Sass," she said with a wry smile, "your little tirade? About how I say my life is hard, I never sleep, I can't get a break, I don't have time for me?"

I nodded, feeling sheepish.

"Other than the stroller and the big butt, those are all things *you* complain about, too, my dear."

I frowned.

"Love you," she said and slapped me on the rear, hard, as she walked away.

"Touché," I called, feeling her words smart as much as the whack on my rear end.

18

A man in reflective sunglasses and a headset motioned for me to roll down my window.

"Hi, there," I said in an alarmingly squeaky voice. I dragged my eyeballs away from the gun in his shoulder strap and said, "I'm Charlie Garrett. Ms. Jacobs and Mr. Rowe are expecting me. To cook. I'm a cook. A chef, actually, of pastries, confections, some candy, chocolate, though chocolate is really finicky—"

Spartacus held up one hand as a very effective silencer. "I've got a five-three and a two-six," he said into a small black wire with a dot on the end. "Garrett, Charlie." He paused, waiting, I suppose, for divine clearance. "Copy that." He produced an iPad and offered me a stylus. "Read this and sign."

I pretended I could read and even understand the five thousand tiny, highly technical words that made up some sort of nondisclosure form. The gist appeared to be that should I take any photos, record any conversations, reveal my whereabouts, or generally appreciate tabloid journalism, I would be sued for all my earthly goods and sent to the gallows.

"Looks good." I couldn't seem to shake the squeak. I signed with a flourish and handed it though the window. "Do I just follow this road up to the house then?"

He pursed his lips and placed the iPad on a black camping chair. "Not yet. Step out of the car, please."

I stared. "What's that?"

He opened the door. "Would you prefer I radio for a female officer for the frisk?"

I stepped out of the car and onto bright white crushed limestone. "No, no, that's not necessary," I said. "I've been frisked plenty of times, almost always by men." I winced and was glad I could not see his eyes behind the reflective glasses. One hates to see oneself disdained by muscular men.

I watched as he unleashed a wand with a red blinking light. "Besides . . ." I couldn't stop talking! "I'm sure you want to keep your job as much as I want to keep mine." I meant it as a joke, but Sparty was not keen on laughing with his subjects. He was done with the frisk before I had the chance to worry aloud if my butt looked lumpy in my chef pants.

"Nero!" he called over a hyperdeveloped deltoid. A German shepherd bounded from behind a spotless black truck. He loped over with an expression that mirrored his master's. Within thirty seconds, he had scoped my car and its trunk. Satisfied that I was only a woman in shapeless clothes and not a terrorist or a photographer, Sparty allowed Nero to return to the truck and me to get back in my car.

"Clear," he said, patting the hood of my car as a final jot of punctuation. I gunned the gas with a tad too much enthusiasm and cringed when I looked in the rearview mirror and saw Sparty checking his ensemble for dust.

I followed the private lane for at least a mile, driving slowly and leaving my window open to breathe in the mountain air. When I crested a final hill and saw the property, I felt like Dorothy entering Oz.

The "house," which seemed such a plebeian word for the structure ahead, perched on the edge of a rise and overlooked a groomed, green lawn that stretched down the mountainside. Trees had been cleared to allow for the lush grass and a heart-squeezing view of Seattle beyond. I could see pockets of seating areas, both on the expansive patio that wrapped around the house, and on the grounds below. Plush outdoor furniture with cushions that were utterly impractical in Seattle's climate clustered around outsized copper bowls serving as fire pits.

I parked my car in an area roped off for staff and walked along a wide path that led to the front of the house and a mammoth set of doors. I pinned my shoulders back, willing the butterflies in my stomach to settle down, and I reached out to grasp the heavy doorknocker. Just as I was about to let it fall, the door opened in a wide arc, pulling the knocker out of my hand and causing me to stumble over the threshold and into the house.

Tiffany Jacobs helped me up, murmuring apologies in her much admired, heavily insured low, scratchy voice. I crouched to gather the bag I had dropped, and my face collided with her long ropes of shiny, black hair.

"I'm so sorry," she said again, then extended a cool, slim hand. "So lovely to see you again, Charlie. I'm glad you could help us out tonight."

"It's my honor," I said, back to squeaking again, a lovely counterpoint to her Lauren Bacallesque voice.

She gestured for me to follow her. "I'll show you to the kitchen, but can you have a glass of wine with me first? Or is that *verboten* when you're about to commandeer a hot oven?" She winked at me, and I followed her like a love-struck puppy dog.

I'm having a glass of wine with Tiffany Jacobs. In her new house. And she's barefoot, which must mean she thinks of me as a close friend! My thoughts chased one another, chastising the ones that recalled I hadn't even known who Tiffany Jacobs was a week prior, and focusing instead on the view that greeted us as we entered the living room.

Ebony wood floors stretched in wide planks from one end of the room to the other, interrupted only by a see-through fireplace that divided the kitchen area from the great room. An oceanic white rug covered much of the living room floor. I got so distracted by the thick pile on that rug, I wanted to take off my clogs and throw them into one of the copper fire pits, then sink my unpedicured toes into the fluff.

"These windows are from Switzerland," Tiffany said as she stopped in front of a curved wall of floor-to-ceiling glass. "I thought they were far too indulgent, but Macintosh insisted, and now I'm so glad he did." I turned and saw a softness in her expression. "He is really, really hot."

As if on cue, Macintosh Sween's crocodile-skin shoes clacked on the hardwood behind us. "Hey, it's the berries and ice cream lady," he said, offering me his hand. I shook it and felt my cheek muscles cramp, my smile was so engaged. "That shot of hot chocolate had Tiff swooning all week." The beginnings of fine lines made delicate jewelry around jarringly green eyes. His teeth shone so white, they were one shade shy of blue.

Tiffany nodded. "Nectar of the gods. Babe, would you bring us the bottle of Tempranillo and the glasses I put out on the counter?" He strode into the kitchen, and she called after him, "Bring another glass, too, if you'd like to join us."

Only after letting my eyes swim in a pool of kitchen-marble-lighting-appliance lust did I force my gaze back to Tiffany, who, by the way, was magazine-ready, too.

Crossing one lithe leg over the other, she studied my face. "I hear you're from the Midwest," she said.

I nodded. "Minnesota."

Mac returned from the kitchen and offered each of us a glass from the Lucite tray he carried.

"Will you stay for some wine, my love?" Tiffany asked. I wondered if she'd had work done on her cheekbones or if they just came like that.

"Can't," Mac said. He leaned down to kiss Tiffany long on the lips. I almost looked away but also felt a bit like I was watching a movie. Surely I was allowed to look, after paying twelve dollars plus popcorn?

"Roger wants to talk about that Berrini script. If I don't call him now, he'll hunt me down at the party tonight." Turning a full-wattage smile in my direction, he said his good-byes and left the room.

I swallowed hard, hoping I didn't look as much like a *Teen Beat* reader as I felt.

"I'm from the Midwest, too," Tiffany said. She pushed a cascade of hair to one side of her head, tilting her chin as she looked at me. "I grew up in Nebraska."

"That's great!" I said with an enthusiasm I had never before felt about the Husker State. I dipped into my glass of wine and sniffed a bouquet of expensive and . . . expensive.

She nodded, a small smile on her lips. "I loved growing up there. Hay rides, football games, church potlucks, even the depressing winters. It was a good, safe place to figure out who you were."

She'd fixed her gaze through the wall of windows, on a faraway point that fell under and away from us. I waited for her to speak again, and when she did, she seemed to be searching my face for the answer to a question.

"You know, I've found people in this business are nothing like the people I grew up with." She frowned slightly but corrected herself at once. I could only imagine what frown lines could do to her script options. "People from our part of the country know how to be discreet. How to keep their mouths shut. How to allow others their privacy."

I nodded, gripping my wine glass with clammy fingers. Had Spartacus the wonder guard radioed up that I was too chatty? Too eager? Too jumpy?

"Actually," she said with a laugh. "That's not true at all. The people in my hometown didn't know how to be discreet at all. They were insufferable gossips. No one kept their mouths shut, and we were all watching each other constantly. I couldn't even buy Advil at the pharmacy without the pharmacist calling my mom and making sure I was having normal periods."

I winced. "I know about that kind of a gossip machine." I laughed to remember. "Once I skipped third-period study hall with my boyfriend to try a cigarette behind the bleachers. By the time we had reached the end of the parking lot, my dad had been called at work by three different people who lived near the school and must have been spying out their windows. My biology teacher asked during the very next class if I'd been paying attention the first time or if I needed one more look at the smoker's lung before I made my decision."

Tiffany groaned in commiseration. "Well, Mac and I have learned the hard way that most people in the entertainment industry would rather throw you under the bus than offer you a bit of privacy. This kind of lifestyle demands a lot from a person."

It does have its perks, I found myself thinking and immediately felt disloyal. I swallowed the last of the wine and placed the glass gently on a nearby burnished bronze table.

"Charlie," Tiffany said. She leaned forward in her chair. "I like you. I like your desserts, I like the way you conduct yourself, and I like your self-assurance. I really enjoyed talking with you at Thrill the other night."

I felt my heart speed up. "I did too. Thank you. I mean thank you for liking me."

She laughed, a low, musical, blockbuster kind of laugh. "You're welcome. I'm hoping that tonight will go very well."

She drew out those last two words, and I nodded, agreeing with her wholeheartedly.

"In fact," she said, still watching for my reaction, "if it does go well, and I'm sure it will, I hope to introduce you to some friends. Powerful friends who would be very grateful for a discreet, hardworking Midwestern chef like you. Friends who appreciate loyalty and the value of a kept secret."

I'm sure my eyes widened, and I hoped to high heaven that I didn't *look* like I was suddenly worried about Tiffany Jacobs's connections to the Mob. She did look a little Mediterranean, now that I thought about it.

"Nothing too intense," she said, apparently picking up on a flicker of my uncertainty. "Parties, personal chef work every now and then. Margot has told me you love your job at Thrill and aren't looking to move on."

"You know Margot?" I hated the way I sounded, so green, so unaccustomed to the networking dance.

"I do," she said after taking a sip of her wine. "We've known each other a long time. She's not a woman to be trifled with." Tiffany arched her sculpted eyebrows. "But she's mostly harmless. As long as you do what she says."

My laugh sounded uneasy and tinny.

"So I know you like working at the restaurant. But I can assure you, if you're interested, you could expand that horizon." She stood and smoothed her shirt with manicured hands. "Well. I'm sure you have plenty of work ahead of you. Shall I show you to the catering kitchen?"

I stood quickly, clutching my bag in both hands, and followed the movie star through her palatial home and back to the area of the house where I felt most comfortable. I air-kissed Tiffany as she walked away, leaving me alone to greet the rush and bustle of the team Avery had assembled from Thrill. They moved in a quiet, controlled manner, all under the watchful attention of the cameras and production crew that had been able to tag along only because of Margot's promise that they would stay in the kitchen for the evening. Now that I knew Margot and Tiffany were old friends, I was sure this evening had been cooked up between the two of them. A pulse of doubt rippled through my thoughts, and I wondered if Tiffany and Mac really had liked what I had served at Thrill, or if it had all been preplanned before they'd set foot in the restaurant.

No matter, I thought as I caught Avery's eye from across the room. *It doesn't matter how I got here, just* that *I'm here.* I steeled my shoulders and walked toward Avery, stepping over a camera cord and a man fiddling with a boom mic. Linoleum-clad kitchens in Minnesota, galley kitchens in New

York, commercial kitchens in Seattle, *Architectural Digest* kitchens in the homes of celebrities—I'd tried them all. And, I thought, as I moved toward the ovens and my crates of supplies, I knew how to make them obey me.

Avery approached. "Ready?" he said, his eyes shining.

I didn't say anything in response. I didn't need to. We both knew the answer to such a silly question.

19

THE following morning, I made a mad dash around my apartment, picking up stray newspapers, empty coffee mugs, shoes, and coats and gave myself a hearty verbal lashing on what a slob I'd become. Since when was it all right to leave little pools of Shiraz in the bottom of a wine glass to be scrubbed out when they became dry and unyielding a day later? When had I decided that flinging a drippy raincoat on the tile was a better option than shaking it out over the sink and hanging it above the tub, like any self-respecting clean freak would do? When, for sweet goodness' sake, had my organic 1 percent milk curdled in a desolate and barren fridge and I *hadn't even noticed*?

Since when?

I felt a smug smile form in response to that question: since I'd started meeting movie stars and cooking for them in their own houses.

I hummed as I continued my clean up, trying to create some sort of order before Kai came over to help with Zara's birthday cupcakes. The images of the TiffanTosh event swam before my eyes as I swept the floor around the kitchen island. I remembered the warm, tawny light of a dining room bedecked with candles; how I felt when the dessert plates came back to the kitchen, practically licked clean; the way Tiffany introduced me to the entire dining party as "Seattle's newest gift" and said that I was "nothing short of a sugar genius." I wanted Kai to see all those memories, to feel them with me, but I knew that by the time I could tell him everything, some of the sheen would be lost, some of the sharpness dulled.

I was deeply involved in this remorse and a vigorous scrub of the kitchen sink when the phone rang from the concierge's line. I pushed the button to allow Kai up, noting with alarm that he was fifteen minutes early. Plus, I'd given Omar the go-ahead to let Kai up without the need for that infernal buzzing. Strange, I thought as I tossed my sponge under the sink and reached for the trash can.

The elevator door opened, and I finished lining the bin with a fresh bag before popping my head above the counter.

I did a double take. "Avery! What are you doing here? I thought—"

"—that I was someone else?" He grinned, looking like a cat who had just enjoyed a plump canary. "I can see that. You never wear your hair down for me."

My hand flew to my hair, self-conscious under his teasing eye.

"But listen," he said, still grinning, "I won't stay long. I brought you these." He held out a dramatic, statuesque bouquet, bursting with birds of paradise, deep purple orchids, fully opened and fragrant roses. I took them and thanked him with a peck on the cheek.

"To the toast of the town," Avery said, sounding a bit like a proud coach. "You absolutely crushed it last night." His eyes shone. "Could you believe it?"

"No!" I said, giddy and relieved not to have to hide it. "The whole night was insane. Could you believe that house?"

"Unreal." He crossed to the kitchen and took a seat along the counter while I rummaged for a vase. "And have you ever seen so many ridiculously beautiful people in one room?"

I shook my head. "It was unbelievable. Willa Olivier was far prettier in person. And so was her date. What was his name again?"

"Christian Bjornberg. Swedish star of *Zeus: Prime Meridian*."

Avery accepted the glass of lemonade I offered. "I want to know every word they said to you. Out with it." He lifted his eyebrows over his glass.

"From what I heard, they loved it all. The cherry almond fritters, the boysenberry brioche pudding—my personal favorite."

I smiled. "Thank you. And the baked whiskey chocolate tortes. Mac asked for a second plate of those." I blushed, remembering how the actor came back to the kitchen to put in his order personally.

"Could you believe it when they asked the two of us to come into the dining room for an after-dinner coffee? I talked with Roger DuPage for, like, twenty minutes. He's the most powerful agent in Hollywood! And he asked me to pass the cream and sugar!"

"I know," I said. "Tiffany introduced me to guests I've only seen in *People* while getting my hair cut. Margot said—"

The light above the elevator door illuminated, and the doors opened. Kai took one step into the apartment and then hesitated, a small bouquet of wildflowers held out awkwardly before him.

"Oh," he said, the boyish grin he'd worn fading quickly. "You're, um, not alone. Omar said I was on the list and I could come on up." He looked like he might just turn around and go back the way he'd come.

I hurried around the counter and to where he stood. Kissing him quickly on the cheek, I said, "You're definitely on the list. I wrote the list myself. Come in."

Still holding the flowers, he let them drop to his side. He walked with purpose toward Avery like a determined, very masculine florist. He held out his hand. "Kai Malloy."

Avery scrambled off the kitchen stool and stood. He pushed his chest up and out, which only made the height difference between him and Kai more noticeable. "Avery Michaels. Great to meet you, buddy."

Kai nodded slowly. "Avery Michaels. Exec chef at Thrill, right?"

Avery tossed his head to the side, looking suddenly like an arrogant filly first time out at the track. "One and the same. I'm afraid Charlie has probably relayed plenty of stories about me." He punched Kai a little too hard on the shoulder. "Sorry, dude, that I've had to keep her out so late and so often." He smiled at Kai, but I could feel the bolt of tension connecting the two.

I cleared my throat, hoping the dance of the strutting roosters would come to its end. "Well, Avery, thanks for coming by. I'll see you at work tonight."

"Definitely," he said and winked at me. "Looking forward to it." He nodded to Kai. "Great to meet you, man. Stop in sometime at the restaurant. I'll hook you up with a free drink at the bar."

Kai said nothing, just stared and flexed his jaw.

I swallowed hard and made big eyes at Avery to remind him where the elevator was. Just before the doors slid to a close, he wiggled his fingers at us in farewell.

"Sorry about that," I said.

"About what?" Kai's tone had hardened. "Just a visit from your boss. At your home. During nonwork hours. What's there to be sorry about?" He wouldn't meet my gaze.

I lifted my chin. "Nothing, I guess. You're right. We're all adults." I glanced at the flowers hanging limp by his side. "Are those for me?"

Kai looked distractedly toward where my eyes had landed. "What? Oh. Yes. I picked them from my backyard." He sounded irritated that he even had a backyard.

I took them from his hand and pulled his other arm around me. "Thank you," I said, standing close to his solid warmth. "I'm kind of disgusted that you are more domestic than I am and able to grow flowers, but I'm also really happy you picked them for me."

Kai leaned into me and kissed me, hard and long on my mouth. When he came up for air, I thought I saw a glint of triumph in his eyes. "The woman who lived in the house before me planted them. I can't really take any credit." He grinned and pulled me to him again. "But I'll take the credit any way. And another kiss."

"Seems like fair payment," I murmured. His touch was softer now, sweeter, lingering. He gathered me into his arms, and I rested my face against his neck. I breathed in his smell, scrubbed clean and with a touch of cologne.

"I missed you this week," he said into my hair.

"Me, too," I said and felt an instant tinge of guilt. In truth, though I had thought about Kai often, I had been running hard and fast all week. Missing him had become a victim of my things-to-worry-about list, and I felt bad about that.

He pulled away. I couldn't read his expression. "I'd love to stand here and hold you for another six hours or so, but I should probably head to work in about an hour. Sunshine is starting to weary of my sudden disappearances."

"I'll bet," I said. Reluctant, but knowing Kai was right to remind me of the time, I returned to the kitchen in search of a second vase. I tried to be discreet as I pushed Avery's gargantuan flower arrangement into a corner. "I hope you aren't telling her you're coming to see me every time you skip out and leave her to run things on her own."

"Of course I tell her," Kai said, an edge creeping back into his voice. "I have nothing to hide."

I paused, my hands hovering above Kai's flowers. "I didn't mean to imply that you did," I said slowly. I matched the intensity of his gaze. "Kai, are we talking about me here, or you?"

He gripped the stool in front of him but didn't sit down. "Sorry. I guess I'm not over it. I think it's weird that you and Avery were hanging out in your apartment. There. I said it." His eyes stayed fixed on mine.

I shoved the flowers into the vase too roughly and two daisy stems broke in half. Sweeping them up with my hands, I said, "Kai, there is absolutely nothing going on between me and Avery. You know that."

He shook his head. "I can't *really* know that, though, right?" He joined me behind the counter and started scrubbing his hands with a healthy lather of soap.

I punched numbers on the double ovens and set them humming to life. "Yes, you *can* know that," I said, starting to retrieve dry ingredients. "You know that because I have told you. That should be enough."

"Listen," he said while opening each cupboard in turn. "It's not just Avery. It's the distance."

"What distance?" I said, exasperated. "And stop slamming doors. The mixing bowls are in the lower cupboard to the right of the oven."

"Thank you," Kai barked. "I'm not talking about physical distance. I'm talking about emotional distance."

"Oh, come on," I said. I was weighing flour, baking soda, baking powder, and salt on my counter scale. "You sound like Oprah."

Kai turned to me abruptly. "That's low. Do not compare me to Oprah just because you can't handle an honest conversation. I am nothing like Oprah."

I pursed my lips but felt laughter rise dangerously within. "You did use the phrase 'your best life' with me once."

He looked indignant. "I did not. I don't even understand what that means!" He jabbed at the air with my whisk, the other hand gripping a Pyrex measuring cup.

Laughter, a hard and snorty one, escaped my lips. It filled the kitchen with my gasps, all the louder in Kai's silence. When I'd regained enough control to have only a few hiccups left, I padded over to Kai, who had turned his back to me and was whisking egg whites with a vengeance.

"I'm sorry," I said, wrapping my arms around him and trying to force him to stop with the bloody whisking. He was doing it far too *violently*. I definitely needed to be in charge of the whisking. "I didn't mean to laugh at you." I hiccupped once and winced.

He sighed and, thank God, put down the whisk. Turning a tight circle to face me without breaking my grip, he studied my face. "I don't like Avery."

I nodded. "I know."

"And I'm pissed he gets to spend so much time with you."

I smiled. "Thanks."

"And I hate your nondisclosure form and that you can tell him stuff you can't tell me."

"Me, too."

"And I'm really proud of you and that people want you on their TV show because you're awesome."

I felt The Splotch making its presence known.

"And I'm very, very ready for you to have a break from the show so we can figure out our normal without Avery Michaels popping his head between us every forty-five seconds."

My sigh came out in a rush. "Yes, yes, and yes. I want that, too."

He paused a minute, appearing to search my eyes for the answer to a question he wasn't asking. "Okay," he said, brushing a strand of hair away from my forehead. "That's all I needed to know." He slapped my rear, hard, as if we were getting ready to go out there and crush the Badgers' offense. "Now let's make some cupcakes." He clapped once and nudged me gently away. "I need space to whisk."

"No, you really don't," I said and commandeered his weapon. "You can fill the cupcake liners."

He scoffed. "Cupcake liners? Are you even kidding me? Woman, I own my own diner. I know how to make a cake."

I rolled my eyes. "Listen, if you are really attentive and you do everything perfectly, I might let you whip the buttercream. But only if you promise not to do something weird and diner-y, like crumbling a slice of crispy bacon on top or something."

He stopped moving. After a moment of silence, he spoke. "That," he said, "is brilliant."

I groaned. "This is never going to work," I said. I watched him search my fridge for bacon, listened to him threaten to go to the store (really quick!) to pick up a pound, and laughed at his sales pitch.

"Seriously," I said again. "This project is doomed."

"No!" he retorted, fist in the air. "This, my dear girl, is the perfect example of your 'best life'! Bacon cupcakes are definitely the best of both our lives put together and then cranked up sixty notches."

I shook my head and laughed at him, betting the cupcakes would not turn out well and hoping our relationship had much better odds.

20

THE dining room at Thrill still shimmered with light, though all the customers had long ago abandoned their clean plates, their soft linens, their empty glasses. The room radiated calm, a delicious irony since the ten hours before the night's end were nothing short of controlled chaos. Standing on weary feet in the middle of the room, I took stock of the day.

I'd had to leave my apartment in disarray after baking cupcakes with Kai, and I cringed to remember the mess that would greet me when I returned home. The cupcakes were finished. Odd but finished.

Kai had won his argument with the bacon, but I conceded only to a monastic crumble of extracrispy bits, as underdone bacon would have violated every personal code I maintained. I forced him to make his own frosting and to include a maple accent, and the bacon/maple combo could only be used on half of the batch. The others, all mine, turned out beautifully and as previously discussed with Manda: strawberry-raspberry cakes with a light and airy lime frosting. I would garnish with a single perfect raspberry right before the party.

Kai was inappropriately confident about his creations, sure they would win the vote he was now prepared to initiate come party time. Honestly, if the man hadn't been so ridiculously good-looking, I would have held fast to my rule never to allow the bacon trend to infect my kitchen. The guy looked amazing in jeans and a T-shirt, and suddenly I'm allowing pork products on my cupcakes? Would the real Charlie Garrett please show herself?

Standing now in the center of Thrill's dining room, I felt every mile I'd walked throughout the day. I let myself down heavily onto the rustic wooden hearth that spanned the length of the fireplace. Its gas flames licked at a row of fake firewood. A tired sigh escaped my lips as I slumped. The elegance and beauty of the room enveloped me and reminded me why I loved working in restaurants. Every so often, I liked to come out to the front of the house. It was so easy to get lost in the abyss of the kitchen and to forget about the world beyond the swinging doors. The people who sat every night in the sea of plush chairs drank in *this* view, this landscape of wood and tile and color and flowers. They didn't get bombarded with the intensity and unforgiving pace of the kitchen. They heard laughter and conversation vibrating around them, not the slamming of metal on metal, the cursing and tempers that flared over and over throughout one evening in the back of the house. The people who ate at Thrill loved this room— and lately, probably the idea that they could possibly make the final cut and appear in one of the episodes.

It was then that I noticed with a start the absence of all the TV production clutter: no cameras, no mics, no thick cords snaking along the floor. The uncomplicated calm was my scene-stealer in that moment. I sat in the chair, trying to bottle the peace of the room, trying to capture the way a patron must feel when waiting for her meal. I closed my eyes and hoped to bottle the serenity and take it with me.

My phone vibrated, and I retrieved it from my pocket.

Kai: Ready to get trounced in the Great Cupcake Throwdown?

I laughed as I typed my response.

Me: It's late and you must already be asleep. Sweet dreams, dear boy. That's the only place you'll be trouncing.
Kai: Where are you?

Me: Just leaving work. Beyond tired and headed to bed. But happy I'll be seeing you in the morning. I'll still want to date you, even though your cupcakes will taste gross.

Kai: You are on some kind of arrogant, pastry chef crack. See you on the battlefield. Sleep well, pretty girl.

The door leading to the kitchen swung open, and I tucked my phone into my pocket before turning to see who was coming into the dining room. Avery picked his way slowly through the tables and chairs. He looked rumpled and every bit as spent as I felt. He offered a tired smile, pulling his chef's hat off as he joined me at the hearth.

"Hey," he said. "Are you as wiped as I am?"

I nodded. "I'm so glad we're almost finished filming. I never thought I'd long for the days of boring old fifty-hour work weeks."

He looked chagrined. "I'm sorry about that, Char," he said. "You came out here for a saner life, and I feel like I've welcomed you into Insanity 2.0."

Even my laughter sounded tired. "If I recall correctly, you were the one who pointed out that I had no friends. Now I finally have a few good ones in town, but they're all irritated with me because I can't ever see them." I shook my head. "I'm not sure what's worse: loneliness or knowing the cure is just out of reach."

"Whoa, there, Aristotle," he said. A smile broke through the deepening lines on his face. "You won't be lonely forever. We'll finish filming, do the promotional stuff, and then you and Wildflower Man can go frolic through all the fields you want. Until next season."

My eyes traveled upward in thought. I let my gaze run along the seam between the ceiling and the wall. "I don't know, Avery. I think I might be one-and-done with this TV thing."

"What?" He leaned toward me. "You're such a natural. And I thought you were having fun. The accolades in the press, the constant requests from patrons to meet the pastry chef, the party at TiffanTosh's place and all the contacts that are sure to open up. You're meant to do this, Char. Admit it." He pulled my hand from my lap and folded it between his palms. I hadn't realized I was cold until the warmth from his grasp cut through my chill. "You're perfect for this job. No one else could do it like you."

We sat in silence, hearing the empty building settle in twinges and moans as it bedded down for the night. Finally, I revealed my confession. "I do like being liked," I admitted softly.

Avery's tone was reflective. "Charlie, I'm pretty sure you have no idea how much you are liked by the people who surround you. You're one of a kind, Char. It was true a decade ago, and it's still true today."

I laid my mop of hair and heavy head on his shoulder. "Thanks, Avery. You have no idea how much I needed to hear that tonight."

The heat from the fireplace warmed my skin through my whites, and I felt myself being pulled into the escape of sleep. I closed my eyes, making myself a feeble promise to just let my eyelids rest a moment. I must have dozed because my eyes would not obey my brain when it told them to open up already. I felt Avery's arm around me, then his hands turning me slowly to face him. When I succeeded in propping my eyelids open, Avery's face was all I could see, and his lips were planted squarely on mine. He kissed me softly at first but quickly graduated to an urgency that shot me straight out of groggy and right into an adrenaline rush.

I pulled away. "Avery," I said, wiping my mouth with my hand. "This is not happening."

"Are you sure?" he said, still close, still staring at my mouth. "We have a lot of history here, Char. And we know we can be great together. This is a low-risk enterprise." He smiled and leaned toward me again.

I put my hand on his chest and pushed him gently but firmly away. "We aren't culinary students any more, Avery. This would never work now. We're too different."

Avery shook his head with a resoluteness mirrored by the set of his jaw. "We are more alike than you want to admit, Charlie Garrett. We could build something that Flower Boy can't even dream of."

"His name is Kai," I said, suddenly chafing in the heat from the fireplace. I stood to find the switch to extinguish the flames.

Avery followed me. He grabbed my hands and turned me toward him. "I can give you what he can't, Char. I understand you. He understands what he wants you to be, not who you really are."

His words sliced through any remaining fog. I cleared my throat. "That might be true," I said slowly. "But I think I'll let him be the one to decide that." I stood, patting my hair where Avery's shoulder had done some damage. "We'd better call it a night."

I walked toward the front door, not turning to respond to his words but feeling them sting just the same.

"My door is always open, Charlie. Just remember that, in case things don't turn out like you've planned."

21

ZARA opened the door with a flourish, somehow managing to twirl even as she pushed the screen door wide.

"Auntie Char! It's my birthday! Do you like my dress? It's new and it's a color called fuchsia which is a weird word and it has sparkles and little hearts everywhere and it's from my Nana Henrick." Her words came out in snippets as she spun away and then toward me. I grabbed her around the waist and lifted her up. She giggled with the giggle reserved only for a birthday girl.

"I love your dress," I said, smacking her cheek with a loud kiss. "You look especially beautiful today." She squirmed in my embrace until I whispered into her ear. The sudden change in volume shocked her into stillness. "You're going to want to open my gift now. And you might want to do it in a corner where your mom isn't watching."

Her eyes got big. She nodded in solemn understanding. "'K. I know right where to go." She took the small wrapped package I offered and scurried up the stairs.

Just in time, too, because Manda the Enforcer came down the hallway with the intensity of a natural disaster.

"Oh, thank God you're here early," she said, gripping me by one hand and pulling me toward the kitchen. "Ten little princesses are about to descend, and I can't find the candles. Jack isn't back from getting the pizza, and Polly won't stop trying to eat the balloons that Dane dropped all over the house. Choking hazard!" She swiped a saliva-coated green balloon from Polly's mouth and swung her up to a hip in one motion. "Dane! Where are you?"

"Here!" Dane called from the family room.

I poked my head around the corner. "Is it okay for him to be pulling every Kleenex out of the box, licking them, and then putting them into one germ-infested pile?" I wrinkled my nose, unwilling to initiate an intervention unless Manda was absolutely over the edge with neediness and wouldn't make a move to do it herself.

"That's perfect, actually," Manda said. She opened and shut drawers with slams and curses. "Kleenexes don't kill people. But I just might if I can't find those damn candles. Sorry, baby," she said into Polly's ear and then kissed her. Polly appeared unaffected by the profanity and the frenetic behavior of her mother.

"I'll take Polly," I said, pulling the baby from Manda. "And I'll run over to Kai's house to see if he can come over now. Maybe he has birthday candles."

I nearly collided with Zara as I was leaving the kitchen. I heard Manda gasp and pause in her rummaging.

"Don't I look beautiful?" Zara said, though it was difficult to distinguish individual words around the generous application of glitter lip-gloss. "My lips are shiny and gorgeous. And my eyeballs have blue powder on them that is *awesome*."

"Good Lord in heaven, help me," Manda muttered. I didn't need to turn to feel the darts she was vaulting my way. "Zara, honey, did Auntie Charlie give you that makeup?"

Zara turned questioning eyes on me. "Maybe," she said slowly, unwilling to betray her source.

I turned, biting my lip to keep from laughing. "I did, yes. And may I just say," I curtseyed to Zara, "you are definitely ready for your birthday ball now."

"I can only imagine the animal by-products in that crap," Manda said to me as I hustled out of the room.

"Mommy said 'crap'!" Zara announced through the swamp on her lips.

Polly and I covered the half block between the Henricks' and Kai's house in short order, but I was still sweating by the time I climbed the stairs to Kai's front porch. The child was a little heat sink, cherubic and gurgling but the temperature of the earth's inner core.

"Hey, ladies," Kai said when he opened the door. His eyes took me in, and I felt my heart do an impressively acrobatic flip. "Do you always look this fantastic for children's birthday parties?"

"You look good yourself," I said as he pulled us into a three-person hug, kissed me on the forehead and Polly on her fat cheek. "And you smell good. And you just shaved."

Pulling one hand across his chin, he led us into his house. "I thought a clean-shaven look would photograph well when I win." He didn't even try to sound like he didn't care. "Victory is mine, Cupcake Queen."

I rolled my eyes and sat with Polly on a worn leather couch. I breathed in deeply, taking in the delicious scent of Kai's house, a mix of vanilla and spice and leather and man deodorant, and I couldn't hide my surprise. "This is really nice."

Kai lowered himself into an oversized chair opposite the couch. His mouth upturned into a wry smile. "I'd love to hear why you are shocked. Did you think I lived in a hovel? Maybe expected more squalor than you're seeing here?"

"No, of course not." The blasted redness in my cheeks betrayed me. "I just figured you were a bachelor and that bachelors don't typically have a close relationship with Pine-Sol. Nor do they frame cool art posters."

Polly started to hunt for something to chew on and settled on a face plant, right into the leather armrest. Kai scooped her up and walked to the kitchen.

"I clean, though not as often or with as much aerobic intensity as some," Kai called over his shoulder. I followed him, loving the creaks of protest that the old hardwood put up as we walked. The light-filled living room gave way to a dining room that showcased a long rectangle table and mismatched chairs. The rooms were tidy, but lived in.

"I do vacuum on occasion," Kai continued. Polly squawked her glee at grabbing two fists full of his hair. "I also brush my teeth. And use the self-cleaning option on my oven about once a year. And I use Q-Tips in my ears to remain wax-free."

I tsked. "You shouldn't do that, you know. Q-Tips only push the wax deeper in."

We'd reached the kitchen, and Kai got Polly happily settled on the shiny wood floor by surrounding her with measuring cups and rubber spatulas. She made lots of happy, grunting noises and then commenced cramming items into her mouth, gumming them with enthusiasm.

Kai leaned against the counter and tugged me toward him. "How are you?" he said.

I had to concentrate fully on his words because his eyes and face and mouth were so much more interesting. "I'm well. You?"

He leaned into me, brushing his mouth on my neck. "My kitchen is a happier place with you in it," he said softly against my hair.

The skin on my arms and neck tingled. "Is that some kind of veiled reference about a woman's place and all that?"

"I'm not very interested in what every other woman is doing right now," he said, feathering soft, indulgent kisses along my jawbone. "But I do think *your* place is absolutely right here."

I swallowed hard and forgot about trying for a witty reply. In fact, I'd forgotten the day of the week and my mother's middle name when we were interrupted by a sharp rap on the front door.

"Hello? Anybody home?" Jack's voice preceded the sound of the screen door opening.

Kai jumped back from me as if burned. His eyes were wide as he called, "Hey, Jack. Be right there."

"Close neighborhood," I hissed while patting my cheeks, hoping they weren't as flushed as they felt.

Kai strode around the corner and into the front hall. I lifted Polly and two spatulas into my arms and walked toward their conversation.

Jack took one look at me and whistled. "You guys were totally making out. Sorry." He took Polly before I lost control of her wild lunging.

"What?" Kai said, trying to look relaxed. "No, listen, we were just getting some things together in the kitchen."

Jack snorted. "Dude, I may be an ancient married man to you, but I still recognize a hormone or two when I see it." He nodded at me, which made my cheeks deepen another two shades. I was going to kill him.

"I'd even say you should go back to the kitchen and carry on, but Manda looked like her head was about to spin off its axis when she sent me over for you two. She says it's time for reinforcements and cupcakes." He turned to go but not before wrestling Kai's spatulas out of Polly's chubby grip. She howled in protest, and Jack had to holler to be heard.

"See you two at the house," he said as he took long strides down Kai's front walk. "Sorry again for the interruption."

Kai left me to go turn off some lights and grab his keys, birthday candles, and the cupcakes off the kitchen table. I waited on the porch and was deadheading a pot of herbs when he took my hand.

"I feel like a teenager caught making out in my parents' basement," Kai laughed.

I set a slow walking pace. The party could wait. The week ahead at Thrill was a going to be a doozy, full of promotional events and industry meet-and-greets. These few steps between Kai's house and a gaggle of screaming kindergartners were likely going to be our only moments of alone time for too many days.

"True," I agreed. "But Jack has also seen me cry off all my makeup, get a bloody nose during a double date then bleed all over my date's white pants, and burn my upper lip into one long mustache scab when Manda and I tried a home waxing kit. He is fully accustomed to seeing me in compromising conditions."

"Wait," Kai said, his hand up to stop my words. "How could you allow yourself to date a man who wore white pants?"

I let him laugh because, honestly, the mental image of Dan Richards and his white trousers was still alarming fifteen years later.

Kai sniffed. "I'm going to assume it was Avery Michaels. Don't even tell me if it wasn't because it's so much more fun to think that it was."

At the mention of Avery's name, I felt some of the blood drain from my fingers, even though they were still cocooned within Kai's warm grasp. My mind filled with images of Avery's face so close to mine, his mouth finding me and pushing hard, the heat of the fireplace on my back and the insistence in Avery's voice and words.

Kai's gentle nudge pulled me out of my silence. "You okay?" he asked. We came to a stop at the edge of the Henricks' sidewalk.

I swallowed. *Tell him*, I thought. *Come clean. He deserves that.*

"Kai," I began.

He waited.

I couldn't. In fact, I reasoned quickly, I *shouldn't*. Avery meant nothing to me, and his weird and sudden affection the night before didn't change that. The tension between Kai and Avery certainly needed no fanning from me. To dredge it all up needlessly would be cruel.

I smiled. "Nothing," I said. "Just wanted to warn you about something."

"What's that?" he said.

"It's the cupcakes." I frowned as if facing a moral dilemma. "You're about to go down." I tried my best to look earnest. "The first step is always acknowledging you have a problem."

Kai's phone chimed the arrival of a text. He narrowed his eyes at me for a retort but glanced down at the screen.

"Good grief," he said while scrolling with his thumb. "It's Dahlia. She's texted about six times, telling me I need to call her. Weird." He furrowed his brow at the phone. "She says she wants to talk with me about you." He dropped his phone unceremoniously into his pocket and shook his head. "Probably already freaking out about our fall festival at the farm and wondering if I'm going to bring you."

I felt my stomach lurch, my close call with total and unnecessary disclosure still fresh. I wanted Kai to like me with no reservations. His sisters, too. I'd almost gotten in the way of that by spilling what didn't need to be spilled. "What will you tell her?" We started up the walk toward a symphony of little girl shrieks.

He pulled me into a side hug as we walked. "That's up to you." He opened the door for me. "But do you think Avery would lend me his white pants?"

I shuddered and he laughed. The thought of Avery sharing anything with Kai—secrets included—sounded like a recipe for disaster.

22

HONESTLY, the limo seemed like overkill. We were in Seattle, after all. The land of Birkenstocks and coffee and impossible parking. But Vic and Margot had insisted.

"But we're only going shopping. For dishes, of all things," I'd said. My protests sounded feeble, particularly with Avery's outsized enthusiasm as my counterpart.

"Carpe limo!" he'd said and dragged me into the back seat across from Vic and Margot.

I sat gingerly at first on the plush velvet, more than a tad embarrassed by all the onlookers who stared as we made our way through town. Weren't stretch limos for proms and sweet sixteens? I felt old and as if I'd come to the party early and overdressed.

"Charlie, Charlie, Charlie," Margot chided when she glimpsed my discomfort. "You must come to peace with your new life." She raised her eyebrows at me.

Vic nodded. "Attention is good. Attention means ratings and advertisers and renewed contracts. Limos attract attention, our corporate sponsors like attention, so we like limos. Even for a trip to University Village to buy dishes."

I sat back into the seat and noted how infinitely more comfortable it was than the one in my decrepit Honda.

"Listen," Avery said quietly, though I couldn't imagine it was quiet enough to escape Margot and Vic's ears. "I'm sorry about the other night."

I scooted a little closer in an attempt to gain some privacy.

Avery took my hand and waited for me to meet his gaze. "Truly. I'm sorry. I was out of line, and I was tired, you were tired." His laugh sounded nervous and forced. "Old habits die hard, right? So, forgive me?"

I could feel Margot and Vic's concentrated attention, even though they were making a point to stare out the long windows.

"It's okay," I said quietly. "Like you said, we're both running on empty. I should have just gone home instead of taking an accidental nap by the fire."

We rode without speaking for a few blocks. The sun played hide-and-seek with the clouds that covered the city. Grand, ominous shadows blanketed our view for long moments and then blew away suddenly, leaving a city gleaming and trembling with light.

"It was a good kiss, though. Admit it." Avery put his hand on my knee and grinned, wagging his eyebrows up and down in clownish suggestion.

I peeled his hand off my knee firmly and with deliberation. "It was sloppy," I said, glad that Avery chuckled and that my heart lightened. Being a part of a world that involved limos and stylists and cameras in my face while torching a line of crèmes brûlée was bizarre enough. The last thing I needed was extra weirdness with an old friend and colleague.

The limo rolled to a stop in front of a high-end kitchen store sandwiched within a block of charming boutiques. Vic unloaded a sheath of postcards into my hands and passed another stack to Avery. They were glossy, black-and-white photos of a woman and a man, both photographed from the neck down. The woman had one hand on her hip and the other pointing with a sassy, painted fingernail to the man's chest. The man faced her, and, though the photo cut off his face and expression, I'm sure he was ogling the woman's open chef's tunic and her burgeoning, healthy bustline, trimmed with just a peek of purple lace. In luscious purple type across the image, the postcards read, THRILL ME. A DELICIOUS NEW SERIES ON SURGE TV.

"Give these to as many people as you can," Vic said, looking uncharacteristically ruffled. "Debut episode airs September 1."

"Sweet," Avery said, taking a close look. "Char, you look great."

I snapped the photo away from his eyeballs, even though a pile remained in his hand. "You and I both know that woman looks nothing like mine."

Margot snickered.

"I mean *me*. Nothing like *me*." I cleared my throat.

The driver opened our door, and Margot motioned for me to get out first. "Smile," she said, without doing so herself.

I obeyed, feeling my fingers curl around the postcards. A few passersby stopped to watch the spectacle of the four of us unfolding from the limo, but most people, I was relieved to note, couldn't appear to care less.

Vic scooted ahead of me to open the door to the Kitchen Collective. He bent to speak into my ear. "They don't know you yet, but they will. Don't worry."

I didn't. But as I stepped into the store and beheld the delights lining the walls and shelves and displays before me, I felt instantly invigorated. Limos were bizarre, but colanders? I spoke colander. These were my people.

The store was crowded with shoppers, and I threaded my way through them on my way to ceramics. The hot chocolate shot I'd concocted for Tif-fanTosh had received a hefty amount of buzz, enough to make it one of our most successful "underground" dishes. One could procure the shot at the restaurant, but one had to know to ask. Avery, in particular, loved the espionage aspect of the dish and refused to add it to the menu, even though it was becoming one of our most requested desserts. To mark its ascent, we were at the Kitchen Collective to find sets of unique glasses and saucers in which to serve the dessert.

Avery squeezed through the throng and joined me at a table piled with deep blue ceramic dishes that caught the overhead lights with their flecks of copper.

"These are wonderful," I said, holding a slender cylinder up to the light. "I think the blue would look great with the interior of Thrill."

"Fantastic, love," Avery said.

Love? I looked at him, but he was opening his arm to a perky, petite woman. She wore a yellow apron printed with the store's logo. Margot and Vic moved through the crowd to stand with us in a little circle.

"Charlie," Avery said, "this is Susie Messenger. She is the owner of the store."

"So fantastic to meet you," Susie said. She seemed to be out of breath. "It's such a great honor to have chefs of your caliber and reputation in our store. Great for business!" She pointed with a quick arc of her finger to the packed store.

I realized many of the shoppers had turned our way. A few of them were taking photos with their phones.

"It's a pleasure to meet you," I said, intentionally speaking more softly than she had. We weren't at a pep rally, for the love of Pete. "These dishes are beautiful. Would you be able to order enough for commercial purposes? We would need, what, Avery? Fifty sets?"

"Hmm?" Avery was smiling at a pretty girl who'd turned her iPhone in his direction.

"Of course," Susie said, nodding. "I'm sure the distributor would be more than happy to help with a larger order. Especially since you two are all over the news! Such great timing for your show!"

I looked at her, uncomprehending.

Margot stepped in. "Charlie," she said, "before you pull the trigger, perhaps you could take a look at the other options? I'm sure Susie would appreciate having photos posted with other items."

"Sure," I said, placing the blue dish down with a slow and careful hand. Walking through the rest of the store was hardly a burden for me, and I was happy to take my time. A kitchen store for me was like a Christmas morning that didn't end. Every new display gave me a little jolt, a visual reminder of why I'd applied to culinary school in the first place. It didn't take long before I was enjoying my role as purveyor and impromptu reviewer of Susie's merchandise. I cooed about a box of Norwegian cheese slicers and ordered several for early Christmas gifts. A cake stand from an artist in Oregon made me swoon, and the shoppers following us around the store also murmured their appreciation.

Susie looked as though she were about to collapse from joy.

The bell on the front door clanged so often, my ears weren't even registering its pitch any more. But one of those bells must have brought the arrival of Kai. When he called my name from the back of the crowd, I looked up, knowing his voice and happy to hear it.

"Kai!" I said. I realized Avery had one hand draped around my waist and had likely had it there for some time. We had very little room to maneuver in the cramped store, and I had not even noticed his closeness after a while.

Now, with Kai's eyes locking on mine, I moved slightly to one side, trying to be discreet as I pushed Avery's fingers off my waist.

A teenager with a long, carefully mussed fishtail braid stepped in front of us, blocking my view of Kai.

"Can I take a quick pic of you two? Really quick. I'll totally post it and totally link it to your site."

"Fabulous idea," Vic said and pushed us together.

"How about a kiss?" the teen asked. "Just for kicks."

The crowd agreed to the brilliance of this idea, and Vic encouraged them with a mischievous lift of his eyebrows.

"No, thanks," I said, more roughly than I'd intended. "A photo's fine, though. If you can take one quickly. I need to talk with someone at the front of the store."

"Aww," the teen said, faking a pout I'm sure her mother abhorred.

Avery and I smiled for her phone, then stayed in position for another fifteen phones brandished for the same purpose. I tried sneaking looks at Kai, and I could see he was still in the store, but I couldn't get a read on his expression because he appeared to be pacing.

Finally, I broke our pose and turned to Avery. "I need to talk with Kai. Be right back."

Avery nodded, busy signing a postcard for a plump woman wearing a denim jumper who was yammering on about her own idea for a cookbook.

I pushed through the gawkers but had an awful time reaching the front of the store. One man wanted to ask me about how I broke into show business. Another woman stopped me to tell me her daughter was a waitress at the Hard Rock Café in Orlando and would I be willing to chat with her about how to move up in the restaurant business? By the time I reached Kai, I felt manhandled.

"This is a lovely surprise," I said, going in for a hug. "What are you doing here?"

I tensed. He wasn't hugging me back.

I backed out of my one-sided embrace.

He stared at the crowd for a moment, his jaw tensing.

"I'm sorry to have this conversation here, but I can't wait for a time when we're both awake and alone."

I felt my heart start to gallop. "What conversation?"

He brandished his phone and pointed the screen at me. "Remember when I said Dahlia was trying to get a hold of me? How she'd been texting and calling all morning yesterday?"

"Yes," I said, struggling to square the intensity of his stare with such a benign question.

"*This*," he said, "is why she was in such a hurry."

I squinted at the photo on the screen, and when my eyes focused, I gasped. "Oh, no," I said. The image was a bit grainy, but anyone could easily make out two figures in front of the fireplace at Thrill, their bodies close, their heads tilted in a heated kiss.

"Kai, this does not tell the whole story," I said. My defenses flared into a quick burn, and the blood started to pound in my head.

"Really?" Kai's tone was incredulous, angry. "You are honestly going to tell me this is some sort of misunderstanding?"

"Keep your voice down," I hissed, noting the sudden quiet in the room.

He shook his head. "No. I can't. This is too important, Charlie. I need you to hear me loud and clear."

I swallowed and wished I were anywhere else. "Kai, I can explain what happened."

He shook his head, unwilling. "Here's the thing, Char. I understand your life is crazy right now. I get crazy. I get long nights and deadlines. I get working like a dog to take hold of your dream. Believe me. I get all that." He took a deep breath and appeared to be grasping for some self-control. "I even get nondisclosure contracts and working with people you used to date. But even with all that, Charlie?"

He paused. I realized I was holding my breath.

"I need to know who you are. And I thought I did." He looked at his phone. The people who were standing around us had gone silent, hanging on every syllable of our conversation. He shook his head. "I do not know who you are. And maybe you don't, either."

"Kai." My voice broke.

"I'm sorry, Char." He backed up, toward the door. "I can't do this. I need clean, direct, honest. I need all of you. And I'm not even close."

He turned and walked out the door. The little bell above the glass chimed a gentle reminder of his exit for seconds afterward. I felt unable to move and likely would not have were it not for the sudden realization that there was a line of phones pointed in my direction.

I turned abruptly, anger climbing over the pile of hurt in my body and gut. "Stop filming," I said. The phone people wouldn't even meet my gaze; they were so intent on watching the scene unfold on their screens.

"I said stop filming! This is real life, not some script!" My words sounded strangled. I backed up and knocked over a display of cake pans and rolling pins. Vic called to me, and I heard Avery say he would follow me, but he didn't. I walked out the door and away from the crowd, away from the confused driver who offered me a ride, and away from the place where I had been the star of my own, unraveling life.

23

BALLET flats are not engineered for long-distance walking, but I put mine to work that afternoon. I turned back in the direction of downtown, the restaurant, my apartment, but really I had no clue where I was. I certainly saw unfamiliar neighborhoods, streets, and restaurants, but I couldn't muster enough interest to get worried. At first, I used all my energy to call Kai's cell and try to repair what I had broken. I left eight voicemails, my words first tilting toward hysterical and repentant, and gradually landing firmly on just depressed and repentant. I tried texting, too. That line of attack wasn't any more effective or dignified, particularly when I resorted to this:

> Me: Kai?
> Me: Kai?
> Me: Kai?

I kept up a harried walking pace, catching glimpses of my reflection in storefront windows. My mother had often accused me of "tromping" instead of walking. She had forced me to attend years of ballet class to try to expunge the tromp. Judging by my reflection in Dottie's Organic Pet Treat Emporium, the ballet fees had been a foolish enterprise. I could feel my phone becoming slippery from the sweat on my palm as I continued to check it compulsively, staring at it and willing it to ring. It did ring once, but I silenced it immediately upon seeing Avery's name on the screen.

Around the time when the arches of my feet began to feel like separate, aching appendages, I realized I had slowed down and commenced some sort of shuffle. My eyes stung, and I felt a bubble of emotion threatening to spill over and onto my cute new dress that had cost more money than I would ever admit to Manda. My lip trembled as the image of Kai's face, hurt and angry, held onto my thoughts with a tenacious grip. I took a shaky breath. Deep within my reverie, I gradually realized that a car traveling along my side of the street was matching the speed of my progress. A glut of vehicles had backed up behind the pacer car, a limo, I now saw, and was raising a wail of protests with honking and shouting. I closed my eyes, on edge to think that I'd have to deal with an Internet scandal, a shocking break-up, *and* a traffic accident, all in one calendar day.

Avery's head was halfway out of the limo's back window.

"I saw you ignore my call," he called.

I kept shuffling.

"I saw you *in action*! Busted!"

I said nothing.

"Are you okay?" He had to shout over the honking.

This question stumped me, and I stopped walking. I stood there mulling over a truthful answer until Margot opened the door next to Avery's and stepped out. For a woman who topped out at barely five feet, she carried herself with the authority of an Amazon tribal chief. She shot a look at the driver directly behind the limo, and he looked like he'd been hit with a stun gun.

"Go on," she said to the men in her jurisdiction. Avery and Vic nodded like privates to their commanding officer. "Charlie and I will see you at the restaurant tomorrow." Without waiting for their input or approval, she stepped onto the curb and clicked toward me in her power heels.

"Let's talk," she said. She pointed to the coffee shop behind me. I glanced at the passel of black wrought-iron chairs and tables and wondered if I would have just kept walking right into them if I hadn't heard Avery's call.

Waving away Margot's offer for a coffee, I lowered myself onto one of the chairs. After Kai's words and his abrupt departure, adrenaline had coursed through me, probably helping me cover a lot of pavement in a short amount of time. Now that I was sitting and still, I felt all the energy that had propelled me to that spot abandon me. My limbs, my heart, my head all felt depleted, even jittery, with exhaustion. I squinted up at the sun, surprised it was out and so irritatingly perky during such a horribly dreary moment.

Margot used her back to push through the shop door to the outside. Returning, she balanced two large coffee cups in her hands. Placing one in front of me, she said, "Drink this. You'll never make it home if you don't."

I looked long at the drink I hadn't wanted, watching steam curl up in delicate ribbons. As soon as the thought occurred to me, I knew with total certainty that it was true. I looked at Margot. "You leaked that photo, didn't you?"

Margot took her time drawing a sip out of her coffee. Steam rose and fogged the frames on her glasses. She sat back in her chair before answering.

"Yes." One word, and that was all she was offering.

I shook my head, anger rising. "You had no right to make such a private moment public."

She raised an eyebrow. "You were in a very well-lit restaurant with all the windows uncovered. Any person walking by could have snapped that photo." She shrugged. "We just happened to have much better lenses at our disposal. And an inkling that we should stick around until both of you had left the building. You and Avery are wild cards when you are together. Makes for great TV."

I clenched my jaw. "Kai broke up with me because of you."

She winced. Drawing one cigarette out of an engraved silver case, she lit it and took a long pull. On the exhale, she returned her gaze to me. "Charlie, please. Do not stoop to playing the victim. It's so unbecoming in a woman of your caliber."

I stood. The table wobbled, and some of the liquid in my full cup sloshed over the rim. "I quit." I pushed the chair back with my foot, but even over the scraping of iron on the sidewalk, I heard Margot's words.

"No, you don't." Her tone was firm, irrefutable.

"Listen, if this is about the contract, I'll pay my way out. I can—"

She sniffed. "Trust me, my dear. You cannot pay your way out of that contract. Not on a chef's salary." She shook her head and took another pull on her cigarette. "But it's not about the contract. It's about you."

I stood, unable or maybe unwilling to move.

She nodded at the chair. "Sit. Your feet won't make it far anyway, and the least you can do is hear me out."

I waited a moment, weighing her words. "Fine," I said finally, in what sounded like the voice of someone on *Saved by the Bell*. I sat carefully on the edge of my chair, as if my body were reserving the option to bolt at any moment.

"I understand you're upset." Margot's voice was measured. "It is unfortunate that the photos caused such an issue in your relationship with Kai."

Hearing her say his name made me newly angry. "Was that an apology? 'It is unfortunate' does not count as an admission of guilt." I tapped my fingers on the top of the table until her stare made me stop.

"I did not apologize." She pointed at me with her cigarette. "And neither should you."

I started to protest, and she shook her head, long earrings swinging into her cheeks.

"Charlie, I allowed those photos to be released because I was doing my job. I'm very, very good at my job." She fixed her eyes on me. "And so are you."

I sat up straighter. "Thank you. But a compliment won't fix this mess."

Margot leaned her slight frame over the table. "Are you feeling guilty, Charlie? I can see on your face that you are. But why? Why should you feel guilty? What have you done wrong? You were working long hours at a job you love, you were tired, and you repelled the advances of an old flame." Her eyes widened. "No offense, honey, but that is not exactly the makings of a sweeping scandal. You're clean as a whistle from my perspective."

Her words hung in the air between us. I rolled them around a bit in my head, testing them for soundness. "I haven't been a very good girlfriend," I said, more meekly than I intended. "I've been working a lot."

At this Margot erupted. "Do you hear yourself?" She stubbed out her cigarette with a vindictive twist. "You work sixty hours a week at a job that is your passion. You have put in years—years, Charlie—getting to this spot in your career. You have defied social norms by excelling as a woman in a profession long dominated by men. Believe me, I know *exactly* how that feels and the kind of commitment it takes." She pulled one of my hands into both of her small ones. I didn't know where to look, so surprised by her uncharacteristic closeness. "Charlie, let me ask you this. What have you dreamed about for the last ten years?"

I answered without hesitation, my response as automatic as the way in which I piped frosting or whipped a mousse. "I've dreamed about having my own pastry kitchen in a premier restaurant."

She nodded slowly, letting me hear my own voice. "Right. And you are so, so close. So close, you should be able to taste the accolades. To feel the power of crafting your own career from here on out. To touch the ink on the menus that bear an embossed imprint of your name. To hear that name bantered about for the next James Beard award, the next Michelin star." She watched my face. My breathing had become shallow.

Her smile was a knowing one. "I can read the desire and the competitiveness on your face as if it were an op-ed in the *Times*."

I didn't even try to deny it. "I've wanted those things for so long. Many, many years."

"And how long have you been dating this Kai?"

I felt my stomach turn. "Three months."

Margot didn't move. She just looked at me and waited for me to know what she already did.

The light had begun to wane, and the cool of a summer evening seemed suddenly chilly. I shivered, wishing I had a sweater. My thoughts turned to the never-used soaking tub in my apartment, and I knew where I wanted to be.

I stood but couldn't find the words to end our meeting.

Margot saved me the trouble. "Sleep on it." She nodded to the other side of the street. "You go ahead and take that cab. I'll call another for me."

I glanced at the waiting taxi and wondered how long it had been sitting there.

"Thank you," I said. I moved away from her, but she had one more thing to say.

"You're welcome. And Charlie?"

I turned.

"You're smart and talented and beautiful and strong. Those are not empty compliments. They are facts." She reached over to my untouched coffee and took a sip. "See you tomorrow."

I walked gingerly on my worn-out feet, and I knew without any further reflection that she had nailed it. After a bath and a good cry and maybe even a movie based on a Nicholas Sparks novel, I would sleep and then, yes, without a doubt, I would see her tomorrow.

24

ALL the inner peace and strong emotional muscles I'd flexed the night before had completely disappeared by the morning. I felt weepy as I showered and got dressed. I never should have watched *The Notebook*. That movie always messed me up for days.

Gulping down a carafe of French press, I talked to myself. My voice was loud in my apartment.

"You're going to be fine," I said to my fridge as I opened it to get the cream. "You just need to get to work early, start in on prep, and act like nothing happened yesterday."

I tried for levity as I brushed my teeth. "Hey," I said through a mouth full of foaming paste. "Who cares? So you had a public breakup! In front of your bosses and a room full of people with smart phones!" I spit out the excess paste. "So Kai won't return your calls or texts! You feel like a loser, right? Well, shake it off! No biggie! Life happens!"

I looked long and hard into my reflection on the elevator door as I waited for it to reach my apartment. "You are a professional. Act like it and people will treat you like one."

That last bit of advice was what helped me gather my courage to open the back door of Thrill and face whatever stood behind it. Turns out, nothing stood behind it right at that second because the kitchen was running at full speed. I frowned at the chaos, confused as to why people were acting as if it were 7:30 p.m. and mid-rush when, in fact, the clock had just inched past noon.

Stepping into the room, I corralled the arm of a passing line cook. "Hey, what's going on?"

The kid could not have been older than twenty-one. He had a beautiful head of black curls and flawless brown skin. I had the fleeting impression I had seen him on a commercial for a men's aftershave. "Hey, Chef Garrett. Sorry about the breakup."

I tried looking dignified, which, in this case, probably meant I looked like I'd sucked on a lemon. I tried repeating my question. "Why is everyone freaking out?"

"Oh," he said, his perfect smile fading into a studied seriousness. "Killian McGuire is supposed to be dining during the first seating tonight."

"Killian McGuire the restaurant critic?" I felt the tips of my fingers tingle at the thought.

"The very one," he said. "Well, we aren't positive, of course, since he made the reservation under a pseudonym. But Chef Michaels is pretty sure it's the same alias he used at Wu Tang and at Bonne Femme, so we're assuming it's McGuire."

I pushed through the crowd, eyes on Avery, who was issuing orders from the pass.

"McGuire?" I said before I'd come to a stop before him. "Are you serious?"

While it was true that any good review from a restaurant critic could double, even triple, a restaurant's exposure, Killian McGuire—feisty, opinionated, and a man with two million followers on Twitter—held unparalleled influence. A good word from him could put a restaurant on a completely different map. In fact, some chefs considered a favorable review from him to be more coveted than a Michelin star. Most twenty-five-to-thirty-five-year-olds—a big chunk of the dining demographic—couldn't care a whit about the stuffy and ancient Michelin guide, but many of them kept track of where McGuire was eating and drinking. And those same people talked incessantly to their friends, furthering his reach. A McGuire endorsement was gold served up on white china.

Avery took my elbow and walked with me toward my station. He lowered his voice. "Vic said that Margot said that Tiffany Jacobs and Macintosh Rowe are good friends of McGuire and that they probably put in a good word." Avery's eyebrows were darting toward his gelled hairline, a long-time habit that marked him as supremely stressed out.

"This is big," I said, my own stress level climbing steadily upward to a jagged spike. We began a slow walk toward my station. "I need to do inventory. I hope he orders the strawberry and sweet wine gelées with candied pistachios. I read somewhere that he has an obsession with strawberries, and the berries we've been getting from Shisler Farms are perfectly—"

"Charlie." Avery stopped just inside the pastry area. No sign of Tova.

I met his gaze.

"I'm sorry about yesterday. I know you really liked Kai."

I swallowed, sorry to remember what I was trying so hard to forget. "Thanks. It just wasn't meant to be." Feeling in my pocket for my phone, I retrieved it as a recently perfected reflex. No message, no voicemail.

"He hasn't called?" Avery spoke quietly, even though the film crew was busy catching the chaos in the main kitchen.

I shook my head. "Not yet. Probably never. I don't know. I guess we don't really know each other that well when it comes down to it."

Avery nodded. "Well, he's missing out. He should at least allow you to explain yourself, right? Nothing happened. Much to my chagrin." His smile was lopsided, and I realized anew Avery was a lot like a lost puppy. A lost, very ambitious puppy.

I punched him playfully in the gut. I meant it to be playful, but I did see him grimace before he could hide it. "Time to impress Killian McGuire. Personal lives are officially dead in the water until he's full, happy, and tweeting to his heart's content. You ready?"

"Born that way." He turned and bumped into Tova, who ducked past him like a lithe cat and approached me with open arms.

"Charlie," she said, burying her face into my hair. "I'm so, so sorry. I saw the whole thing on *Sparkle Online*."

"Thanks," I said awkwardly. My arms were pinned to my sides within her embrace.

"Go ahead and cry." She petted my hair. "Emote. Feel. Be present. This is a safe place."

"Probably not," I muttered, eyes on the distant cameras. "Listen, Tova," I said more loudly. "We have a lot to do today. Did you hear Killian McGuire is coming to Thrill tonight?"

She pulled back. Her ginormous eyes looked soulful, maybe even thoughtful. Hard to tell with the mascara. "I heard about some reviewer guy. Never heard of him. But Charlie . . ." She gripped my hands. "I want you to know I'm here for you whenever you need to talk. And I totally understand heartache. I've been dumped many, many times."

I pursed my lips. "It's a harsh word, *dumped*."

She clapped her hands and reached for her apron. "I know you, Charlie Garrett, and I know you are a worker bee. Work can be a great distraction against feeling like yesterday's trash, so let's get to it. What do I do first, Captain?" She threw off a mock salute.

Trying to focus on Tova and not the all-star pastry team I wished I had for a visit from McGuire, I pointed to a crate of strawberries. "Wash those thoroughly. I'm pretty sure he'll order the gelée, and I want to be ready."

We set to work and literally kept our heads down for the next six hours. Tova was not going to win any awards for her technique, but she did seem to genuinely want to please me and help me do well. Perhaps pity was driving her to work harder than I'd seen her work before. She did offer several times to "hug it out" with me, a concept I found both frightening and inefficient. The third time she brought it up, I told her just that.

"Say what you want," she said, unaffected by my blunt refusal. "But I know that deep underneath that heart of ice, you do have feelings, and those feelings are hurt. When you are ready to face the hurt, Charlie, I'm here. You know," she said as she returned to cutting butter into cubes, "I've taught hot yoga for, like, three years. I know tension and pain when I see it."

I snorted my cynicism and she shrugged. But by the time I'd prepped for two services, torn into a BLT during a hasty family dinner, and scrubbed down my station for the fifteenth time, I was certainly tense and certainly in pain. My fingers were kneading one particularly large lump in my neck when Avery flew around the corner.

"He's here." A fine bead of sweat lay along the edge of his chef's cap.

Tova squealed. "I'm so excited! Is he gorgeous?"

Avery glanced at her as if she was some sort of noise pollution he had just then noticed. He zeroed in on my face again, and I saw his eyebrows shake. "We can do this. Right?"

I nodded. "We can and we will. Tell me as soon as you can what he has ordered for first and second courses so I can be ready."

The rest of the restaurant filled up quickly, and those people wanted food, too. I charged through the orders that Chet hollered from the main kitchen.

"Fire two crème brûlées, one gelée!"

"Yes, Chef!"

"Fire one flourless chocolate, one gelée, and one nut tart!"

"Yes, Chef!"

Chet barked, we answered and cranked out dessert after dessert. I kept my eye on the gelées, pleased to see them selling so well but beginning to worry we would sell out before Killian McGuire had a chance to order.

"How many people are in McGuire's party?" I asked Tova, knowing she would not hesitate to gather intel. A few moments later, she returned from her errand.

"Mike the camera guy says Mr. McGuire is dining with three other people." She became very serious and lowered her voice. "I want you to know that Mike is trustworthy. I know this because I'm unofficially dating him. Today's our three-day anniversary. Don't tell Margot."

My laugh was sharp. "Your secret is safe with me. Believe me, you don't want Margot involved in your dating relationships. Gets very crowded very fast."

She turned toward the ice cream maker. "I can't see us lasting anyway," she said above the noise of the machine. "He's already seeming like the jealous type. But he does look really cute in a headset."

I joined her at the machine, making sure the speed of the paddles remained at what I'd recommended. I'd mixed the custard four hours prior, using my time-tested recipe with heavy cream, whole milk, sugar, vanilla beans, egg yolks, and just a pinch of kosher salt. Tova and I stood together, watching it come together in the chilled bowl. I looked at my watch.

"Should be done soon."

"We have some of this in the freezer, you know." Tova pointed to the walk-in. "You made it yesterday, so isn't it still fresh?"

I tossed a sheet pan of pistachios with a drizzle of maple syrup, readying them to toast for the next round of gelées. "It's fresh, yes, but I want fresh*est* for tonight. Plus," I reasoned, "it won't matter anyway. He's not going to want the ice cream."

Avery delivered McGuire's order himself. He gripped the metal shelving next to the threshold. "He wants the ice cream sandwich."

I was already halfway to the refrigerator to retrieve the gelées. I turned on my heel. "What? What do you mean he wants the ice cream sandwich? After the asparagus soup, the peach salad, and the snapper, he wants two chocolate cookies with cherry-bourbon ice cream in between?" My hands were starting to shake at the wrongness of it all. "That's too rich! It will ruin what's left of the meal on his palate."

Avery shook his head. "We can't tell him what to do, Charlie. The man knows palates and he knows food and he wants the sandwich. And no one else at his table even ordered dessert." He was already walking away.

I stared at the beautiful gelée in my hand, bursting with fresh strawberries and sweet wine and ready to be christened with maple-syrup-kissed pistachios.

Tova tsked when I moaned. "Charlie, the Jell-O is good, but that ice cream sandwich is wicked." The timer on the ice cream maker beeped. "Done!" Tova said and handed me a scoop.

I sighed. "Not yet. We'll bake the cookies and make the cherry bourbon mixture, *then* scoop." My nose at counter-top level, I sliced a half-dozen thin cookies from the log I'd chilled in the walk-in and put them in the oven to bake. Four extras, in case of breakage. I could feel Tova watching me as I gently stirred the pitted cherries into a saucepan of sugar and water.

"A splash of bourbon when this is done," I said, though she knew I wasn't asking her to do the splashing. Tonight was all on me, and we felt the division of labor as strongly as though there were a rope dividing her half of the kitchen from mine.

I watched the oven timer while doing my best to keep us out of the weeds as other orders kept piling in. Avery popped his head into our space four times in the space of fifteen minutes.

"I'm going as fast as I can!" I finally snapped, shaking a dusting of confectioner's sugar over a tart. "Back off, Malachowski."

He grunted and walked away.

"What did you call him?" Tova asked, but I ignored her, too. The cookies were out and cooled enough to handle. Carefully folding in the cherry mixture, I formed the ice cream into a precise square and gently settled it between two cookies. A garnish of mint and a thin line of chocolate on the side of the plate and I stepped back. Avery came out from his lurking position and whisked the plate away from me.

"Looks perfect." He was out the door before I let out the breath I'd been holding.

"Nice work," Tova said, her eyes admiring. "You really know how to work under pressure, even when you've been discarded by the man you love only a day before."

The thought of Kai, even a fleeting one, made me want to emotionally eat, and I reached for a spoon. The extra ice cream from McGuire's sandwich beckoned me in ragged stripes left on the chilled bowl. I handed another spoon to Tova.

"To us." I pulled a generous tablespoon's worth off the edge and put it in my mouth. After the initial coldness softened, I felt my eyes grow big. I spit the ice cream out of my mouth, some of it landing just below Tova's chin.

"No!" I ran out of the pastry kitchen, past a line of cooks and hot stoves and out the swinging door to the dining room. I heard Mike the cameraman hustling behind me.

After a quick sweep of the restaurant, I spotted him. I jogged through the packed tables to a cozy four-top in the back corner. Keeping my gaze trained on McGuire as I ran, I watched him laugh with one of his dining partners and then lift a heaping spoonful of ice cream sandwich to his lips. Just as he opened his mouth, ready to gather cookie, ice cream, cherries, and bourbon into his mouth, I lunged for the table and swatted the spoon out of his hand. A perfect little scoop of ice cream rocketed away and, by the mercy of a loving God, did not hit anyone before landing on the wood floor with an unceremonious splat.

McGuire, his spoon mid-air, stared at me. I thrust my hand into the space between us.

"Hello, Mr. McGuire. I'm Charlie Garrett. Pastry chef here at Thrill."

He looked over a pair of reading glasses with bright red frames. Slowly, he lowered his spoon to the table but did not offer his hand. His voice, when he finally used it, was higher pitched than I'd imagined, particularly coming from a man of his girth. "Chef Garrett, you are a lovely woman. I've seen the press photos, but I dare say you are more attractive in person."

I pulled my neglected hand out of the air. "Thank you," I said. I could feel the Splotch gathering steam.

"Nevertheless," he said, "I am here to investigate your work as a chef, not to critique your physical appearance. Would you care to explain why you just attacked me?"

Clearing my throat, I waited for an ingenious lie to emerge, something that would absolve me of my guilt and put all aright. Nothing came. Not a dangerous, dark lie, not a white lie, not even a fib. All I could think about was the taste of the ice cream in my mouth. Margot shifted slightly from her position behind a camera. I tried matching the determination I saw in her face with the certainty in my voice.

"Sir, I needed you not to eat that particular serving of ice cream."

A waifish woman next to him *hmphed* her disapproval, but he kept his focus on me. "And why is that?"

I swallowed. The room was absolutely silent but for the quiet strains of an indie duet on the speakers and the raucous thumping of my heart in my ears. "I must have used salt instead of sugar. I've been distracted and—" I stopped myself, hating the direction I was headed. "It doesn't matter. I made a very big mistake, and the dessert is inedible. I'm sorry."

McGuire put his nose close to the plate and inhaled. After a moment, he resumed a straight back. "I have some extra time this evening, Chef Garrett. While it is unorthodox to accept a second attempt, I do admire your fortitude and your chutzpah." His mouth twitched. "Not to mention your backhand."

"Thank you, Mr. McGuire." I bowed slightly, feeling every bit the serf to his ruling class, and I turned back toward the kitchen. Walking with my nose upturned as a counterpoint to my humiliation, I reached the kitchen door and nearly collapsed when it shut behind me.

"Brilliant!" Avery was slapping me on the back hard enough to cut through my fog. "You were amazing! Best episode ever!"

I leaned into the tile wall for support. "Best episodes seem to come at my expense, Avery," I said. He didn't hear me because the kitchen was cheering.

Gathering my reserves and still shaking with adrenaline, I made my way through the kitchen, the thumbs up, the backslapping, and the high-fiving. When I reached Tova, I pointed to the walk-in.

"Yesterday's ice cream, please. The one that tastes like ice cream."

"Got it," she beamed. "Heard you rocked it out there, Charlie. I can't wait to see it on screen."

I shook my head and willed my hands to stop shaking long enough to refresh the bourbon sauce. Second chances didn't come along often in my line of work, and as I lined up a series of tasting spoons, I tried not to think about what this one had cost.

25

Manda pushed the iPad across her kitchen table and grinned. "Nice recovery," she said. "My favorite part was how they used slow motion for your facial expressions as you raised your hand to bat the spoon out of the guy's fingers. That was gripping."

I rummaged in my bag for the microfiber cloth I used to clean my phone. "At least McGuire loved the second try. That's my only consolation." I wiped at the iPad screen. "How did you even *see* the video on this screen? Have you ever cleaned this thing?"

Manda looked as though she were disappointed in my inability to grasp even the most basic of ideas. "That iPad has been used by six very young, very slobbery hands within the last twenty-four hours. When I need to choose between a clean screen and a technology-induced coma for my children while waiting in the doctor's office, I choose the coma."

I rubbed at a dried chunk of something oatmeal-ish in color and consistency. "Are you sure he's not there?"

Manda leaned the top half of her body toward the window in her front room. Polly was on her lap so she leaned, too, and giggled. "Still no. And you're getting paranoid and weird."

"I am not," I protested, setting the tablet on the coffee table. "I'm just not ready to see Kai yet. It's too fresh."

"Moooommmm!" Zara called from upstairs. "Dane is eating crayons!"

Manda tipped her chin toward the stairs. "Dane, honey, don't eat crayons," she called.

I stood. "Should we go up there? Aren't crayons toxic?"

She shrugged and pried a lock of her hair out of Polly's dimpled fingers. "Nah. Crayola would be out of business by now. Plus Zara will ruin his fun faster than I can get to the second floor. She's a total killjoy. Typical firstborn."

I cradled the cup of coffee Manda had brewed upon my arrival. "Thanks for this. I'm sorry it's so early, but I needed to just hang out with you and remember what normal feels like."

After a long pull of her green tea, she stretched to set it on a shelf out of Polly's reach. "First, this is not early. We've been up since the crack. Zara is already on her fourth costume change." She set Polly on the floor and nudged over a few brightly colored toys with her toe. "Second, let's just be honest that the early hour is so you can avoid seeing Kai."

"Is he there?" I asked again, feeling my heart stutter at the thought.

"No," she said without looking. Her complete unwillingness to even play along reminded me of how long she'd been parenting. "So you've finished filming, right? Pretty soon I'll be able to watch the whole thing and not just whatever gets passed along to the media?"

"Right," I said. The warmth from the cup reached into my fingers, which retained a chill from the damp summer morning. August marched onward and that morning had dipped one tiptoe into cool fall temperatures. "We have some publicity things still on our contracts, but we're getting close to the debut episode."

"Ooh," she said, eyes sparkling. "Sounds like a party. Should I host one here? Can I have the star in our midst?" Her voice was inching up in excitement.

I frowned. "I wish. They're having a party at Thrill. I have to be there. But after that, we can watch the show every week together." I winced. "Or not. I'm not looking forward to seeing myself on screen."

Polly had gotten onto all fours and was rocking back and forth in a kind of burlesque-meets-downward-facing-dog.

"Are you still feeling like you did the right thing?" Manda studied my face.

"What, with the show? Yes. Definitely." I nodded. "I haven't decided about a second season, but I know this season has been great exposure, great for branding."

"Branding." Manda said the word as a statement, but I knew what she was asking.

"You know, marketing. Making my face a household image, building an audience. That kind of thing." I stopped, hearing a lot of Vic and Margot in my words and not much Charlie. "Anyway, I've worked a long time to get here and it's nice to see things finally taking off."

"What about Kai?" Manda tucked her feet under her as she adjusted in her chair. "And no, he's not home."

As if I were going to ask that again. "He never called back," I said, shrugging back into my victim's stance. "I never even got to explain myself and prove I wasn't guilty of anything. I've decided we were just wrong for each other."

Manda said nothing, her posture waiting for me to explain.

I sighed. "Manda, Kai is great. He is. But I'm going through a time in my life when I need to focus all my attention on work. And if he can't handle that, well . . ."

She nodded slowly. "I see. That was a horrid little speech and totally canned. Try again and this time tell me the truth."

I opened my mouth, locked and ready for reload, but Zara's voice interrupted.

"Moooooommmm!" she called, sounding more frantic than before. "Dane is eating a Sharpie!"

"A Sharpie!" Manda scooped up Polly. "Sharpies are permanent! How on earth did he get a Sharpie? If he got it on the walls or the floors . . ."

Her footsteps on the stairs were receding down the upstairs hall when I heard a cheerful knock at the door.

I leaned toward the window and fell out of one of Manda's kitchen chairs. "Shit, shit, shit, shit." I was muttering and crawling over to hide behind the couch, but the Henricks had a door with a mammoth glass cutout so Kai could easily see me crouching behind the furniture. I managed a weak smile and tried to look nonchalant as I walked to the door.

"Hey," I said, trying for breezy. "How's it going, Kai?"

He cocked his head to one side and narrowed his eyes. "Been better. You?"

I shrugged. "Not bad, not bad. How can I help you?" I sounded like the Target cashier.

He ran a hand through his already tousled hair. His eyes were annoyingly bright and beautiful. I found myself wishing he would look at me like he had the day we spent at Forsythia Farms.

Holding out a piece of notebook paper, he gestured for me to take it. "This is the neighborhood sign-up sheet for the block party next month. I came home to grab some things for Howie's and remembered I was supposed to pass it along to Jack and Manda last night."

I took the page from him and studied it like I really cared about bringing a side dish, salad, or dessert.

Kai cleared his throat. I looked up from where I was reading the words *broccoli and raisin salad* over and over.

"Listen," he said, voice lowered. "Charlie. I'm sorry I haven't called you back." I noticed a day's worth of whiskers cropping up on his jaw and chin and wanted desperately to feel their rough texture on my cheek.

"I understand," I said, hating that I sounded so clinical. "I can see how you were upset. It has to be hard dating someone who is a part of a publicity machine." I laughed, but my heart was hammering out a primal rhythm in my chest.

"It was," he said, looking more relaxed. "Really weird, to tell you the truth."

I nodded.

He nodded.

I willed him to move closer, thinking if he'd just take one small step, I could close the distance and kiss his whiskered cheeks and full bottom lip and we could start over.

But he moved in the opposite direction, taking a step back toward the front door. "Well, it's good to see you. I'm glad we could resolve things, you know, since we'll probably run into each other around here every now and then."

I swallowed hard and pulled my mouth into a wide smile. "Totally. Good to be on the same page."

"Exactly." His eyes lingered on mine, his right hand paused on the door knob.

Manda came clambering down the stairs at an unsteady gait. She held Polly in one hand and gripped Dane's fingers in the other. A long and spindly Sharpie mustache curled over his mouth, one curlicue arching all the way to his earlobe.

Manda's cloudy expression lifted instantly when she glimpsed Kai in her foyer.

"Kai! How delightful to see you! We were just talking about you." As soon as the words rang into the space we shared, Manda clamped her mouth shut.

"Is that right?" Kai's mouth pulled into a half-smile. "Then I wish I would have shown up a few minutes earlier." He looked at me again, but not for long. "I was just stopping by with the sign-up for the block party. Charlie has it."

Never one to miss a cue, I waved the sheet in the air like a banner. Manda raised her eyebrows at my enthusiasm. I stopped waving.

"You ladies enjoy your day. The weather should make it easy." Kai opened the door and stepped onto the porch.

"Yes, it's beautiful out! Feels like fall!" I couldn't stop myself! The exclamation points! The fake smile! The seasonal update!

Manda waved to Kai while I stayed rooted to my spot in the middle of the entryway. Dane tried to squirm out of Manda's vise grip but to no avail.

"You are sitting with me for a while, mister," she said, pulling her entire entourage to the family room. She called over her shoulder, "Char? You okay?"

I groaned long and loudly. Dane giggled and said, "Auntie Char cweepy."

"We resorted to *the weather*," I said. My shoulders sagged as I padded toward Manda and the kids.

"That bad, huh?" Manda looked at me with compassion while maintaining an impressive hold on her son's wiggling torso. "What did you feel?"

I shook my head, trying to filter out the topmost emotions. "I felt sad. And nervous. And like I wished we could back the truck up a few days." I frowned at her. "I don't like feeling like I'm not in control. And that man makes me feel like I'm spiraling in a fixed point *away* from control."

She bit her lower lip to contain the smile. "God forbid you relinquish control."

"Exactly!" Exasperation bubbled forth and I *let* it bubble. "This is just what I've been saying. A relationship like that is absolutely impossible right now. I'm so close to getting what I want, and I can't afford to be distracted."

Manda pulled Polly's leggings out a bit to investigate the diaper situation.

I nodded, readily convinced by my own persuasion. "I'm a chef. And chefs make sacrifices to get to the top. The top is within an arm's length, Manda, and I owe it to myself to get there. I need focus. Calm. Direction. A clear head." I slapped the arm of my chair with each directive.

Manda wore a thoughtful expression, all the more impressive because Dane was jumping across her lap with squeals and varying degrees of success. "I don't think I'm one to talk about how to achieve focus and calm," she said finally. "I'm about to take a Magic Eraser to my son's skin. Using one toxic substance to rid him of another." She closed her eyes. "Please don't ever tell my Earth Moms support group."

I thought of the noxious fumes that had arisen a week prior when I'd attacked the deep sink at Thrill with something called Kill It. "You're safe here."

Manda opened her eyes. "Char, you're a smart girl. Very capable, very bright, and very, very good at what you do." She smiled. "You know what you're doing." She stood and stopped Dane from performing a frontwards flip. Walking over to me, she leaned down and planted a kiss on my cheek, then waited for Polly and Dane to do the same.

"Trust yourself," she said, and I waited for the next sentence but nothing came.

I wiped child spit off my cheek and said, "But what? What aren't you saying? Why the diplomacy?"

She feigned ignorance. "I don't have the slightest idea what you're talking about. Unless you mean I should go in for the hard sell on why Kai is one in a million and how he would be a great husband and dad and that maybe, just maybe, your goal in life should not be to control everyone and everything around you."

I pulled a face. "Right. That's what was missing in this conversation."

She laughed. "Listen, I knew when we were in fifth grade and you had me sleep over for the first time that we were not exactly cut from the same cloth. Any eleven-year-old who thinks it's fun to alphabetize her *Popstar!* magazines according to the last name of the guy on the cover is definitely going to do things in life I will not." She squeezed my shoulder, her warmth and long-time support of me filling any doubt I'd carved out between us. "Love you, Char. Go knock 'em dead, just like you always do."

I nodded, feeling suddenly emotional. "Thanks, Manda."

"Now," she said as she turned toward the kitchen. "Let's get your face back, Dane. You're much more handsome without facial hair."

"Hair is cweepy!" Dane said, triumphant in his new knowledge.

I watched them walk away and blinked away the love I had for this motley crew. A full breath and a quick glance to make sure Kai's car was really gone, I opened the door and walked out with new resolve to prove myself worthy of all the support I'd been given. *Time to finish what you've started*, I said to myself, and I quickened my step on my way to face the workday.

26

THE next week at Thrill, the cameras were gone, and I cooked like a woman on fire. No rush was too daunting, no special order too inconvenient. When the production crew left, Tova was granted a few days off, and I barely noticed having to pull extra weight in her absence. Free to do what I knew best without anyone watching, I threw myself into the work. The prepping, the measuring, the scoring, the seasoning, the baking, the scouring—I saw nothing but the *doing*. From the first moment I arrived at Thrill to the second before my body made an easy surrender to sleep, I pushed every nonwork thought out of my mind, particularly those involving men who named diners after their grandfathers, and focused solely on running the pastry kitchen that was soon to be mine without any strings attached.

The exodus of Margot, Vic, and their posse had the opposite effect on Avery. After a harrowing weekend of packed tables and constant demands, we met Monday morning to share the ride to a photo shoot in a loft downtown. The driver opened the back door of the dark sedan, and I slipped in next to Avery, who was sitting with his head resting on the backseat, eyes closed.

"Are you sick?" I tried to be discreet as I scooted as far away from him and his pallid complexion as I could.

"No," he said without opening his eyes. The car eased forward and into traffic. "I feel great."

I whistled. "You'd better start looking alive or Margot will take drastic measures. I've heard she is a fan of spray tanning."

"I'd be open to a little sunshine in a can," he said, rubbing his face with one hand. "This week killed me. I'd forgotten how hard it was to work in a restaurant." His expression was sheepish. "I can't wait until next season when all the support staff comes back. And I can roam around the restaurant looking for story lines instead of being married to the stove all night."

I frowned. "I thought you liked being married to the stove. The stove is a great spouse."

Avery sniffed his disagreement. "I've seen the light, Charlie. And I'm not going back. Food media is where it's at for me. Thrill is just a launching pad."

A sidewalk folk band caught my eye out the tinted window, and I listened to muted strains of a Marvine Gaye cover as we drove past. The vibrancy of Seattle unfolded as we made our way through the city. The trees were just beginning to turn, and I saw glimpses of yellow amid the deep green. A chatty group of teenagers filled one section of sidewalk, joined at the arms and blocking anyone else's passage.

When the car slowed to a stop, I craned my neck to look upward. I could glimpse a few stories of weathered red brick and the name on a small sign. In a vintage font, the lettering read Back Door Events. The driver opened my door and instructed us to go to the third floor, where Vic met us with a clipboard tucked under his arm and two glasses of champagne.

He offered the drinks to us but was so distracted, he could have been handing us our Costco receipts with a streak of highlighter down the middle. "Hi, guys. Drink these and try to relax. You'll take better photos." His eyes settled on Avery. "Good God, man, do you sleep? Head over to makeup and see if they can bring some color into your face. And don't let Margot see you until they're done or we'll get way behind schedule waiting for you to go to Bronze Bodies."

I nudged Avery in the ribs. He took a quick sip of his champagne before striding over to the makeup corner.

Vic was already moving in the opposite direction, but he called to me. "Charlie, they're ready for you in Hair."

A line of mirrors and black folding chairs flanked the back of the room, and I squinted to find Lolo. Making my way through the crowd, I greeted the faces that had become familiar to me throughout weeks of shooting. A smattering of line cooks, the hostess, a dishwasher, and Chet the sous chef nodded as I walked by. I sipped my champagne, gathering from the happy hum of the room that the rest of the gang already had a head start on the relaxed vibe.

Lolo's voice lifted just a smidge from her characteristic monotone. "Thank the dear Lord the day has come," she drawled. "I finally get the chance to do more than a slicked-back ponytail."

"Really?" I said. "What's the plan?"

She pulled my makeshift ponytail out of the elastic and felt my hair with practiced fingers. "The plan," she said, "is volume."

Lolo's prediction, it turned out, applied to more than just my hair. By the time I was done in her chair, then with makeup and styling, I had to stare to recognize myself. Margot called me over to a white backdrop, lit up and luminous with the help of suspended professional lighting. A smattering of slow whistles moved through the crowd that parted as I walked.

I rolled my eyes. "Seriously, guys. This isn't me."

"Baby, I beg to differ," someone said. "You look more *you* than you've ever looked."

I scowled into the dark room but couldn't pick out who was talking among all the laughs and catcalls.

Avery evaluated me as I walked into the light. He stood with both hands on his hips, his hair carefully styled and some kind of magical makeup enabling him to look fully awake for the first time that day. He smiled in a way that made me want to ask for a trench coat.

Margot looked me up and down, then up again. She nodded. "Nice work, Lolo, Sebastian. This is just what I wanted."

"I look like a hooker," I said, quietly, to discourage any more comments from the peanut gallery.

"You don't," Margot said, her eyes on a screen next to the photographer's camera. "But I will tell you that hookers are great for ratings. We'll have to work one in next season."

I caught a reflection of myself from the back wall. "My hair is huge. And these jeans are so tight, I'm having difficulty taking a full breath."

"Flat hair is for makeover shows, medical dramas, and any show involving a university." Margot sounded bored. "Believe me, Charlie. I know publicity campaigns, and *Thrill Me* is definitely big hair."

I shifted in my heels, feeling the beginnings of a blister. The group behind the camera conferred in whispered conversations but none too loud to divert attention from Margot. She consulted briefly with the photographer, a short, angular man with a Mohawk and a facial tattoo. He nodded and turned to his assistant, who handed him what looked like a chocolate macaron. Popping the entire cookie into his mouth, he chewed and waited for Margot to speak.

Margot's voice filled the room. "All right, people. Since Charlie and Avery are already basking in the light, we'll warm up with a few shots of them. And then we'll move to the large group shots before tackling smaller ensembles like the line cooks, the pastry people, and the serving staff. Let's get some great photos, everybody."

"Did she say basking? I definitely don't feel like I'm basking," I muttered to Avery and his ridiculous smile.

"Picture your face and hot bod on the billboards right off I-5. Or in a full-color pull-out in next month's *InStyle*. Or lining the checkout shelves at the grocery store." Avery looked as if he wanted to make out with the huge lens trained on his face. "If that thought doesn't make you work it, I don't know what will."

I tried to inflate my lungs with a calming, yoga-ish breath but the waistline of my pants was like a denim tourniquet.

"Charlie," Margot said over her glasses. "You're going to need to step closer to Avery."

I teetered over in my heels and stood shoulder to shoulder with him.

She frowned. "Now you look like you're taking National Honor Society photos for the yearbook."

Avery chuckled. "I was never in the National Honor Society, I promise you."

I'd been treasurer of the Edenton High School chapter, but I wasn't about to point that out.

The Mohawk man, who claimed his mother had named him Dash, approached us with a solemn expression. He nodded to his assistant, who flipped the switch on an mp3 player and cranked the speakers. Stevie Nicks sang out with a tight vibrato.

"Charlie," Dash said. "Trust me. You're stunning. Avery, man, you are gorgeous."

"Thanks," Avery said, his grin somehow managing to expand.

Dash turned us to face each other. "I want you to take a moment and look into each other's souls. Find the soul."

I bit my bottom lip. "Finding souls has never been easy for me."

Dash inched us closer together and waited. I looked, but all I could seem to find was Avery's normal, eager gaze with a bit of eyeliner on the upper lid. I was just about to break the pose when Dash's voice came from behind the camera.

"Now!" he said. "Avery, don't move, and Charlie, look at me."

I turned and I could hear Dash's shutter start clicking.

"Great, great. Now Charlie, pretend I've told you a delicious secret and you can't tell anyone else. And then whisper that secret into Avery's ear."

I leaned into Avery, and I heard a new round of catcalls.

"Open one more button on your shirt, Charlie," Margot called. The shutter continued to click on Dash's camera. "You look Amish."

I frowned into the darkness behind the bright lights. "You can't be serious."

Margot came into the light, holding a very full glass of champagne and wearing an expression that I believed was an attempt at patience.

"Charlie," she said softly, then paused to wave Avery away for a moment of privacy. "Drink this and become a seductress. A clean one, mind you. This is Surge TV, not Showtime. But remember you're selling smart, capable, and sexy. We need images that show *that* Charlie, not the one who looks like she's never walked in high heels and is worried she's late for curfew."

I worried my lower lip with my teeth. "I don't really think of myself as sexy. And besides," I straightened in my heels but had a difficult time pulling it off, "I don't remember deciding 'sexy' was a part of my branding campaign."

Margot smirked. "'Sexy' is always a part of the branding campaign," she said. "Charlie, trust me." Her tone was more placating. "I won't do anything to embarrass you. We're just looking for a playful, tantalizing glimpse into the relationships on the show." She clapped her hands, signaling the end of our discussion. "Now, let's get to work."

I gulped down half the champagne and gave the glass to Mohawk's waiting assistant. Turning to Avery, I tugged on his collar and raised my eyebrows. "You got me into this, you know."

Avery looked like he'd won a jackpot, but Dash was the one who shouted. "Perfect!"

When I left the loft hours later, little droplets of water hung in the air somewhere between a traditional rainstorm and early evening mist off the Sound. Lolo met me on the way out of the building. She stood by the front door, huddled in a flimsy jacket and pulling on a cigarette.

"Hey, lady," she said. She nodded her chin at me. "Hair still looks amazing."

I touched the top of my head gingerly, still amazed at how much taller I was after Lolo's work. "Thanks. I'm afraid it won't look too great after I take a walk in this humidity."

Lolo dropped her cigarette on the ground, stubbed it out with a metal-studded platform wedge, and picked it up with two careful fingers. She tossed it in a nearby trash bin and nodded down the street. "I'm parked a few blocks away. Want a ride home?"

I shook my head. "Thank you for the offer, but I want to stretch out the sad and depressed muscles in my feet." Gesturing to her shoes, I said, "I don't know how you wear those things. I feel like crying, and I only had to wear heels when I was in front of the camera."

She laughed quietly, her voice raspy with the aftereffects of tobacco. "I'm a slave to fashion, baby. In my line of work, I have no other option. And listen," she said as she started down the street, "don't give in to the crying," she said. "I told you Margot will hate you for it."

I watched her for a while, the spikes of her newly blue hair catching the light every time she passed under a street lamp. Gathering a long, deep breath into my lungs, I enjoyed anew my yoga pants and their willingness to let me inhale and exhale at will. The quiet of the night pulled close around me as I started to walk, the slow silence only punctuated by the polite rumble of fuel-efficient cars every now and then and sound bites of conversations I picked up from the scant foot traffic.

After a day full to the brim with lots of people and lots of big personalities, I found the solitude invigorating. Images of Mohawks, piercings, tattooes, heavy makeup, and, most disturbingly, my own Photoshopped cleavage on an editing screen began to fade the farther I got from the studio. Soon the stiffness in my back and shoulders loosened, and I swung my arms as I walked.

When I reached a crosswalk and was forced to stop for a red light, I realized I was breathing quickly with the exertion. I frowned at my slacker cardio health and resolved to do better starting soon, but then felt the frown dissipate into a nervous smile when I realized where I was. Across the street, a red and turquoise sign was still illuminated above the striped canopy, though a small rectangular sign hanging on the front door proclaimed Howie's closed for the evening.

I stood through an entire cycle of red-yellow-green, squinting at the café, wondering if he was there, wondering what he was doing, and wondering if I dared walk over and see. After a considerable amount of self-talk, I decided the chances of Kai being at work so late were very rare and thus, I did have the nerve to just walk over and peek inside. I stepped into the street when the light turned in my favor. I approached the glass, knowing that I just wanted to be close to a place that used to mean uncomplicated happiness to me. No angle, no Photoshop, no branding campaign. Just really good pancakes and Motown and the hope that the cute short-order cook might stop by my table.

I stopped in front of the center window, ran my fingers across lettering that proclaimed, YOU LOOK HUNGRY. BETTER COME ON IN. My eyes swept the room, the shiny countertops and floors, the neat stack of napkins and vintage red-and-white salt and pepper shakers at each table. The lights in the kitchen were off, but the Mason jar fixtures above each table were illuminated. In my periphery, I saw movement at the edge of the room, and I let my gaze seek out what it was. I gasped, then jumped backward into shadow.

Kai and Sunshine sat with their backs to me, their bodies taking up a small section of a booth that hugged the wall. Kai had his arm around Sunshine, and she was leaning into him. He pulled her close to him, and she let her head fall onto his shoulder. Her dreads splayed out along her back and onto Kai. I stood, fixed to the spot, mouth open and heart hammering. When Sunshine lifted her face, I saw such overwhelming tenderness on it, I stopped breathing. Kai moved in to kiss her cheek and I backed up, stumbling, unable to watch anymore. I ran into the street without looking and nearly got run over by a Prius.

"What are you doing, lady?" the cab driver said out his open window. "I could have killed you!"

I scurried around to the side door and flung it open, desperate to be inside and invisible.

"I need to go home. I can't walk anymore," I said, feeling my heart beat in my neck, my wrists, my chest.

"Okay, all right," the driver said, his tone implying he'd worked with his fair share of deranged lunatics and knew that arguing would be of no use to anyone.

I gave him the address of my apartment and let my body slink down until I could barely see out of the windows. Forcing my eyes to focus on the opposite side of the street, I didn't look back at Howie's, or the warmth within, or the people sitting in the booth. I didn't see anything but the blur of streetlights and the fat droplets of rain that had finally begun to fall.

27

THE following morning, I stood at the edge of my day and steeled myself for what it held. Avery and I were booked to appear on the morning news program, *Rise and Shine, America*, and while I did not exactly feel risen and shiny at present, I forced my face into a cheery expression. A nationally televised interview was just the colossal-sized distraction I needed to push out of my mind the image of Kai leaning into Sunshine. I'd keep to the party line, I'd do what I had promised, and I'd be one step closer to my long-awaited professional freedom.

The outdoor set of *Rise and Shine, America* pulsed with activity. Avery and I hovered around the edges of all the commotion. Vic and Margot flanked us on either side. A man in jeans and a flannel shirt was perched on a ladder in front of us. He fiddled with a light above the stage, an elevated platform set up on a lookout high above the city. The Space Needle soared in the distance, and the Sound beyond brooded in the struggling morning light. A pale woman with a skinny ponytail frowned at a small but elegant flower arrangement she'd placed on a low coffee table. In front of the stage was a large digital clock, its red numbers serving as a ruthless town crier proclaiming six minutes and forty-eight seconds remained until airtime. I watched all the action and chewed on the inside of my cheek until it started to hurt. Then I moved to my fingernails.

"Stop that." Margot spoke to me through a smile she directed toward a man in a headset standing near the craft service table. "Look confident."

I yanked my finger out of my mouth and glued it to my side. "This is so nerve-wracking," I said, voice timid. "I'm just not used to the chaos and tension, I guess."

Vic laughed. "What are you talking about? I've seen Thrill's kitchen during a rush, and this is like an Enya concert by comparison."

"Not the rush." I willed my voice to be louder under Margot's gaze. "The live TV. I didn't realize how much I take the editing room for granted."

"Here come Stan and Bunny," Vic said, striding to meet the couple as they approached. The men slapped each other on the back and jabbed each other in the ribs for enough time that I heard Margot release an impatient sigh. The woman stood with a pleasant, fixed expression while the boys duked it out. Finally the three turned to our little huddle.

"Margot, lovely to see you again, just lovely," the man said into Margot's ear as they exchanged a sterile embrace. The woman shook Margot's hand but kept stealing glances at Avery.

"Stan, Bunny," Vic said, unveiling us like the new car behind Door Number Three, "I'd like to introduce you to the brilliant duo that has brought *Thrill Me* to life. Avery Michaels and Charlie Garrett. Folks, the morning hosts who need no introduction, Mr. Stan Traynor and Ms. Bunny Lancaster."

We shook hands in turn, Stan murmuring niceties while flashing a mouth full of teeth that looked a size too big for his face.

"Great to meet you all, splendid to meet you," he said after air-kissing me near my earlobe. "Looking forward to the debut."

Vic wiggled crossed his fingers in an exaggerated display of nerves. "This weekend! I can't believe it's already here."

Bunny put her arm on Margot, who appeared to dislike having Bunny involved in her personal space. "Oh, you guys will be *great*. Just spectacular! Really!" She pointed to the clock. "But we'll talk about that on camera, right, Stanners?"

With that, we were herded over to the set and directed to take our places.

Stanners gave one more punch to Vic's arm. "Arteaga, you haven't changed at all since college. Remember that Chi Alpha ski trip?" He whistled. "That night alone should have put a few years on you." When Stan laughed, I thought of a sea lion.

The next few minutes left me breathless and full of questions as we were decorated with lapel mics, given the run-down of the four-minute interview, and encouraged to relax! Not to worry! Only five million people were watching! This fact was followed closely by another sea lion laugh.

A sizeable crowd had gathered outside a line of portable fencing separating them from the filming area. Production assistants wearing headsets and badges raised their clipboards in a sudden rush of forced enthusiasm, and the crowd responded with whoops and hollers. The cameraman closest to us held his hand under the teleprompter and motioned for three, two, one, then a finger pointing to Bunny.

"Welcome back, Seattle," Bunny said, waiting appreciatively for the shouts of adulation to continue while the clipboard people jumped up and down like rabid cheerleaders. "What a great crowd here in the Emerald City!"

This educed another wave of shouting and general giddiness. I smiled at a spot beyond the camera, trying to glean some relaxed joy from a woman in the front row of bystanders. She waved a fluorescent green sign that said, SAY WA? SEATTLE LOVES RISE AND SHINE!

Stan waved to the crowd and said with all earnestness, "A little liquid sunshine won't keep these good folks away!"

Bunny nodded and grinned at the rain that had started to fall beyond our protective canopy. A row of perfectly trimmed blond bangs framed her forehead. "So true! So true! Stan, I am so excited to have a convo with our next guests. Can you believe how lucky we are to have these two with us this morning?"

Stan gave a low chuckle, remarkably different from the sea lion approach. "Bunny, as always, you are 100 percent on the money. We are lucky indeed to welcome to the show today two illustrious chefs and the stars of a new reality show on Surge TV. Charlie Garrett and Avery Michaels, welcome."

"Thanks!" Avery said, his hands gripping his knees, a wide smile pushing his cheeks high enough to make his eyes squint. "Honored to be here."

I smiled and said hello. "Thank you for having us."

Bunny began. "So? Are you so, so excited for the debut of *Thrill Me* this weekend?"

"Great name, great name," Stan said in his sonorous voice. "Catchy."

I saw Vic do a fist bump behind the camera.

"Totally excited. Honored. Blessed. Humbled. Stoked." Avery appeared to be caught in some sort of one-word vortex.

Bunny tried another volley. "Now, you two have known each other a long time, right? Charlie, is it true that you and Avery went to culinary school together?"

"Yes, we both attended the Culinary Institute of America in Hyde Park." I tried one of Stan's low laughs on for size but it came across as a little skanky. I quickly cleared my throat. "A long time ago."

Bunny threw back her head in a giggle, but her hair didn't move. "I can hardly believe it was *that* long ago, my dear. You're a spring chicken! But talk to *me* about a long time ago, and I'll be picking up what you're putting down!"

Avery roused. "You look great. Bunny. Super. Awesome."

I saw a flicker of hesitation in Stan's eyes, but it was gone as fast as it had appeared. "You two are a dynamite pair, you know that? I've watched some of the footage from *Thrill Me*, and . . ." He shook his head and raised two groomed eyebrows. "Can we talk about the heat?"

Bunny shook her head and tsked. "No kidding, Stan. How do you two keep up that pace in the kitchen, night after night?"

Avery became serious. "Not easy. Difficult. Exhausting."

I sat up in my chair. "Avery and I are both very committed to creating meals that people enjoy." I tried to obey Margot's instructions to speak slowly, trying to act as though I were having coffee with a friend. "We try to give our guests memorable food, and we hope the show really gives a good behind-the-scenes peek of a premier kitchen. Kind of a peeping Tom's view into the real story behind delicious food."

Bunny pounced. "Speaking of heat and of peeping Toms, a little birdie told me that someone has been spying on you two. And that you might have been building a little heat of your own. Let's take a look."

I opened my mouth, shut my mouth, tried to formulate a response to the photo that had taken over the image on all the monitors within viewing distance, and therefore, within the contiguous United States of America. It was a photo of Avery and me on the fireplace night, to be sure, but this version was enhanced, very well focused, and taken from an angle that showed me surrendering fully to Avery's kiss. In fact, though I could not remember doing it, I had an urgent arm draped around his neck.

An arm with a hand that had a manicure.

I didn't get manicures.

I could feel The Splotch forming along the neckline of my shirt, up to my ears, along my jaw. This was a rapid-fire Splotch, and it was showing off for *FIVE MILLION PEOPLE.*

"Mmmm," Bunny said with a mischievous lilt in her voice. "Looks like those ties run deep between you."

Avery put up his hands in defense. "Now, now. That was an accident. Really. Broke up. Long time ago."

I gathered myself enough to say, "We're just good friends."

Stan snorted. "I wish I had a friend that good." Before we could respond, he pushed through to the next bullet point on his index card. "Charlie, I'm glad you brought this up."

I brought nothing up! I felt my jaw clench at the mounting injustices.

"You mentioned you and Avery have had struggles in your relationship but that you are friends to the end."

What was going on? I said nothing of the sort! I leaned forward in my chair and glimpsed Margot shooting me with laser eyeballs from behind the camera.

Bunny picked up the line of questioning. "How do you achieve a balance between work and relationships in such a demanding profession?"

"Well," I said, trying to draw out the word as I scrambled for a good answer that wasn't blatantly a lie. "I'm still learning how to strike a good balance. I have good days and bad days, I suppose."

Stan nodded, suddenly solemn. "I can imagine it's difficult, particularly when people can be so spiteful. So hateful, really."

Bunny sighed, her eyes widened in concern for me, her new best friend. "Charlie, what would you say to your detractors who have implied that to be a woman in your position, you must have, shall we say, compromised your integrity?"

I felt the bile in my stomach rising up through my esophagus. "I'm not sure where you are getting your information, but—"

"Charlie is a good woman," Avery interrupted, his brow furrowed. "She deserves her position at Thrill and has worked for years to get there."

Bunny sighed. Her false eyelashes batted once as she took in the man who was finally able to speak in full sentences. "What a beautiful defense of someone you truly care about."

I stared at the woman. Was she actually *getting misty*? If my fingers gripped any more ferociously to the sides of my fancy modern chair, I would rip off the veneer and be left with metal rods.

Stan nodded and slapped his knee with his index card, as though grateful to have made it through such a harrowing interview. "America, if you're anywhere but in front of your television this Saturday night at nine o'clock, eight central, you are missing out. I'm telling you, these two people and, heck, the whole team of *Thrill Me* are going to knock your socks off. Thanks for coming in today, guys. Avery Michaels and Charlie Garrett, everybody!"

The crowd cheered, and peppy theme music played in the background. Bunny held my hand in hers as she turned to the camera. "Join us after the break when we get down and dirty about the growing back-to-school epidemic: cyberbullying. Back in a moment!"

The cameraman waved us off, and I saw the monitors cut to a commercial for a bathroom cleaner. Two production people were on us like flies, removing our mics and directing us off the stage.

"Thanks, kids," Stan said. He clicked his tongue to his cheek and made a pistol with his fingers, which he fired at a grinning Vic.

"Come back and cook for us sometime," Bunny said, though her words were swallowed by a woman who was standing in front of her and touching up her lipstick.

Margot took one look at my face and intercepted me with a grip on my elbow. She guided me to our waiting car while Avery and Vic stopped to talk with a gaggle of shrieking middle-aged women.

"That was horrible! Ridiculous! And insulting!" I fumed as she shoved me not very gently into the back seat of the limo. I could barely sit on the upholstery, I was so amped up. "Who said I slept my way to the top? I want to know! Sexist pigs!" I wasn't finished. "And that photo! You have an entire *team* devoted to our nondisclosure contracts and yet you can't keep one photo under wraps? You seem to haul out that privacy clause only when it suits *you*."

Margot looked entirely relaxed as she crossed her legs and draped one arm along the back of the seat.

I launched into another round. "And just so we're all clear, I did *not* sign up for this," I said, pointing past her ringlets to the set. "I am a *chef*. Not a—a doll you bring out for networking purposes. I have a brain! Opinions! A voice!"

By this point, my breathing was shallow. Little spots danced along the edge of my vision.

Margot appeared unfazed by my shouting. She cocked her head, as if studying a still life. "First of all, the interview went well. Good job. You kept your composure when the Charlie of a few months ago would have crumbled under the pressure." She opened the minifridge and removed two chilled waters. She nestled one into the seat beside me even though I had certainly not indicated I wanted a refreshment.

"I have no idea who said the bit about your career trajectory." She shrugged. "Someone online? An old high school classmate who's bitter you were homecoming queen?"

I drew in a sharp breath. "I was never homecoming queen."

Margot kept talking as if she couldn't hear me. "Could have been a question Bunny or Stan formed on their own, under the general guise of 'detractors.'" She lifted one hand and let it drop onto her lap in complete resignation. "Who cares? Idiots will be idiots. You can't worry about them."

Realizing my mouth had gone dry, I cranked open the top of the water bottle with excessive force and some of it sloshed onto my lap. After a long gulp, I wiped my mouth with the back of my hand. My heart still hammered in my chest. "So I'm just supposed to forget it? Ignore the fact that I had my integrity questioned on national television?"

Margo turned slightly toward me. Her petite frame seemed childlike in the expansive car. Her feet barely skimmed the floor mats. "You don't have to forget it. In fact, if you're smart, you'll use that slight as a rallying cry for all women who have felt like you do right now. You could turn it into a fantastic tweet and watch the conversation take on a life of its own."

"But it's not true." I implored her with my gaze to understand. "I'm not that person. And even associating my name with that idea makes me want to rip someone's head off."

Margot chuckled. "That kind of reaction can make for good press, actually. Righteous rage could really work for you. We can start scheduling follow-up interviews today." She mused aloud about some possible headlines. "'Reality show star takes on sexism in the workplace.' Too self-important. What about 'Reality show sweetheart takes a stand on sexism.' That's better."

I gritted my teeth. "I don't want a rallying cry. I just want to work."

Margot paused a beat before speaking. Her tone softened slightly. "Charlie, I know this kind of thing isn't what you thought you'd be doing in Seattle."

I sniffed my disdain.

"However," she said, "you have a platform *now*. People are listening *now*. You say you have a brain and opinions and a voice. Well, use them. Take this moment when the world is stopping to listen and tell them what's on your mind. Believe me, they'll be on to the next curiosity soon enough."

The driver opened the door, and Avery and Vic got in.

"Those women were crazy," Avery said, shaking his head in what I supposed was the joy of a million male fantasies. "Autographs, selfies, videos. They couldn't get enough. You should have stayed, Charlie. They were totally asking for you."

I clung to my water bottle, my head spinning.

Vic must have noticed my silence because he reached over and patted my arm. "Charlie, don't worry about that photo. We had to use it because it's invaluable for debut publicity, but it had a shelf life and I think that shelf life is over. Don't you, Margot?"

Margot nodded. She squinted outside at a burst of sunlight. Sliding her sunglasses over her nose, she agreed. "We won't use it again. The public will do more with it now than we ever could."

My throat remained parched. I guzzled the rest of my water bottle and gestured for Avery to hand me another. He obliged, but a shadow of worry crossed his easily readable face.

"Don't worry about her," Margot assured him when she noticed his gaze. "Charlie has a few things to ponder." She looked me with a thoughtful expression. "She'll figure it out."

I drank long and deep from the water bottle, surprised to find it was still unable to quench my thirst.

28

It's not that I didn't fume. Oh, I fumed. I fumed for a good three days. And I got really proficient at fuming. But after my anger subsided, I had to accept the truth in Margot's words. This was a moment, just one moment. I could push through, and maybe even use all the attention to further my own goals. Nationally recognized as an excellent pastry chef? Ready to launch her own line of products? Already thinking about her first cookbook? Check, check, and check. I could play the game, I realized, and at the end, I could be the winner.

Plus, in my most shallow self, I had to admit that a little retail therapy never hurt.

For all of the discussions at Thrill surrounding what I would wear, what Avery would wear, his tux, my dress, when I finally got ready on the night of the debut episode, I did so without fanfare in my quiet apartment. I stood in front of my bed and fingered the gown that lay before me. I studied the winner of the mini-election held by all interested parties at Thrill earlier in the week. The comments of the Dress Parliament returned to my thoughts:

Sebastian the stylist: Refined and elegant without looking like you're going to stop by the country club for a round of bridge.

Avery: Hot.

Lolo: Deliciously perfect.

Margot: Finally. Don't forget to wear lipstick.

Tova: The absolute opposite of prom. I *so* hated prom, didn't you? You look amazing, Charlie! Seriously! I can't believe you have those arms without ever even trying CrossFit. I want to hate you, but I can't when you're wearing that dress!

The deep emerald of the dress shone richly against the soft grays of my bedding. I ran my hands gently along the bodice and felt the comforting weight of the fabric, hoping that its permanence would steel the butterflies in my stomach and scatter my second thoughts about the evening ahead.

Lolo had indulged me with a home visit earlier in the afternoon, and the result of her time and effort had made my hair and makeup look relaxed and pretty while still living up to the dress.

When it was time to get dressed, I carefully lifted the garment over my head and let it fall over my hips. After some maneuvering, I managed to coax the zipper up the back; I turned to my full-length mirror. For once in my life, I didn't feel the need to critique each inch of my body, each imperfection on my face. The dress hugged in all the right parts and made me feel very grateful to be a woman. The bodice was figure-formed but modest, a direct response to my request after seeing the publicity photos and being aghast that my breasts appeared to have perked up, grown up, and pushed out, all in the space of one photo session. But as a beautiful counterpoint to the smooth cover of fabric on top, a slit ran in a clean and dangerous line up to the middle of my right thigh. I pivoted before the mirror, unapologetic in my admiration of legs that never saw daylight. Turns out, running in a kitchen at all hours was at least good for the calves.

My phone vibrated as I was slipping on the strappy heels Sebastian had chosen for me. Tova was texting their arrival at my apartment building. The limo was waiting out front. Tova had really worked hard for me over the past several weeks, and as a thank-you I'd suggested that we share a limo to the party. Needless to say, Tova was in favor of that kind of carpool.

I fidgeted with my new clutch during the elevator ride down but knew as soon as I stepped into Omar's view that I'd done all right.

"Ms. Garrett," he said with a slight bow. "You are ravishing."

"Thank you, Omar," I said. "You are kind to say so."

He shook his head, opening the towering glass door with a distinguished air. "Kind, perhaps, but honest, as well." He smiled and watched from the door as the driver helped me into the car, shutting the door with careful precision and then pulling slowly away.

"Charlie!" Tova said, reaching over the space between our seats. "You look so gorge! I can't stand it." She was practically vibrating within a swath of sequins. "Charlie, this is my date, Donny Chu."

One look at Donny and I could guess Tova hadn't chosen him for this honor because of his membership in Mensa. He looked at me with what appeared to be a practiced expression. Unless I'd missed my guess, Donny's Botox injections and new cheek implants were responsible for his look of faux thoughtfulness.

"Lovely to meet you, Donny," I said. His fingers were long and clammy.

Tova leaned over to speak in a stage whisper, as though in addition to the burden of looking like an Asian Greek god, Donny also struggled with hearing problems. "He's an underwear model!" She gave me a thumbs-up. I smiled in return, wondering how recently Mike the cameraman had gotten the axe and predicting Donny would suffer the same fate momentarily.

Tova and Donny engaged in what only could be described as tonsil exploration, and I turned my back to them as much as I could without ripping a slit into the other side of my dress.

The streets of Seattle flashed by my window, and as we made our way through the city, I felt a deep and abiding loneliness settle in my chest. The night felt auspicious, and like something that should be shared with the people I loved. I thought with longing of the intimate party Manda had suggested hosting long before she knew I was expected at tonight's command performance. On an impulse, I knocked on the window separating our seating from the driver.

"Can we make a quick pit stop before going to the restaurant?"

A few minutes later, Tova and Donny barely came up for air when the car rolled to a stop outside Manda's house. My heels clicked with optimism as I hurried up the steps of the Henricks' front porch. When Manda came to the door, her hands flew up to her mouth.

"Oh, wow. Wow, wow, wow, wow, and wow." She reached for me and gathered me into an aggressive, spine-mangling hug. "Charlie," she said into my hair, "you are so beautiful." She snapped back to attention. "But what are you doing here? You're supposed to be at the debut party."

I nodded toward the limo. "We're on our way. I made them take a quick detour." I grabbed her shoulders. "Can you come with me, Manda? Please? Just put on your favorite dress or pants or whatever and come."

"Charlie—"

I shook her shoulders a bit. "Manda, please. Tova is making out with an underwear model in the backseat of that limo, and I want to be with someone who knows me and loves me tonight."

Zara wiggled out from under the arm Manda was using to prop open the door. "Holy smokes," she breathed. "Auntie Charlie, you look like a movie star." She peeked behind me. "Is that a limousine? Am I dreaming this moment?"

Manda pulled her daughter back toward the house. "Charlie, I'm so sorry. I would love to come, but I can't." Her eyes were mournful. "Zara has her school open house tonight. They're putting on a little play, and she's the lead alien."

I looked down and noticed for the first time that Zara was in a purple leotard with matching tights. Her hair was pulled into severe Princess Leia cinnamon roll braids. My spirits sank.

"Of course you can't go," I said, forcing a brave smile. "I shouldn't have waited so long to think of it."

Manda looked as if she were about to throw herself in front of the limo as penance. "I'm so sorry, Charlie."

"Don't think one more minute about it." The resolve had returned to my voice. "I'm sorry to make you feel sorry. Now give me a hug, you Henrick women, and wish me luck on my grand ball."

Zara swooned into the skirt of my dress. "My auntie is going to a ball. This is the best day of my life." She pulled back abruptly. "Where's the prince?"

I made a face. "Gross. Who needs a prince? Princesses are totally capable of having fantastic times at balls without having princes along."

Manda had grown conspicuously silent and was staring at a point beyond me. I turned and felt my stomach drop.

"Have a great time," Manda whispered, herding a protesting Zara back into the house before shutting the door with a definitive click.

I kept a vigilant focus on my feet as I descended the porch stairs. Kai waited for me on the sidewalk. He leaned against the worn pickets of the Henricks' fence. One side of his mouth pulled upward in a wry smile.

"Chef Garrett."

"Chef Malloy," I said, chin tilting upward at his cool tone.

"I'm assuming you're not headed in for prep work in that get-up."

I met his gaze and fired back as much ammo as I could muster, which was no small feat considering what his eyes could still do to me. "Tonight is the debut episode. There's a party at Thrill. I think we talked about it a while ago, but I . . ."

"Ahh," he said, nodding. "The debut episode. I remember. I'll be sure to set the DVR. See what you've been up to."

The cut of those words was intentional, I was sure. My chest rose and fell with rapid breathing. "I'd better go." My legs felt wobbly as I teetered away, all the afternoon's practice walking in heels a wash as I pushed toward the limo.

"Charlie, you look beautiful." His words sounded pained, but I didn't dare look back. Our damage was done.

"Say hello to Sunshine for me." The lilt of my voice made my meaning unmistakable. I allowed myself to turn as the driver opened the door to the back seat.

Kai's brow was creased. "Sunshine?"

I nodded but said no more. *How does it feel*, I wanted to fire off, *getting spied on? At least your private moment wasn't broadcast nationally.* Climbing into the limo, my hands shook as I took a glass of champagne from Tova. She grinned at me, cheeks flushed.

"Here's to the best night ever!" Donny was too busy downing what was left in his glass to clink with Tova and me.

I held my champagne flute in clammy fingers, letting the amber liquid grow warm before finally choking it down.

29

THRILL had been transformed—from the security staff behind the velvet ropes, to the hired catering staff, to the restaurant itself. The bones of the place were still there—my nemesis, the fireplace, still crackled with a warmth that easily dispelled the fall chill. The long window on one side still framed the pretty courtyard view of the tree, glowing now with leaves dipped into autumnal gold. I was pretty sure the light fixtures in the dining room were the same as they'd been the day before. But everything else was different, sparkling, and new. All the tables and chairs had been moved out of the space, and some patient and burly souls had replaced them with dozens of clustered seating groups. Chairs covered in tailored white fabric huddled around inlaid wooden tables set with dishes of tapas and small desserts. I didn't recognize any of the food, much less any of the beautiful people hovering around it.

Tova came from behind me and linked her arm through mine. "Charlie," she said, her voice low and loose after two flutes of champagne, "this is officially blowing my mind."

I smiled at a beautifully groomed couple who stood across the room, watching us. "I think those are famous people," I said through my smile. "Try not to be too obvious."

"What? Who?" The volume and pitch of Tova's voice would have been well placed in a physical education class. "Oh, you are *not* serious." Her acrylic nails were starting to pinch through the fabric of my dress. "That's Damarius Reynolds and Emma Cary. I can't believe they're here! And together! Last week's *USWeekly* said they'd broken up."

I'd almost forgotten Donny was there, but he spoke up. He shifted slightly but retained his practiced sullen expression. "Damarius Reynolds is legend. He was so ripped in *Revenge of Revenge*. His ab definition was unbelievable."

"We are so going over there." Tova shook out the sequins on her skirt and smoothed her waistline. "Come on, Donny. Destiny calls."

I watched her walk away, Donny doing his best catwalk swagger behind her, and felt Avery's arm slide around my waist. He spoke into my ear, and I noticed I was taller than him in my heels.

"This is it," he said. "I about keeled over from a panic attack in the car. Damn Margot and Vic for making us arrive separately. I could have used your calming influence." He pulled away, and I marveled that he could square his shoulders and be faux relaxed after such a confession of nerves. "You look amazing," he said. I couldn't help feeling as if his compliment, along with the way he took a step back to appraise me, were for the benefit of those around us and not me.

"You cleaned up well, too," I said, still sporting a version of the smile I'd offered the Ripped Ab couple across the room.

Margot stepped into the admiration circle, and we exchanged the briefest pleasantries ever before she began guiding me around the room, introducing me to industry people. Grateful I'd brought along a clutch, I filled it quickly with business cards from her favorite agents (one talent, one literary who specialized in celebrity cookbooks), four different TV execs who had garnered thirty-nine Emmys among them, a personal trainer to the stars ("I make Photoshop obsolete"), and a red carpet's worth of celebrities. My mind spun in circles, and I tried my utmost to remain engaged with each person, though after a while the perfect faces started to run together. I couldn't remember if Celia or Frances was the distant cousin of Sophia Loren, if Mateo or Spike was the guy who had a new surfing reality show on the WB, or if it was neither of those guys and the show wasn't about surfing at all but about snowboarding naked. Someone had said something about naked extreme sports, that much I did know.

Vic called the room to attention just as I was getting to know an earnest woman named Midge who worked at some sort of political e-magazine and wanted to know what I thought about Russia. In general. I was grateful to hear Vic clapping his hands for attention.

"Welcome, everyone, to this evening's event. We are proud and grateful such a star-studded group of people has joined us for the debut of the most-talked-about show of the season, *Thrill Me*."

The room pulsed with applause. I felt eyes studying me as Avery came again to stand by my side. Midge looked miffed to have been displaced.

"Tonight is all about indulgence," Vic continued. "The food, the wine, our beautiful surroundings, all you attractive people." An appreciative chuckle rose from the room, though no one looked particularly surprised by Vic's compliment. "We want you to enjoy yourself. We hope you feel as if this room and this moment is an escape from the harsh reality of the world outside. After all, in our business, we make shows about other people's realities so you don't have to face your own."

This comment educed an enthusiastic round of applause. One of the naked surfers/snowboarders even raised his glass to me from across the room.

"So settle into this evening," Vic said. "Find your seat, relax, and embrace all we have done to leave you feeling nothing short of *thrilled*."

"Nice," Avery said appreciatively as he tipped his chin to Vic. "Working a crowd like that. Pipe dream for me. One day, maybe."

I followed him through the crowd to the table by the fireplace that he'd pointed out as being reserved for us. I winced a little inside—this was the last place I wanted to spend any time. "Are you familiar with the concept of verbs?"

He made a face while he gestured for me to take one of the white chairs. "I'm sure that's a really great insult, but I don't know grammar. So it doesn't even work on me."

I sipped from a glass of wine offered to me by one of the hired staff. The thought came to me unbidden, but I couldn't help noting Kai would have appreciated my joke. Kicking off my ghastly heels, I tucked them out of sight and reached for a plate of food to begin my emotional eating.

But moments after I'd successfully pushed him out of my mind, Kai returned and with a vengeance. TiffanTosh had found their way to our table, settling themselves on one of the cozy couches. I sat next to them in a wing chair, while Avery took one of two seats on another couch. We had been given very clear marching orders from Margot that Avery and I should spend a good part of the evening in close proximity, but we were not to act like a couple. When I reminded her that would not be an obstacle, as we were not, in fact, a couple, she shrugged.

"These things are fluid," she said. "There's no harm in letting people wonder."

Avery and I had begun a discussion about the food on the table and what each dish might contain when a server approached our table and stood behind our only empty chair. "Miss," she said to me, "are we still waiting for this gentleman?"

I glanced up from a plate of figs and goat cheese. "Which gentleman?"

The server consulted her electronic tablet. "My guest list indicates we are to expect one more in this party. Kai Malloy."

I swallowed. Avery stopped talking midsentence.

"No," I said coolly. "I'm afraid Mr. Malloy won't be joining us tonight."

"All right," the girl said, drawing out her words. Her forehead creased. "I'll mark it down here then. Change to party of *four*." She looked doubtful, as though she suspected I was in the habit of lying about seating arrangements.

"That was weird," Avery said, his voice forcibly perky. "I thought you told Margot about the change in reservation a few weeks ago."

"So, party of four then." The server still hovered by the empty chair. She appeared to be having trouble with her stylus and kept tapping the tablet with increased irritation.

"Party of five." Tova sat down in the empty space on Avery's couch in one, sparkly motion. "You don't mind, do you?"

I was pretty sure Tova's eyelashes were fake, but I was entirely certain there was a reason she was batting them at Avery's surprised face. I'd merely have to hang around long enough to find out.

"Yes. I mean, no. Of course we don't mind. I certainly don't. Do you?" Avery's question, I supposed, was intended for the rest of us, but he kept his eyes on Tova as if they were meeting for the first time.

"Tova," I said, my mouth full of chocolate hazelnut bread pudding. "Where is Donny?" *Let's get that underwear model over here to fill that chair!*

"Oh, Donny," she said with a one-shouldered shrug. Already the name sounded foreign on her lips. "He's talking shop with a Victoria's Secret model." Tova appeared to be much less bothered by that statement than the average American woman.

I was grateful when the overhead lights dimmed a few minutes later. I sank back into the cushions of my chair and willed myself to stop looking at the empty chair directly across from me. *Time to watch our crowning achievement*, I said to myself. *Look alive. Look happy. Look like you've earned this moment.*

The theme music for the show played, and I found myself transfixed by the intro. One by one, the main "characters" filled the outsized flat screen that had been rented for the occasion. First our faces appeared, expertly made-up, followed by our first names in sleek white lettering. Avery and Tova huddled together, whispering to each other about what was happening on the screen. Avery did lean across Tova to nudge me when my name and face appeared during the opening sequence, but after a few minutes in, I knew that my viewing pleasure was going to be a solitary one.

In Vic and Margot terminology, the "story arc" of the first episode centered on how I came to join the crew at Thrill. I saw Avery as he'd looked when he approached Chet with the idea of bringing me on board. Unknown to me at the time, cameras had rolled when Avery had called me in New York. They caught every part of his reaction and my voice on speakerphone as I'd opened the rhubarb tart, the label maker, the boxes. It all seemed like a lifetime ago. Watching it unfold in front of me, seeing the smug triumph on Avery's face when I said yes, I felt the joy of that moment whittle down to a feeling I recognized as regret.

Tova squealed after seeing her first interview, educing an appreciative round of laughter and applause from the other viewers in the room. When she and I met for the first time, some hidden camera had captured the look on my face, one of surprise and maybe a smidge of annoyance.

"But you grew to love her, didn't you, Char?" Macintosh Rowe asked loudly, and the room again rumbled with laughter. Tova hid her face in Avery's shoulder in mock embarrassment.

I watched the rest of the episode, marveling that all the people around me, and all the people sitting at home in front of their TVs, were witnessing scenes from *my* life. Edited scenes, for sure. Pretty-haired scenes with sweeping sound effects. Scenes where I was courted, wooed, and brought to a new place without realizing the whole thing would be replayed in front of millions. Scenes that represented a part of me, certainly. But *scenes*. Chapters. A few sentences here and there. I stole a glance at the empty chair, wishing someone who knew the whole story could sit here with me and remind me who I really was.

Full lights came on again, and the room erupted in cheering and applause. I smiled and kept smiling when Avery stood and pulled me to my feet beside him. Tova looked up at us, grinning and clapping. TiffanTosh, looking impossibly elegant as they draped limbs around each other, clapped appreciatively.

Some idiot at the back of the room started chanting for a speech, and the idea took hold. Avery looked at me with bug-eyes, and I knew he was not going to be the one to address the crowd, at least not without another stiff drink and a tranquilizer.

I turned my face toward the group, feeling my cheek muscles twinge after so much smiling.

"Thank you," I said. "Avery has nominated me to talk, as he's suffering from a bit of stage fright these days. Did anyone catch us on *Rise and Shine, America* last week?"

Avery laughed and made a silencing motion with his hand. "Quarantined," he said and was rewarded with hearty laughter.

"Thanks for coming out tonight, everyone," I said. "It's great to have you all here to celebrate with us." The empty chair was staring me down, so I lifted my gaze to where Margot stood in the back of the room. Her somber expression had a way of jolting me back into the importance of this situation. "Many of you know what it feels like to work hard and finally get to the place you've devoted so much time and so much of yourself to."

My throat tightened. I took a deep breath and smiled. "I've been working in kitchens for a long time. Some of them were large and impressive and intimidating." I remembered the feeling of despair when I'd arrived at L'Ombre and thought I'd never get the hang of how to roll out a single pastry much less please Felix and Alain. "And some of those kitchens were out-dated, cramped, and crawling with the sturdiest of all creatures, the Manhattan cockroach."

I saw a few nods of recognition. Margot remained immovable, focused on me.

"And all this time I've been working toward achieving a view like this, a view from the top of a long, hard climb."

I paused. My cheeks trembled with the effort of keeping the smile in place. I looked at the expectant faces gazing my way and realized I'd stopped talking for too long. Margot made a sign for me to wrap it up.

"So now I have my view," I said. Macintosh cleared his throat. I looked down but couldn't seem to focus on what he was trying to tell me.

"Char," Avery whispered. I turned to him, startled when I realized I was crying. "Are those happy tears, Charlie?"

I shook my head, tears falling freely now. I wiped one cheek with the back of my hand and saw streaks of mascara smeared on my fingers. Looking across the crowd, I felt utterly, completely, irrepressibly alone. My gaze stopped on Margot, who was making no attempt to hide her disappointment.

"What does a girl do," I said, the words choking me, "when she doesn't like the view?"

The question hung in the air—even the music of wine glasses and china stilled for a moment. I picked up my clutch, heavy with the business cards of people who now watched me with wide eyes as I walked out the door.

It took me two blocks to realize I'd left my shoes behind.

30

"**NOT** bad," I said aloud to my empty apartment. "Seven extra grams of grated nutmeg makes all the difference. Best cinnamon-streusel pumpkin muffin ever. Or at least so far." I opened my eyes, making a slow assessment of my kitchen. Four other batches of pumpkin muffins littered the countertop, many of them on their sides after I took one bite and impatiently tossed them aside. This batch, the fifth, was the queen of the bunch.

"I do have some reservations about the pecans." My fluffy panda-head slippers slapped on the wood floors as I walked back to the oven. Holding my butter-smudged working recipe up to the light, I considered the next round of alterations. "I wonder about almonds. Or no! Pistachios!" I made a hasty note and groaned when I heard the buzzer announcing I had a visitor who wanted to come up the elevator.

"I told Omar no visitors," I muttered while walking to the phone. "What?" I snarled. "Avery, I'm tired of this conversation. The answer is no second season. No. *Non. Nyet. Nada.*"

"Listen, *nada* is Spanish for 'nothing.' If you're going to freak out, at least get your vocab right." Manda sounded as if she were about to put me in time-out. "Let me up. Omar is giving me the evil eye."

Knowing I had to face the Manda music at some point, I pushed the button to allow her entry and remained slumped against the counter when the elevator door opened.

"Heavenly days," she breathed when she saw me. "You're worse than last week." She pointed her finger at my face and spoke sternly. "Did you watch the episode last night after all? I thought you said you weren't going to watch the rest of the season because it made you want to commit crimes."

I rolled my eyes and made a face, which, apparently, did not help because Manda recoiled. "What?" I pulled my fingers through my hair. "So I haven't showered for a couple days."

She put her hands on her hips.

"Okay, more than a couple days. And no, I did not watch last night's episode, thank you very much. Though I'm sure all my Facebook besties from high school did and will be messaging me all day to get the inside scoop on my awesome life. So many friends, none of them real." I swallowed the ire rising in my throat.

Manda nodded at the counters. "Pumpkin cupcakes?"

"Muffins. With streusel." I plucked one from the most recent batch and tossed it to her. "This is the best so far. You know, baking is really fun when you don't have to worry about snotty people in the dining room, or a crazy boss, or camera crews or restaurant critics." I bit into my second muffin and chewed around the buttery crumbs in my mouth. "I'm pretty good at it."

Manda chewed thoughtfully. "You are. You're right. These are delicious. So were last week's apple turnovers."

"Mmm. The puff pastry was wicked good."

"And the rum chocolate cakes from the week before."

"I loved those. I should make more of those."

Manda snagged my third muffin while it was on its way to my mouth. "Slow down, there, tiger. You're going to feel sick again, like after the cheesecake bites last weekend. Too much of a good thing can be a bad thing." She turned my shoulders toward the master bedroom. "You go take some time to scrub the grime off your skin and hair while I clean up out here. And then we will talk."

"I can talk with greasy hair. It's easy," I whined. Showering sounded like a lot of work, and I was onto something with the pistachios. I just needed a few more hours.

"But I'd rather look at you when you don't appear to be in need of social services. Go."

I muttered something about being prejudiced against the homeless, but I obeyed Manda's orders. The walk-in shower steamed up quickly with hot water, and I stood under the spray for a long time with my eyes closed, chin raised. By the time I had washed every inch of skin, shampooed twice, and shaved an astonishing amount of hair off my legs, I felt dizzy with the expended effort. I kept my hair wrapped in a towel when I walked back to the kitchen in a clean T-shirt and jeans.

"This role reversal is chilling," I said, taking in the image of Manda dumping a stack of old newspaper into the recycling bin.

"Tell me about it," she said, picking up a browned apple core from a table by the couch and disposing of it. "I never thought I'd live to see the day when my neurotic best friend leaves an empty coffee cup unattended so long the dregs turn to mold."

"No!" I gasped.

"Yes. And I'm happy to see you are repulsed." She sat down heavily on the couch and patted the cushion next to her. "Come sit. I made you tea."

My feet on the ottoman and settled under the blanket I'd dragged off my bed days before, I took the mug she offered. My nose wrinkled on the first inhale. "What is this stuff?"

She pursed her lips. "Kava. It's good for anxiety and depression. Just in case you're experiencing one of those things."

I took a cautious sip. The tea tasted better than it smelled. "Cardamom, cinnamon . . . " I took another sip. "Maybe some licorice."

"Charlie." Manda tilted her head, her eyes large and penetrating. "Tell me how you are."

I shrugged. My fingers drew warmth from the ceramic in my hands. "I'm all right. Getting my head back on straight, I guess." My whole body felt tired. "It's taking some time."

"Have you talked with anyone at the restaurant?"

I shook my head. "Not really. I still grant phone interviews to keep Margot and Vic happy, but mostly, I'm out of the picture." I took a long pull of my tea and shuddered when it scalded my tongue. "Tova and Avery have been hitting the media circuit, which turns out to be better for everyone."

"I saw them talking with Kelly Ripa yesterday." Manda couldn't help looking guilty. "Sorry. They did great. Avery did a cooking spot, and Tova had everyone eating out of her hand with her self-deprecating comments and perky boobs."

I searched my heart of hearts but could not summon even a spark of jealousy. "I'm happy for them. They're getting exactly what they wanted."

Manda adjusted the blanket to cover her legs, too. "And what do you want, Char?"

I stared out the wall of windows that soared just beyond where we were sitting. After all my months in Seattle, the vista from my couch still took my breath away. I inhaled slowly, then exhaled in a rush. Pulling my gaze away from the mountains, the Sound, the clouds that seemed to be floating just beyond my fingertips, I looked at my best friend.

"I'm moving back to New York."

She swallowed, and I could see her trying to control her reaction. "Why?" She fingered the fringe on the blanket. "I'm pretty sure I know the answer to that question, but I think it would be good for me to hear you say it. Closure. You know? Like an open casket."

My eyebrows arched. "Nice comparison. I'm moving to Manhattan, not to the morgue. Though some have made comparisons."

Manda pressed on. "But why are you moving back? You finally have the top spot in the pastry kitchen at Thrill. Can't you just go to work and not be a part of the second season? Or take a sabbatical whenever they're shooting?"

I smiled. "Sounds reasonable. But I'm afraid it's totally impractical. Margot and Vic would never go for it, not to mention how Avery would feel about it." I shook my head. "I can't go back there."

We were quiet for a moment until Manda spoke again, likely knowing the answer before she'd even finished her question. "What about working somewhere else? We have lots of restaurants in this city, you know."

"I know." I smoothed my wet hair with one hand, avoiding her gaze. "I think it would be better to make a clean break. New York is a great place to become anonymous again."

Manda nodded, and I could see it pained her.

I cleared my throat and tried for a cheery tone. "But listen. I have great news. Alain called from L'Ombre, and he offered me Felix's job."

Some of the gloom lifted from Manda's eyes. "Seriously? That's fantastic, Char. So Alain finally made good on his promise, eh?"

I threw the blanket off my legs, suddenly feeling too warm. "Can you believe it? Felix actually retired and they're holding the position open for me." I walked to the window and cranked a handle off to one side. "Look at this," I said as the window creaked. "I found this a few days ago when I burned a batch of madeleines and the exhaust fan wasn't keeping up. This window opens." I looked back at Manda, victorious.

She frowned. "Charlie, that is the smallest crack of fresh air I have ever seen. It's pathetic."

I frowned. "Well, at least it's something." I leaned into the crack and took a deep, long sniff. "Pretty soon I'll be back in the city where my only choices will be recycled indoor air pollution or outside air pollution. I'll be yearning for a breathful of this."

Manda came to stand next to me and tugged me into a hug. We stood, arms around each other, friends through school dramas, birthed babies, heartbreak, lost jobs, lost loves, gained weight, lost weight, and many, many years of days all piled up into a big ball of affection and friendship and fidelity.

"Are you sad you moved out here in the first place?" Manda's voice sounded small.

I kept my cheek on her shoulder. "Not at all," I said. "I've loved living close to you, even if we never saw each other as much as we wanted."

She sighed but kept me in her grasp for a while longer. Just when I thought she had no more to say, she reminded me of the man who, for better or worse, had come to represent Seattle to me. "I liked you two together."

I bit the inside of my cheek, trying to tease out a platitude or a wise, accepting response. It was no use.

"I did, too," I said.

31

ZARA sat next to me on the couch, tulle skirts gathering in exuberant sprays around her knobby knees. She held my face with care, her blue eyes roaming slowly across my forehead, down my cheeks, and around my mouth.

"I'm taking a picture in my brain since I won't see you in Seattle forever after."

My spirit continued its downward spiral. I was becoming accustomed to its weight after the last few days of packing and planning. The movers were on schedule to arrive the following day, and I had stopped by the Henricks for a final goodbye before flying to JFK the next morning.

I put my arm around her tiny shoulders. "Not forever. I'll be back."

"But not in time for my dance recital. And you won't be at our house for Thanksgiving. I heard Mommy and Daddy talking about it and Daddy said he was depressed because you make good pies, but Mommy's pies are healthy."

I winced. Dane clambered up to sit on my other side. He shoved his pudgy fist in front of my face, too close for me to recognize the small vehicle it held. He named it for me and I gasped.

He said it again.

"Dumb *what?*" I said. I knew Jack had his flaws, but I couldn't imagine he'd taught his young son one of the most deplorable words in the English language.

Zara looked at my uncomprehending face and stepped effortlessly into her role as older sister interpreter. "*Dump truck.* It's his favorite."

As if to prove her point, Dane began to chant the name of his favorite construction vehicle, which also, conveniently, could serve as a devastating insult if the need arose later on in his life.

His foul language reminded me of New York, and I slumped my shoulders again, fussing with the wrapping on the package in front of me.

"Is that your lunch for the airplane?" Zara asked.

I stared at the package so long, I jumped when Zara nudged me and asked her question again.

"No," I said. "It's a gift for someone."

Manda came around the corner holding Polly, who was naked but for a fresh diaper. Manda had called her most recent explosion a "ten-wipe blow-out." I had begged off tagging along for the wardrobe change.

"Char, you have to do it." Manda's voice was kind but firm. "If you don't, you'll always feel like you should have. Don't add regret to a cross-country move."

"You're right." I stood, resolved. "I've sat here long enough. You're sure he isn't home?"

Manda cocked her head at me, eyebrows raised. "I believe you've asked me to clarify that eighteen times since you got here an hour ago."

I sucked air into my teeth. "So he could have come back within the last hour."

Manda shoved me from behind. "Help me out, kids," she said to Zara and Dane. "Auntie Charlie needs a gentle push out to the porch."

Jack met us on the front walk, where he was gathering leaves into a pile. "Go get 'em, Char." He punched me lightly on the arm. "We'll all watch to make sure you don't run and that you feel as uncomfortable as possible during your private moment." He grinned at my scowl.

I walked up the sidewalk as quickly as I could, newly worried that Kai might return home at any second. Taking the front steps two at a time, I crossed the wood slats of the porch floor, stepping around a group of irregular white and blue-black pumpkins flanking either side of the door. I paused, looking over to the Henricks for moral support. Manda and Jack gave me thumbs-up, while Zara called, "Give Mr. Malloy the cupcakes, Aunt Charlie! He loves bacon cupcakes! They were the grand prize winners at my party!"

I nodded, ignoring the jab. "Okay," I said quietly, positioning the short but no-less-agonized-over note I'd written on top of the cupcakes. "This is it then." I was crouched, staring at the cupcakes, my hands hovering over the package.

"Wait." The sound of my voice bounced off the bare wood floor. "What am I doing?" I was muttering, hands still on the package. "I'm a fool. This is crazy. I can't do this." I stood up abruptly and saw spots dancing between me and the Henricks. Running down the steps, I shouted to Manda and Jack.

"Where is he?"

Manda looked at me like I was nuts. "Charlie, I told you. He's not here. Just leave the cupcakes—"

I shook my head, impatient for her to understand. "I need to find him. Right now. I leave tomorrow morning and I've been an idiot and I have to find him. Now."

I saw the light dawn in Manda's eyes. She smiled.

"Oooh," Zara said. She shook her finger at me. "Auntie Charlie said 'idiot.' That's an automatic time-out."

"Sometimes the shoe fits, honey," Manda said distractedly. She called to her husband. "Honey, did Kai tell you where he was off to this morning?"

Jack paused, two gloved hands on the top of his rake. I gave him four full seconds before hollering.

"A little faster, Jack! This is an emergency!"

He twisted his mouth to one side. "I don't think he said where he was going." He squinted, frowned. "I just remember him saying some lame joke about jumping off a cliff. I told him suicide was never a laughing matter—"

"Jumping off . . . a cliff! I know where he is!" I ran toward the Henricks' minivan, which was parked along the curb. I pulled on the sliding door handle and groaned to find it locked. My body twisted with one hand still on the car. I looked back toward the house. No one had moved.

"I have to find him," I said, feeling more sure of those words than anything I'd felt in months. "And I need you to help me. I don't know how to get anywhere in this city."

Manda frowned. "Now, that is just sad, Charlie."

"It's true!" I was starting to shriek. "Everybody in the van! Auntie Charlie needs help on a treasure hunt or Auntie Charlie is going to have a nervous breakdown."

"Awesome," Jack called. He jogged to the driver's side door, his entourage hot on his trail. "This is like geo-caching only more urgent. I love it."

I nearly had to breathe in a paper bag while waiting for Manda and Jack to buckle three car seats, particularly when Dane began weeping inconsolably about something involving his tennis shoes (a hateful choice, apparently) and his snow boots (too small, but eventually retrieved from his closet so we could leave in peace).

After an intense debate between Jack and Manda, they decided on the general location of the cliff where Kai and I had accidentally fallen asleep all those months ago. Once he had his coordinates, Jack raced into every busy intersection as if he were in a high-speed chase, tires squealing and kids giggling with delight. Manda clamped white knuckles on her armrests and occasionally exclaimed in disbelief.

"You didn't speed like this when I was in labor!"

"Just close your eyes, Manda!"

As we rounded a corner, the kids squealed and Manda turned to the backseat. "Kids, stop encouraging your father!"

Jack pushed even harder on the gas pedal when she added, "You are not a stunt driver and never will be!"

We drove more slowly once we reached the neighborhood where Manda and Jack suspected Kai and I had walked. When we passed a dilapidated wire fence with a narrow path beyond, I yelled for Jack to stop. The brake action was so swift and severe, I tumbled between the front two seats.

"Thanks," I said, yanking open the infernally slow slider. "Wish me luck." I was jogging by the time I heard the door close behind me.

The path was steeper than I'd remembered and overgrown with branches after a full summer's worth of rain and sun. Lines of shallow scratch marks traced pink stripes on my arms, and, at one turn, I tripped over a rock and went sprawling on my hands and knees. When I cleared the final curve and stepped onto the soft grass, I was panting.

I scanned the clearing quickly, the rush of blood in my ears louder than the surf that crashed on the rocks below. The trees moved in the breeze, the music of their leaves a crisp lullaby in the fall air. My body tensed at the sound of movement, but all I found was a squirrel running along an outcropping of rock.

Kai wasn't there.

I stood, chest heaving, thoughts returning with an unforgiving thud of truth. Of course he wasn't there. Letting my legs give beneath me, I lowered myself to sit facing the sea. Why on God's green earth had I thought he *would* be here? Seattle was an enormous city.

I stared out at the water, feeling every bit the ridiculous fool I was. Balancing my elbows on my knees, I closed my eyes and felt a cold mist from the ocean tickle my face.

I was too late.

"Charlie."

I turned around, my hand clutching my chest. Kai stood with rumpled hair, eyes intense.

I rose to my feet, slipping a bit on the wet grass. "You're here," I said, surprise and relief filling me in equal parts.

Kai remained still, his eyes on mine. "I was on a walk." He nodded to a path behind him.

I blinked. "I didn't know the path continued."

A half smile. "We didn't exactly get that far." He shook his head a bit, as if to clear it. "Jack said you're moving back to New York. Tomorrow."

I nodded. "Yes." My toes and fingers suddenly felt numb with cold. "About that." I paused, willing him to hear my heart, even if I mangled what I was about to say. "Kai, I was hoping you'd be here so I could talk with you in person before I left."

He waited. His eyes looked more gray than blue surrounded by the sky and sea.

"I'm sorry." I rushed ahead, scared that if I stopped talking, I'd chicken out and walk away. "We had something good and true and . . ." I paused, searching until I found the right word. "Hopeful. We had something hopeful. And I screwed it up." My words caught in my throat, but I pushed on. "You were good to me and very, very patient. And I squandered it all because I could only see one thing."

His face remained unmoved, but I watched his jaw tense.

"I could only see the goal that I had set for myself and I didn't want anything to trip me up. Anything or any*one*." I sighed, feeling a deep exhaustion start to settle in my bones when Kai crossed his arms in front of his chest.

"I expected you to wait," I continued, my voice quiet. "Wait to see me on my nonexistent days off, wait to talk to me on the phone until the middle of the night, wait to hear me acknowledge I was falling in love with you until it was convenient for me."

I was sure he could see my heart doing gymnastics under the buttons of my coat. "I shouldn't have waited. And I'm sorry. Maybe you can't do it today, but I hope you can forgive me."

Kai took three steps toward me, and the grit in his gaze was enough to make me take a step backward toward the cliff.

"You are infuriating."

I swallowed hard but met his gaze. "I know."

"And difficult."

"I agree."

"And you're an elitist," he said, finger pointing at my nose. "About stone fruits. And flowers. And butter, for the love of God! You're very weird about butter."

I nodded. I knew.

He let out an exasperated sigh. Hands shoved in his pockets, he shook his head.

"You are a total mess about wanting any kind of personal life, Charlie. I just can't see how it would ever have worked."

The big lump in my throat that I'd been intent on ignoring made my cheeks burn with the effort. My eyes stung and I shut them against the salty spray in the air, the heart-stopping view of rock and sea, the truth written so clearly on Kai's face.

"There are so many reasons for us to walk away." Kai lowered his voice.

I opened my eyes to watch his mouth form the words.

"I rehearse all those reasons at night when I can't sleep, but I'm always distracted. I keep thinking of the way your smile makes my chest physically hurt."

He was pacing now.

"I've made lists—actual lists, with bullet points, like I'm going grocery shopping or something—when I'm at work and all I can think about is the way your eyes get deeper green when it's raining or the crazy passion you bring to making a damn cupcake."

I thought to smile but couldn't seem to breathe.

Pulling his hands out of his pockets, he ran one hand through his mussed hair.

"And this morning, I finally convinced myself that the lists are right and that none of the other stuff mattered. Not that you can make me laugh hard enough that I beg for mercy, or that every other woman looks uninteresting and dull to me now, or that you are, without question, the most beautiful woman I've ever known." His words tumbled out in a rush, as if he were trying to keep up with them. "None of that mattered this morning. I was ready to be done with the girl from New York who came here and ruined everything."

Kai lifted his hands and slowly, gently, he took my face between them.

"You ruined everything," he said, leaning in.

"I know, but—"

He reached for me and gathered what felt like every inch of me into his arms. He kissed me long and deep, a take-no-prisoners kind of kiss with his hands in my hair and my feet barely touching the damp earth.

It required all my remaining self-control, but I pulled away, shook my head. "This isn't fair to Sunshine." I pressed my fingers to my lips. They still tingled after his touch. "We have to talk about her before we go one step further."

Kai's forehead creased, but he didn't loosen his arms around my waist. "Sunshine. You mean Sunshine who worked at the diner."

I pulled a face. "Please tell me you don't know more than one woman named Sunshine."

He tilted his chin, daring me to continue. "Why would I need to consult Sunshine before kissing you?"

I raised my eyebrows. "I saw you together. One night, about a month ago, when you and Sunshine were sharing a booth at Howie's." I gulped. "You were sitting very close. You had your arm around her, you leaned into her, and, well, I couldn't stand being there any longer, but we both know what happened."

Kai waited a full, interminable beat before bursting into laughter. "Garrett, for being a woman who alphabetizes her spice rack, you have a remarkable imagination." He laughed again, and now I was getting annoyed.

"I saw the way she looked at you," I said, stepping backward and out of his arms.

He pulled me back to him and waited until I met his gaze. "You may have seen something on Sunshine's face, but you didn't look too closely at mine. She came in that night to say good-bye." His eyes sparked with amusement. "Sunshine moved to Montana last month to live in a yurt and raise her own goats."

I attacked him that time, my hands wrapped around his neck and my mouth peppering his face with kisses.

"What's a yurt?" I said, feeling the scratch of his whiskers on my cheek.

He froze and pointed to the grove of trees behind us. I heard branches snapping followed by an insistent "Shh!"

"Mommy?" Zara sounded forlorn. "How long do we have to watch Auntie Charlie and Mr. Malloy kissy-face? Also, Dane just ate the last carob chip."

EPILOGUE

I had seen very few sunrises in the previous ten years but, even so, the one that spread across the sky above Forsythia Farms that Saturday morning had to have set some kind of record for captivating beauty. The last three months had been crazy-busy, between canceling the movers and finding a new apartment and convincing Alain that I really was not returning to L'Ombre. I'd fully acclimated to getting a full night of sleep and not staggering in the door just before dawn. I'd made a fairly seamless transition from constantly harried to only occasionally neurotic. Still, the slower pace of my new life and perks like getting to watch the sunrise had the power to stop me where I was and make me take notice.

"Staring directly at the sun causes permanent damage to your eyes, you know." Kai ducked under the white canopy he'd built for the little baked goods stand we'd cobbled together with an old farm table, stepladders for shelving, and big bunches of wildflowers. He handed me a steaming cup of apple cider, one stick of cinnamon bobbing along the caramel surface. "I've always thought your eyes were rather pretty, so I'd hate for you to go blind. Especially during the last market day of the season."

I sipped my cider. "Thank you for your thoughtfulness." Pointing to the sky, I said, "Is this kind of divine showing off a normal sight for people who don't work from noon until two in the morning?"

Kai stepped back, appearing to evaluate the sunrise on a sliding scale. "Yep." He nodded. "This is normal. Spectacular, but normal. I have to say, it reminds me, again, that I'm so glad you quit that job. Smart woman, you."

I rearranged a stack of chocolate-pecan cookies that formed a neat line along the front of the table. "At least for a while. Maybe I'll get super bored with jaw-dropping sunsets and you'll have to push me into a cab and send me to the nearest high-pressure commercial kitchen."

"Like an intervention," Kai said.

"Exactly. An intervention. Maybe too much rest and general well-being will make me crazy. You never know."

He didn't speak for a few moments, and I looked up from where I had squatted next to a ladder. My hands were on a tall glass rectangular jar filled with a tower of scones.

"There are different kinds of crazy," he said, looking at me over the rim of his mug. "Lucky for you I'm helping you with the 'can't handle it when one scone is two centimeters to the left' kind of crazy. That's a particularly scary kind, but I feel you are making progress."

I narrowed my eyes at him as I rose. "I never would have agreed to help out at your little family market this fall if I'd known the kind of workplace harassment I would have to endure." I could hear the smile in my voice as I tucked my cold hands into the warm folds of Kai's coat and let them settle there.

He leaned down, offering parts of sentences between each kiss. "Garrett, you have no idea (upper lip) the kind of harassment (lower lip) I can inflict on arrogant pastry chefs (moving resolutely in the direction of my neck)."

A chorus of clearing throats made me jump backward, knocking the farm table hard with my rear end. Dahlia, Gemma, and Tom Breyon stood just under the canopy. Tom laughed.

"It's barely daybreak, young lovers," he said with a wink. "We have a long day of hard work ahead of us."

"All the better reason to fortify oneself," Kai said as he wrapped his arms around me from behind.

Dahlia's lips were set in a line, where they had stubbornly remained since I'd arrived during the first weekend market at Forsythia Farms eleven Saturdays ago. I watched her intently, hoping today would be the day that would thaw her distrust of the woman who had publicly broken her brother's heart and had even gotten paid for it.

"I brought you two some blankets, in case we have a light crowd and the sun doesn't warm us up for a few hours." She set a stack of blankets on a nearby chair.

Gemma nodded at Tom as she spoke. "I'm going to guess they won't need any extra heat." The two giggled like school children until Dahlia groaned.

"All right, prepubescent teens. Back to work." Leading the way with a determined stride, Dahlia herded Tom and Gemma back to the barn, where visitors would soon arrive to buy donuts, cider, and the remaining bushels of apples from the family orchard. Gemma turned around and caught my eye. She smiled and then rolled her eyes at Dahlia.

I smiled in return but felt my shoulders sag.

Kai noticed. "Dahlia still loves you," he said, his arms still around me. I leaned my back into his warmth. "She just has to punish you for a while so you know she cares. Give her time."

"How much time, would you guess?"

"When I put the pages of her diary through Dad's paper shredder, she didn't forgive me for roughly one calendar year."

I groaned.

"But don't worry. I'm sure she has matured significantly since seventh grade." He stopped to correct himself. "Well, seventh and eighth grade, if you're counting the full twelve months."

I whimpered but stopped abruptly when our first customers approached the table, a couple taking turns pushing a running stroller. The woman wore a voluminous stocking hat with a bright pink pom-pom that flopped on top. Beside her a lanky, bespectacled man walked, one hand commandeering the stroller and the other cradling a stainless steel carafe. Under a mountain of fleece blankets, two chubby cheeks poked out of the cocoon.

"Are you guys open?" The woman had dark circles under her eyes but wore a cheery smile. "We've been up for a while and will probably be ready for a nap by nine. Do you mind if we shop now?"

"Not at all." I smiled, marveling at their early morning gumption and thinking Manda and Jack and their kids would probably not make it out to the farm until after noon.

Parking the stroller at the edge of the stand, the woman perused the cupcakes, the muffins, the glass hurricane filled with a rainbow of macarons.

"Everything looks and smells amazing." I could hear awe and hunger in her voice. She looked at me with wide eyes. "Did you bake all this?"

"She absolutely did." Kai sounded as if he wanted to beat his chest in victory. "She's pretty much incredible."

I felt my cheeks heat up underneath the pink caused by the cold morning. "I'm used to large quantities and quick turnaround. This has been just for fun, to help out at the farm." I unfastened a striped round tin I'd placed on the table. "I have samples of the pumpkin streusel muffin. Would you like to try some?"

"Absolutely." The woman daintily plucked two samples from the tin and held out one for her husband, who was standing before one of my displays with a studied expression on his face. "Here, Mitch. Better eat this before I do."

He ambled over and took the muffin from her hand.

The woman's eyelids dropped sometime during her first bite. "This is exactly what I want to eat every day of autumn. And winter. And most of spring." She grinned. "I'll take a dozen. Does this woman cook for you? If so, you're a lucky man." She directed her words to Kai.

He shook his head. "She has control issues in the kitchen. I cook for her."

Mitch snorted from his resumed position by my display. "Lizzie, maybe you two should be friends."

"I might have one or two control issues," I said to her.

Kai's turn to snort.

I ignored him. "But I bake things for him all the time."

"Four times, actually," Kai said. "And one of them was a bribe to take her back. So that doesn't really count as kindhearted baking."

I cocked my head at him and stared. "You are—"

"Well," the woman interrupted with a laugh. "You were right, Mitch. The ambience and banter are just as delightful as the baked goods."

I looked at Mitch. He saw the question mark on my face and shook his head. "I definitely did not use the word *delightful*." He put his hand out to shake mine. "Mitch Shapiro. I'm a repeat customer."

I swallowed hard as I shook his hand. "Mitch Shapiro, the Seattle real estate man?"

Lizzie straightened from feeding a morsel of muffin into the chubby cheeks. "Please do not recognize him. It's so annoying. And it inflates an already healthy ego."

Mitch continued. "I've been out here three other times this fall because of a project nearby, and each time I've gone home wishing I'd bought more of what I ate from your booth."

Lizzie licked streusel off her finger. "I believe the word would be *mooning*."

I didn't have much time to get flustered from the compliment because Mitch jumped right in. "Listen, I think you have something here. I've read up on you, on your experience as a chef, your good press from L'Ombre in New York, the TV show gig here with Thrill."

I winced. "Not some of my finest moments."

Mitch waved away my concerns with one hand. "All press can be turned to one's advantage. Particularly if you give some things time. Plus, you have name recognition before you even sign the lease. That's a huge advantage."

My eyes widened. "Sign what lease?"

He grinned for the first time, revealing two deep dimples in his slender face. "Chef Garrett, I think you should set up shop in my new loft development in Seattle. Premium real estate, built-in customer base full to brimming with folks who want delicious cakes, muffins, and cookies, and a generous investment toward start-up costs for a small share in the business." He took another muffin bite from the tin. "As long as you keep baking like this, you're going to have more business than you know what to do with."

My head was spinning. Kai had slipped behind Lizzie and the stroller and was giving me hysterical thumbs-ups and mouthing the word "Yeeeeeeessss!" over and over.

"I'm flattered," I stuttered. "And floored."

He laughed and slapped his business card on the table. "Think about it. Everything's negotiable. Just let me know when you want to go for coffee, and we can get things rolling."

The little guy in the stroller was starting to fuss. Lizzie pointed to the jar of scones and, widening her eyes, said, "Nap time approaches, people. I'll need some of those. And a half dozen of the Kitchen Sink cookies."

Kai hustled to help me as I gathered Lizzie's order.

She tore a bite off a chocolate chip and toffee scone. Closing her eyes, she said, "Don't think too long about Mitch's offer. This is delicious."

I watched Kai bundle up the Shapiros' packages and place them gently underneath the carriage of the stroller. We exchanged friendly goodbyes, Mitch taking one more appreciative look of my displays, and Kai and I watched as they made their way toward the cider, Lizzie's hat bouncing with each step.

"That was awesome," Kai said, lifting me off the ground when he hugged me. "You can't help being famous, can you?"

I slugged him, but gently and punctuated with a loud kiss on his cheek. I caught a glimpse of the riot of orange and purple behind him. Turning us both toward the light, I said, "Look."

We stood together watching the cashmere colors of dawn touch the fields and spread over the house and barn. Kai enveloped my hand in his, and we stepped forward into a slant of sunshine that had spilled onto the ground in front of us.

Lifting my face, I saw the morning light was gradually unveiling a pale blue expanse in the swath of sky right above us. I closed my eyes and simply enjoyed the building warmth of an autumnal sun, the feeling of Kai's fingers entwined with mine, and the heady promise of the new days ahead.

Kai's voice was soft and deep, just the kind of voice a girl could happily hear as perfect bookends to her days. "I'm glad you're here."

My head on his chest, I felt his heart beating through his coat.

"Me, too," I said.

ACKNOWLEDGMENTS

AUTHORS are wise to admit that books aren't created in a vacuum, that they are labors of love by many, not one. This is entirely true, but you should know that mostly I wrote this book while in my pajamas, pacing a room, yelling at the computer screen, and in dire need of concealer. I was alone, and this was best for everyone. Nevertheless, these people absolutely spurred me on, loved me, and, on occasion, were tactful enough to pass me a hand mirror before leaving my house.

Thank you to:

My Seattle advisory team, Jason Pace, Dawn Bilyeu, Laurel and Rick Ballinger, for their ready willingness to make Seattle into a three-dimensional home for Charlie.

My panel of culinary experts, Chef Robert Lewis and Chef George Formaro. Both of these gifted gentlemen are far too well adjusted and not nearly narcissistic enough to have worked in any of Charlie's kitchens. Thanks to both of you for letting me peek behind the curtain. Also, please start following me around and cooking for me all the time.

The Nicoles (Frail and Mele), Brianna Scharfenberg, and the entire Skyhorse team. What a lovely process, working with you people! Thanks for asking me to join in the adventure.

Heather Gudenkauf, who is gracious and kind and very, very generous. You went out of your way to help me move into this next stage, Heather, and I am one grateful Iowa girl.

Valerie Gray, who saw what I couldn't and then was kind enough to destroy the first version of this story. Thank you for pushing me to write the story I wanted to write and to do it with confidence. You gave me a tremendous gift.

The intrepid women of our writing group: Wendy Delsol, Dawn Mooradian, Carol Spaulding-Kruse, and Kali VanBaale. My writing has flourished, stretched, and grown under your care, as have the friendships we have built together. Each of you is dear to me.

Chip MacGregor, who is the definition of loyal and true. He's also the definition of an unparalleled literary agent. And of a witty kilt wearer.

Ann, Deanna, Makila, Sarah, and Sarah for deep friendship and a willingness to enter in, no matter the cost.

Ryan, Betsy, Olivia, and Jonah Beach. My life is rich and beautiful and full of shimmying and interpretive dance because of you.

My extended family for buying my books even if you never read them. It's okay. I barely read your Christmas letters, so we're even.

My parents for assuming I can and then cheering like maniacs when I do.

My children, Ana, Mitch, and Thea, for loving good stories and for encouraging me to write my own. Also, sorry about the times I threw unsolicited hissy fits about how I did, in fact, have a "real" job and couldn't help you right that second with the bagel slicer. I understand your confusion. It's hard to take a woman seriously when she's in her PJs.

My husband, Marc, who loves me with a tenacity I do not deserve and who still laughs at most of my jokes.

God, the Beginning and End of all the greatest stories and the Author of the kind of love that changes everything.